The Migraine Mafia

a novel

by

Maia Sepp

www.maiasepp.com
Cover by Theresa Rose - Lucky Bat Books

ISBN-13: 978-1494315931
ISBN-10: 1494315939

For John

(Bringer of the ice packs)

CONTENTS

1 – Urban Sainthood

In retrospect, Sidney Dott's bowtie should have warned me that something was terribly wrong. It was one I'd never seen before, dyed his signature power colour, a red-orange, burning-tar-tinted blend he refers to as "funky sunrise," a freakish mix that probably elevates Sid's endorphins. Sid is our chief technical officer, my boss's boss, and he's famously fond of wearing power colours to difficult meetings. From what I hear, he's even more enamoured of his endorphins.

I had run into Sid in the hallway after snagging my second Coke of the morning from the break room, and he had deftly steered me towards my office. My boss, Elliot, our vice president of technology, fell in step beside me, and within seconds the three of us were all having what I thought at the start was an impromptu meeting. But I was distracted by Sid's bowtie and his shiny grey three-piece suit, his cowlick so aggressive today it left him looking more than a little surprised. So maybe that's why it took me a few minutes to realize that the meeting was actually about me.

When Sid said, the first time, "You're definitely not fired," I started paying attention. He repeats it again, now, probably because I haven't said anything in response.

"No, definitely not," Elliot echoes. Elliot is business-casual, bald-egg bald, nerdy, plump, and proud of it. Today, as ever, his shoes are spit-polished.

"Really?" I ask, even though all I can hear is that one word echoing in my head: *fired.*

"Definitely," they answer at the same time, an off-key duet.

"So I can come to work tomorrow?" I try not to sound too eager.

"Yes, of course," Sid says, before smiling in that inscrutable way of his.

The squeeze in my chest eases as I exhale and slowly move back in my seat. "And next week?"

The look that runs between the two of them is an *I told you so.* "Uh…no." Sid lifts his shoulders in a kind-of-but-not-really apologetic shrug. "So, Viive," he says, mangling my name the same way he always does: Vee-*vie* instead of Vee-*veh*. "We know you've been under a huge amount of pressure lately, and we want you to take some time to get yourself together."

I take a sip of my Coke to try to ease the moment, but that small swallow manages to turn itself into a cough that won't stop. Another look passes between the two of them, one that makes my stomach hurt. When I finally get a hold of myself, I say, "Sure, the Dagobah project was a lot of work, but we're up and running now. Everything's fine."

"Well, here's the thing, Viive," Elliot says. Elliot starts a lot of conversations like this, and it's generally not a prelude to anything pleasant. "Sid and I have noticed over the last few months that morale in your team is down, and you've missed…how many?" He turns to Sid.

"Six," Sid says succinctly, pulling on his bowtie, a little tic he has.

"Six management meetings," Elliot says, while he holds his hands out in a *well there you have it* kind of a way. "And you were late for the conference call with Spiegel & Spiegel earlier this week–"

"I was dealing with an emergency that day, and I had one of my guys take that call. Unfortunately he was waylaid by an executive assistant–" (I don't say who did the waylaying, because we all know it was Sid's corporate helpmate, a pouty twenty-something blonde who breaks into a little dance that looks like she needs to pee whenever she wants something.)

Sid coughs.

I continue, "…who needed help with her printer. Like we've discussed before, I run a technical team, but we don't fix printers." I pause for a minute before adding, "And with all the overtime lately, everyone's morale is down these days."

"I respect what you're saying," Sid says, a nothing answer that means he has no intention of asking his assistant, Bethie, to stop doing the little pee dance. "But it's not really the point."

"I hear you've been lying down in the nurse's office every day at lunch," Elliot adds.

"I did that, like, once, weeks ago, late on a Friday night," I say. The muscles on the back of my neck are ratcheting tighter by the minute, and I'm starting to get a headache, a dull nudge behind my ears that's hard to ignore. Since all these headaches are the reason we're having this little meeting, I decide not to mention it.

"You just don't seem your usual self, lately." Elliot shrugs.

"Well, I…I've been having a few challenges, but everything will be fine," I say. "Everything *is* fine." I hope neither one of them notices that my right hand has slipped under my desk, that my fingers are now crossed. I try to ignore the slight tremble in my wrist as I do it.

"Look," Elliot says, "you haven't taken any vacation since you started working here, which is four years ago, right? There's a policy coming in the new year–if you don't take your vacation, you're going to lose it. You have twelve weeks saved up–"

"You want me to take off *three months*?" There's a jagged, nervous energy in the room now, and I have to put both hands against my desk to try to steady myself.

"No," Elliot says, looking at Sid. "No one is saying that."

"Why don't you take…?" Sid fingers his goatee in the creepy way he does, taking his index finger and running it through his beard. "A month."

"A month! Come on, guys," I say, my throat suddenly parched. I take another sip of my Coke while I consider my next words, and the can empties with an unexpected slurp. "I appreciate your concern, but like I said, I hit a rough patch a while back, and everything's fine now. And even when I'm a little under the weather, I'm still here longer hours than most people."

Elliot glances at Sid, who's still rummaging through his goatee. "She's right, you know."

Sid nods before shrugging. "Can you pass me your pen, please, Viive?"

I hand it over, wondering why his request bothers me so much, and then I realize I've never heard Sid say *please* before. It seems so wasteful of him, to throw away a *please* on such a nothing comment.

Sid scribbles in the little notebook he keeps while Elliot says, "We're only trying to help, Viive."

"I appreciate that, guys," I say, forcing a smile to materialize on my face. "I really do."

"So, three weeks?" Sid says.

After looking at my face, Elliot says, "Okay, two weeks. You go, get back on your feet, and come back all rested up."

"Sure," Sid says. "Hell, take your husband on a trip. Go to Bali. It's great this time of year."

Relief swells in my veins; two weeks suddenly sounds like something to celebrate, like winning a Pulitzer or a bake-off.

"And then come back with a note from your doctor saying you're able to work," Sid says.

"What?" I ask, the relief draining out of me.

"We'll need a note from your doctor," Sid repeats.

"What if I don't get a note from my doctor? I mean, I barely even have a doctor."

"Viive," Sid says, pinching the bridge of his nose, his eyes closed. "How is it possible that you have a chronic illness but no doctor?"

"Oh, come on," I say, forcing a smile to my face. "It's hardly a chronic illness."

"My wife read in the newspaper last week that migraine is one of the most debilitating diseases in the world," Sid says.

I've never liked his wife.

"What happens if I can't get a note?" I ask.

"We've been heading this way for a while, Viive," Elliot says.

"We have?"

"We're all busy," Sid says. "And keeping your shit straight is really your job, don't you think?"

Elliot looks past my shoulder for a minute, focusing on something there. He looks older than his forty years. But Sid looks pretty happy, one hand resting on his lapel, the other exploring his neck. Sometimes it seems like Sid can barely keep his hands off himself.

The two of them make a few noncommittal noises and then go, leaving me with dark thoughts about strangling Sid with his bowtie. After I run through a few more revenge fantasies, I sit back in my chair, my nerves still pulled tight, a jumpy twang in my bones. I exhale, my breath an exhausted sigh. There's work to do, but I can't focus on the buzz of my cell phone, or anything remotely productive. Instead I look around my office, like the walls will give me an answer. It's really nothing but a glorified cubicle, four walls with a door but no ceiling; a sham of an office. I can't even have a private phone call in this not-quite-a-room. The walls are grimly positive, with posters made by our creative department extolling the virtues of being AGILE, TEAMWORKY, and IMPACTFUL. My desk is cut-rate Scandinavian chic, my chair a beige colour that's supposed to be reassuring, and the floor is circa late 1800s concrete, when this loft was an industrial business that probably employed child labourers. The space is huge—twenty thousand square feet over two floors, tucked into a corner of Toronto's Adelaide and Spadina neighbourhood in Chinatown—and open-concept cool, sleek and modern and old-school all at the same time. It's also drafty, cold, and uncomfortable. I have to wear sneakers most of the time because walking around on concrete kills my ankles. But the execs think the floor looks nice, which, I guess, is the point.

It doesn't seem like much, not something to get so upset over and want to hang on to. But the overclocked thump of my heart against my chest reminds me that it is. I like working with Elliot. Up until now he's been supportive of me and my career. And I need this job, for a lot of reasons.

Of course, this is the kind of place where everyone's always on the lookout for someone to topple from their post, for blood in the water. We all try to be casual about it, but that doesn't mean it's not there. Getting fired is not unheard of, and if it becomes common knowledge I've been asked to take some time off, it'll poison everything for me here. *Here* is an über-competitive tech start-up, with the regular mix of ego and talent and nonsense that comes with newfangled new business ideas. We're a digital solutions agency, which means we build code, host computer infrastructure, and wrap it all up in the marketing voodoo we use to entrap clients.

And I don't have a problem, I tell myself, but it's hard to ignore the moment when the sharp, hard current in my head makes me a liar. I press against my left temple with my thumb. After a few minutes I lean back in my chair, wincing when it pinches my ass yet again, before opening my bottom right drawer. It's a mini-migraine rescue centre, full of caffeine-packed pop, pain-relief gel, over-the-counter pain killers, and near the back, some prescription meds doled out by my general practitioner, a twitchy woman in her sixties who's just making time until retirement. I pick up the water bottle on my desk—empty. I dry-swallow two white pills, acetaminophen with a dash of codeine–helpfully behind the counter in Canada–and pull out a small pack of saltines.

My gaze falls on the back of the drawer, where my nameplate is perched, almost as if it belongs there. My husband, Nate, had it made for me two years ago when I was promoted. I have a degree in engineering, and a career record of computer infrastructure design, implementation, and alchemy, which is how I was promoted to senior manager of technology, a role that's a stepping stone to where I really want to be.

The nameplate has been missing for about a week now, and I palm it, tracing the letters of my name absently with the fingers on my other hand. Non-Estonians are perpetually befuddled by it, a product of my parents' mixed marriage, meaning that my mother is Estonian and my father is not. All this cross-cultural canoodling left me with a ridiculous name: Viive McBroom, a goofy Canadian mash-up of Scots-Irish and something foreign. The *something foreign* is a Scandinavian-ish former Soviet-Bloc country perched on the Baltic Sea, where they speak a language jam-packed with vowels but without a future tense, which I've always found vaguely comforting. We have no idea if tomorrow will really come, after all. In any case, my mother and father insist they just wanted to name me after family, which is how I ended up with the same moniker as my great-grandmother. I wanted a nice, Canadian, pronounceable name. My mother admitted once, after getting too deeply into the vodka at an Estonian Independence Day party, that perhaps something simpler would have been a better choice, a conversation she denies to this day. My little brother got off scot-free with *Martin*, which he's been holding over my head since the seventies.

I put the nameplate back on my desk and sigh.

The package tears as I open the crackers, spilling crumbs onto my desk that I can't help but stare at. If I had to think about it, could I count all the saltines I've had over the years? Probably not. They're the perfect sickness buddy, the ultimate go-to when you need to match medication with food. I should know, I learned to speak early and must have learned how to complain directly afterward. I was diagnosed with migraine by five, an icepack connoisseur by eight. I grew up with restrictions on everything: my sleep (not too much, not too little, no sleeping in on the weekends, not even on your birthday), what I ate (no chocolate, no cheese, no fun), where I went (routine is a migraine girl's best friend), everything except for the bland comfort of saltines. And then it got worse: a few years after I left home, my brother Martin got me referred to a pain clinic downtown, a cult-like clan of pain specialists who infused me with hope and then probed and injected and drugged me to within an inch of my life, torturing me for two years before I finally missed an appointment and never went back. Now I only ever talk to people–including Elliot–about my migraines in mumbles, which means that these days living with pain is my normal, and I'm managing it all just fine, thankyouverymuch.

"Up to no good again?"

I look up. Otis, one of my best friends and the manager of User Experience, a department that spends its time optimizing websites and luring customers, is standing there with two coffees in his hands. He has the office beside me, and since he doesn't deserve a ceiling either, we sometimes throw things to each other (mostly junk food, particularly Ding Dongs, but sometimes Ho Hos). Otis is loud, with a booming British voice and a laugh you can hear clear across the office, and he's tall, rangy, and perpetually smirking at something. He has shag carpet in his apartment, over in The Junction, and an aggressive puffball toy poodle named Gloria, who goes to a doggie daycare that has a pool. In his spare time, Otis is trying to convince his wife to try polyamory. There's a 98% chance he's the one who hid my nameplate in my drawer.

"A little," I say, as he makes his way over to my desk, handing me one of the coffees before plopping down in the same chair Sid recently vacated. "Thanks."

"Anything for you, luv," he says, with what's a Manchester accent, or so he claims. Frankly I wouldn't be surprised if Otis is really from New Jersey. "Want to tell me what's going on?" he asks.

I give him a look. "How do you–"

He points to the not-a-ceiling.

I run my fingers through my hair and exhale a heavy sigh. "Basically…" I pull the lid off the coffee and sniff before taking a sip. It's flavoured–buttered pecan–with cream and just the right amount of sugar. God, I love Otis. "Elliot and Sid want me to take some time off."

"Any particular reason?"

"I missed some management meetings, and–"

"Nobody goes to those."

"Right, of course not. But they said they've heard some muttering about me being burnt out. Someone told them I've been lying down in the nurse's room all the time, which is total bullshit."

Otis squints. "Who would say something like that?"

"An excellent question." I pull the back of my Converse sneaker off my left foot and massage my ankle, which is sore again from these stupid floors. After a minute, I reach into my desk drawer. I peruse the contents—a few Kit Kat and Milky Way bars, some Godiva for really bad days—and then pull out a box of M&Ms. "Want some?" I say, as Otis reaches forward to take a handful. The two of us pop a few in our mouths at the same time, and I let the chocolate dissolve on my tongue with a happy sigh (imagine how irritated I was, a few years ago, to discover that the food sensitivities everyone associates with migraine don't affect me at all, and that I can eat all the chocolate I want).

"Otis?" The marketing manager is standing in my doorway. "We have a problem."

"On it," Otis replies. After he's gone I lean back in my chair again. Half the conversations in the office are interrupted in this panicky kind of way. Everything is an emergency; no one can wait for anything.

After a few minutes my thoughts drift back to the day Elliot hired me. His buffed shoes and equally shiny head had all emanated confidence. He shook my hand and told me we were going to do great things together. He didn't mention I'd have to miss Christmas dinner three years in a row, or do maintenance at four in the morning, or untangle problems with a favoured client's shitty network when Nate and I were supposed to be at a cottage during the most perfect July long weekend on record. He didn't need to–in this line of work you go home when the job is done, and that's just the way it works. But that loyalty comes with its own rewards: respect, security, opportunities. Opportunities like the promotion Elliot has been promising me for the last year.

And so maybe that's why, sitting here, a ball of anxiety still rumbling around my stomach, all I can think is: *It wasn't supposed to be like this.*

"So, here's the thing," I say the next morning, as I look around the small meeting room, a forced smile on my face. "I'm going to be taking some time off."

Every Friday at ten a.m. I have a mini-management meeting with my team leads and seniors, before taking them all out for lunch. I have two leads: Manjit, who runs the customer-facing group (we design and build complex computer hosting solutions and software for clients; our coolest is an interactive menu site for a catering company that makes and delivers gourmet meals for start-ups like ours. In what can only be defined as not surprising, our office doesn't subscribe to this service), and Brian, who's in charge of our internal testbed, where all the code our development team builds is put through its paces. Both the seniors, Jeff and Tran, work with Manjit, but the four of them collaborate on everything, like a tiny little nerdy family. I run a team of twenty people—two teams, really, fifteen in Manjit's, five in Brian's. Our service-level agreement for both is 24/7, because, as Sid would say, *we're so very agile.*

"You can do that, take time off?" Brian says. Brian is a perpetual wisecracker, on the cusp of thirty, a tireless, brainy worker with an endless capacity for creative problem solving, a riot of spiky brown hair, and a veritable Louvre of tattoos on his arms.

The other guys laugh, nudge each other.

"Starting when?" Manjit asks. Manjit is decked out in a collared shirt and dress pants as usual, his brown eyes thoughtful. He's studious and reserved, and doesn't talk unless he has something important to say. The two of us once stayed up for thirty-two hours while we moved our gear to a new data centre. I brought both him and Brian over from my last job.

"Starting now." I try to smile.

"Right on, boss lady," Brian says, even though I've been asking him for years to stop calling me that. After I give him a look he shrugs: *Who, me?*

"And how long?" Manjit asks.

"Two weeks," I say, which silences them all for a bit.

"You can do that?" Jeff asks, and he looks like he's only half kidding. "What if we need something?"

I try to sound positive. "I'll be on call, like usual. Just text me. Okay, let's get started." It's hard not to worry, looking at everything to do; as usual, there are so many things that could go wrong. The five of us start slogging through all of it. I lose track of how many times I say *just in case* and *don't forget.* Just in case, I'll do it before I go. Don't forget to turn up this, and turn down that, and do this maintenance, and oh yeah, this client is crazy so call him directly. All of this is punctuated by the never-ending buzzing and checking of all of our phones, the eternal ballet of corporate crisis management. We finally come to the end of the to-do list, and everyone looks around the room, expecting more, but it's one-thirty already and everyone is about as paranoid as I want them to be, so it's not a bad time to break.

"I think we're done," I say.

"Cool," Brian says. "Okay, lunch? 'Cause I'm starvin'."

"Sure," I say, pretending I don't see Manjit's quiet eyes on me.

As the guys pack up, everyone except Manjit exchanges barbs and a few well-timed mom jokes, and then we all go back to our desks to divest ourselves of our laptops before lunch. I'm doing a quick check on my email to make sure nothing is pressing, when Susie careens around my office door, decked out in a pink monstrosity that's part dress, part fashion crime; too short, too tight, too ridiculous. If she sneezes she'll fly out of it.

"Hi Viive," she says. Her voice is cutesy-breathy in a practiced sort of a way and she's pronounced it "Veeev," the way she always does. I want to like Susie, who was recommended by Brian and has worked for me for three months, but she squeezes herself into shirts so low that someone dropped a pen in her cleavage last week during a cross-functional planning meeting. Not someone from my team, but still.

"Viive," I say.

"Veeev," she agrees, nodding. Her smile is beatific.

"What are you wearing?" I gesture at the taffeta train wreck in front of me.

"Retro party," she says, giving me two thumbs-up.

"It's two-thirty in the afternoon."

"Party's right after work, didn't want to be late."

"Aren't you supposed to be racking the new servers in the testbed right now?" I ask.

"Yup."

"Then you need to wear something appropriate, please."

Susie looks like she might–and I'm not making this up–cry.

"I don't want your dress to snag on something. I don't want you to get hurt." I don't want to say that the spectacle of Susie's pink meringue will convince Sid that my vacation should last forever and ever.

Susie still looks as if she's deciding whether to weep or not. The truth is that lately she's started crying if she doesn't get what she wants, a tactic which has been more successful than I'd like to admit. "So, can you please change?" I ask.

And then she flounces–I swear to God, flounces–out of my office. I've been thinking I might need to fire Susie, but I've managed to make it this far in my career without letting someone go, and I'd rather not start now, what with all the other things going on. Because with me maybe being fired and all, I kind of have my hands full.

The day drags on, as bad days do, and after work I make my way to my sister-in-law's place via a combination of subway and GO train that does nothing to improve my mood. Right now I'm sitting in her kitchen, wondering if I could ever be the kind of person who makes their own salad dressing, because Nate's sister, Avery, is whisking vinaigrette with the frenzy of a circus performer, and just watching her is exhausting. I'm observing her from my perch and sipping soda water and ice from an impossible-to-spill tumbler; Avery has given me kiddie glasses ever since an unfortunate grape juice incident six years ago. She can hold a grudge, that Avery. On the other hand, she does it in a smiley kind of a way that's hard to hold against her. If I had to think of one word for Avery, it would be *pert.*

Sometimes I wonder what pert becomes when you get older.

She stops what she's doing and beams at me while walking over to the fridge. Avery is compact, her hair caramel-coloured just like Nate's; shoulder-length, stick-straight, and well-behaved. (I like to think that her hair is scared into submission.) Her eyes are the same green as Nate's, and she's a lot shorter than I am, maybe a smidge over five feet. Big neck, tiny feet. It's funny, the details you notice about people. Tonight she's wearing that awful perfume again, and I lean back as subtly as I can, to stay out of her orbit, but she notices anyway; narrows her eyes. Avery is excellent at noticing things.

The guests for dinner tonight are a fusion of my family and Nate's: my mom, Nate and I, but not Avery's husband, Patrick, who was called away at the last minute to deal with a problem in their Calgary office. Nate's parents are living in Seattle these days, and they come as often as they're able, which everyone agrees is never often enough. My dad is in the U.K. right now, working on a never-ending merger/acquisition/accounting thing, and my younger brother Martin refuses to leave the downtown core on a Friday.

I roll the ice cubes around in my glass while I watch Avery put the finishing touches on dinner. It's a small kitchen for such a big house; a monster home in Ajax with a tiny yard and two SUVs in the garage. The fan over the stove, turned on to dilute the smoke from something smelted to one of the burners, is blowing Avery's perfume around, eau de migraine. I might not have any food sensitivities, but I do sometimes have a problem with scents. Nate and I have been asking her to stop wearing this particular perfume for years.

Right now, my headache is in that muted, dangerous stage where it could go either way; get better, or rampage around my skull like a tantruming toddler. This stage, I like to think of as the squeeze; solid, steady, tortuous pressure. My skin is humming with it.

"I'm glad we were finally able to get together," Avery says, her shoulders hunched in the way of short angry people.

I press my hand against my forehead. "Hmm?" I glance up from my glass to meet her gaze.

"Last time you cancelled at the last minute, so we had to reschedule, remember?"

I do remember. I had a major outage at work which was punctuated by a whopper of a migraine. I've always wondered how Avery can stay irritated at such trivial things for ages when Nate forgets slights the minute they happen.

"Remember?" she repeats. She's holding the spatula in her hand a little like it's a weapon.

"Work stuff," I mumble. "I'm sorry."

"One of your headaches again," she corrects. "I really wish you'd try harder to come to family get-togethers."

"It's dinner, Avery," I say. "It's essentially an excuse to eat a ham."

"It's so much more than that."

"Okay, it's a really *good* excuse to eat a ham." I try to smile at her, to lighten the mood in the tiny room.

Avery stops what she's doing, leaving the oven door open, letting the warmth leak into the already overheated kitchen. It's so close and crowded that it's getting hard to breathe. I pick up the designer purse she gave me for Christmas, which I only use when I come to see her–it's bedazzled–and root around for my all-purpose bottle of pills. If I ever actually packed all the bottles from all the different medications I take there'd be no room for anything else in any of my handbags, so every once in a while I top up a portable pillbox, which, because it's made out of a clear plastic, ends up looking colourful and faintly cheerful. I search for a while before finding the two I want. I usually think of my pills in terms of colour. These ones are blues; over-the-counter, only-sometimes-work blues.

"What are those pills?" Avery leans against the wall and pours herself a glass of wine.

"Nothing." Why, I wonder, didn't I just go to the bathroom and take them there? *Idiot.*

"Doesn't look like nothing."

I sigh. "Your perfume is giving me a headache."

"Don't be ridiculous, smells don't cause headaches." Avery refuses to believe even the most basic science about migraines; she once told me the reason I get them is because I sometimes go to bed at night with my hair wet.

I reach back into my bag and pull out my phone, so I can text Nate to see how much longer he's going to take. After that, I wash the pills down with the soda water. The light in the kitchen is getting brighter, and Avery is starting to look small and far away, like I'm seeing her through a pinhole, and the realization turns my stomach into knots. *Shit.* The tunnel vision and nausea are excellent signs a migraine is on the way. I cover my eyes for a minute, kneading my forehead before running my hand slowly down my face. I try to calm my breathing, smother my worry. Stress always makes things worse.

"You should have a glass of wine, you'll feel better."

Booze with a maybe-migraine? Also not awesome, which Avery's well aware of. "No thank you."

My phone buzzes, and I pull it out of my purse. There's a text from Nate, saying, "Picking up your mom now. There soon."

I don't think I can survive any more time alone with Avery, a thought that makes me sad, albeit briefly. When Nate first brought me home to meet his parents–back when they were in Toronto and Avery was still living with them–she and I got along great. We used to do fun stuff together, go out for drinks every once in a while, have lunch. But I missed returning too many phone calls. Too much work, too many headaches. She finally gave up after I couldn't make her thirtieth birthday party. I always have the best intentions when I see Avery, to get along, to try to spark our old friendship back up. The truth is, I miss her. I glance down; I'm holding onto my glass so tightly my fingers hurt. I transfer it to my left hand and flex out the fingers on my right. Then I take a sip of soda, which lingers in my mouth a lot longer than it should. It's getting hard to swallow now, and all I can think is: *Please don't get worse, please don't throw up, fall down, make a scene.*

"I have a friend at work who used to have migraines," Avery says. "He's totally fixed now! I could get the name of his neurologist."

I try not to sigh. "Sure."

"I'll call him for you." Avery starts chopping onions on a board in her brisk, no-nonsense way. The noise of the knife against the wood is too loud, just too much for the small room. Something rotten darts around my stomach and I shiver. And that's when I know I'm going to be sick.

"Excuse me," I say.

Avery exhales loudly as I walk away. We're not allowed to wear our shoes in her house, so I can feel the nap of the carpet against my feet like sandpaper as I go. Every sensation is amplified now; louder, shinier, squishier than it should be. Instead of using the powder room on the main floor, I go upstairs so Avery won't hear me, and I barely get the door shut before I'm heaving, my face in my hands, my insides burning, my arms shaking. After I'm done throwing up I rinse my mouth out and sit on the side of the bathtub. My legs are so weak I can't stand.

There's a moment where it's just me and the bathroom, cocooned against the world in general and Avery specifically. I put my head down on the bathroom counter, an oasis of cool pressed against my head.

And I wait.

Eventually I root around in my purse to get some Gravol and some yellows–ergotamine–a migraine drug cooked up by a faceless pharmaceutical conglomerate fat off Viagra. I swallow the Gravol, dry, one at a time. And then I hold the two yellows in my hand while I sit there, trying to calm my breathing, waiting to see if I'm going to be sick again, my head full of medication mumbo-jumbo: If I take this now, will it work? Do I need to go home to bed? How much medication do I have left for the rest of the month? Will I be okay this evening if I don't take it? If I take one now, what if I really need two and it's too late? Can I take a chance on tonight if Avery doesn't take off her perfume? (Probably not, but miracles do happen.) What if I eat something? That might work. And I might feel better now that I've been sick. What if I take two more of the blues and give it a half hour and see what happens?

I hate this, the exhausting migraine logistics that are part and parcel of this stage. It's sort of like those choose-your-own-adventure books you read when you were a kid, only a lot less fun and with a lot more drugs. Taking the heavy-hitting migraine meds might knock the misery out of my brain, but it'll also probably knock me on my ass. And there's only so many of these you can have a month, so if you don't really need them and you take some, you're about as screwed as screwed can get. On the other hand, to actually work, you need to take migraine meds at the first sign of an attack. If I'm really honest with myself–no crossed fingers under my desk this time–do I really need them?

Breathe. Don't ruin dinner. You can do this.

I stand up, examine myself in the mirror. My eyes are bloodshot, my brain thumping with pain. All I want is an icepack and a bed and ten hours of silence, but since I can't have that, I adjust my shirt, a black blouse with long sleeves over black jeans, and try to ready myself for the outside world. I wash my hands, run some toothpaste over my teeth with my finger and turn to leave, but the room tilts away from me and I have to steady myself on the bathroom counter. *Shit.* There are bad signs and very bad signs, and if I'm having balance problems, that's a *very very* bad sign. Waiting another half hour could be too late and then I'll end up spending the whole weekend in bed.

I try not to think about what Avery is doing in the kitchen while I'm up here, what snide comments she's going to pelt me with when I finally come back downstairs, while my left temple bangs against the inside of my skull like it does when it's about to really get going. I try to remember the last family dinner I didn't ruin in some way, a thought that brings tears to my eyes. And that's when I pull out two yellows and swallow them, with water cupped in my hand this time. Instantly, I feel like I've made the wrong decision, and a sweaty sort of guilt runs through me. If I use all the meds all up before the end of the month, I won't be able to go to Thanksgiving dinner. Plus, the yellows make everything blurry around the edges, like I'm not really there. How many do I have left anyway? I look at the yellows in the bottle and mentally count the ones still at home. Only four left.

I try to calm my breathing and not think about anything but getting through the next five minutes, and then surviving the five after that until I can finally run the clock out on the evening. Finally, I get up, run some cold water over my wrists, and head back downstairs. Nate and my mom are taking off their coats in the entranceway.

"Hi, sweetheart," Nate says when he sees me. He kisses me on the lips before giving me a hug that squeezes every inch of me, the first relief I've felt in hours. Nate looks, as always, boyishly charming, with messy caramel hair I have to pat back into place all the time, a formerly thin frame that's starting to plump up, beautiful green eyes, a lazy, gorgeous smile. I kiss him back.

My mom stands there, a little off to the side like always, before putting her arms out for a hug. The two of us are about the same height, but she's just a smidge taller; five nine-ish, maybe. Viking-sized. We have almost the same colouring, too, the same blue eyes, the same wintery pale skin. Her chin-length blonde bob has always been a little too severe for my taste, though; my same straw-coloured hair is a lot longer, snaking past my shoulders in a boring sort of a way. She puts one of her hands under my jaw and looks me in the eyes.

"You have a migraine," she says, in Estonian.

"Ei, on korras," I say. *No, I'm fine.*

"What did you do?" she asks.

"I don't know. I didn't really eat much at lunch–"

"Mmmhmmm," she says.

"And Avery's perfume is making me sick," I finish.

Nate sighs. "I'll go talk to her." He kisses me again before heading to the kitchen, a bottle of wine crooked in his arm.

My mom is clutching some flowers and a *kringel*, a sugared braid of Estonian bread, in one hand. I crane my neck to see the label of the DVD that's in her other, eventually realizing it's a documentary about the Brooklyn Bridge. You'd better believe we're going to watch it before the night is over; my mom is a civil engineer, a partner at her firm, and has been smitten with bridges as long as I can remember. I'm the only kid I know whose summer trips consisted of visits to nowhere. I've been to more viaducts, suspension bridges, and causeways than anyone I've ever met, except for Martin, who slept through most of it.

"You have to eat," she says. "I gave you those protein bars. Have you been carrying them with you?"

"They taste horrible, *Ema*."

"Don't 'Mom' me. When I was growing up–"

"You walked uphill both ways. I know, Ema."

"Vaata," my mom says with an eyeroll, a catch-all Estonian phrase that means, literally, "look," but can stand in for such diverse meanings as: *oh my God, no way*, or sometimes simply, *shit*.

Nate and Avery, in the kitchen, are speaking in raised voices.

"Ema–"

She sighs in the put-upon way of mothers from every culture. "Ma ütlen ainult–"

"You're only saying what?" Nate asks, back from the kitchen. Nate's been plugging away at Estonian classes for the last few years, which have been paying off in wonderful ways, since my mom has a bad habit of talking about people in front of them, Nate included. He learned mostly to make her stop, and now my mom is both proud of him and stymied by his actions, which, I have to say, is one of the neatest checkmates I've ever seen. Nate is exactly like this.

My mom hooks her arm under his and pats him with her other hand. "Viive didn't have lunch again."

Nate untangles his arm so he can put it around me. "Really?"

"I got paged while I was eating," I mumble, guilt worming its way through me.

Avery calls us in to dinner then, and my mom and I sit together on one side of Avery's long, rectangular table. Nate sits at the end, and Avery across from the two of us. I glance at Nate and then my mom; the four of us look like an unlikely bunch, sun-deprived Scandinavians beside hearty Canadians.

"Can you carve, please?" Avery asks Nate. Her face is squished like she's an eight-year-old; her makeup has disappeared and she looks furiously scrubbed. I sniff, tentatively, to see if she's still wearing the perfume. I can't smell anything, and I'm immediately sorry I took those yellows. Briefly, I rest my forehead in my palm. I'm going to need them later this month, I just know it. I try to ignore the sweat dotting the back of my neck.

"Don't you think, Viive?" Avery asks, mispronouncing my name in her special way, elongating the Is and dropping her voice at the start so it sounds like a car starting: ViiiiiVEH.

"I'm sorry, what?"

She purses her lips. "Don't you think we should talk about how our days went?"

My mom says, "I got stuck in a five-hour meeting, and I am very grateful for this delicious dinner. Thanks so much, Avery. It looks like you did loads of work."

And it does. There's a ham, three kinds of potatoes, and green beans with what looks like slivered almonds. Canadian food. I adore it, but I have to force myself not to flinch when Avery serves. She always gives everyone huge portions, and my mom is absolutely not someone you can waste food in front of.

"Just a little bit of everything, please," I say. My stomach seems less upset, but my head is getting heavier, partly because of the almost-migraine, partly because of the medication that's supposed to fix it.

"It's delicious," Avery says, and she can't hide the gleam in her eyes.

"I'm sure it is," I say, more firmly. "But I'm not that hungry."

"I thought you said she didn't eat lunch," Avery says to my mom.

"My stomach is just a little queasy. I'll be fine in a few minutes."

"Really, Viive, can't we have one family get-together which doesn't revolve around you and your…" Avery sniffs. "Problems?"

"Absolutely," I say, trying to keep my teeth from grinding against each other. "Let's talk about something else. Anything else."

My mom smiles sweetly and says, "Viive isn't healthy like you, Avery." She puts her plate out for Avery to serve. "And I would love some food, please."

My mouth is beginning to feel like it's full of cotton, and the room is taking on a fishbowl-like glow. Maybe I took the yellows too late, after all. I try to muffle the fear hiccupping inside me.

God, there are so many ways to be wrong.

Avery serves my mom and sits down with a thump.

"Avery," Nate says, probably more sharply than he meant to. Then he holds out a serving spoon. I take it in my hand and focus on getting it from the bowl of potatoes to my plate without my hand shaking. I do not want to spill something. Once all the food is safely shuttled to my dish, I take a small bite. I chew while the three of them talk over me, like I'm here, but not really here. Finally finished, I take another bite of potato. Bland food is always easier to eat after being sick.

A little later, my mom squeezes my hand with a smile, before putting her knife and fork on her plate, exactly at four o'clock. Her napkin follows. She looks interested as Nate chats to her about his latest project at work, and when she thinks no one's watching, she lifts the napkin to make sure the cutlery is still in the right spot.

After dinner we eat the *kringel* my mom has baked (delicious, chewy, and sweetly ethnic), and talk about safe, polite things: gardening, work, the weather. While we're having tea and coffee, we watch the documentary about the bridge, which, as bridge documentaries go–and I've seen a lot–is excellent. When we get up to leave, my legs falter a little, and Nate puts his arm under mine easily, like he does this all the time, which he does. Sometimes it feels like I can't walk without him.

"How are you feeling?" he asks.

"I'm fine." It's a sneaky kind of a moment, when I pretend to be okay, and Nate pretends to believe me. To push past it I say, "I'm sorry."

"Nothing to be sorry for, sweetheart." He holds my elbow tighter. But I am sorry, and it seems like I'm always sorry lately. Every once in a while I wonder what our marriage would be like if I wasn't sorry all the time. But right now it's time to figure out how to put one foot in front of the other and get to the car. Every step costs me something, and my feet are clumsy with medicine and sickness, my equilibrium is on hiatus, and the street lights are fun-house bright and jagged like knives.

While Nate drives home, he and my mom chat while I try to follow the ins and outs of their conversation, but it all seems so complicated, even though they're only talking about people at work, things my mom wants to do this weekend. Everything is blurry around the edges, like everything is far away and happening to someone else. When we drop my mom at home, she kisses me on my forehead and gives me a stern-but-loving motherly look that I've never seen on anyone else's mother, and then she's gone.

Nate heads toward our place, and when he turns onto our street he says, "One of my co-workers is having a maternity leave drink-thing tomorrow night. Want to come?"

"Which one?"

"The kleptomaniac. Karen."

I have to search my memory for who Karen is, and when I finally remember I feel like an idiot, because Karen the klepto has figured prominently in Nate's workplace shenanigans over the past year. She's an executive assistant who "borrows" things off people's desks. She doesn't usually take anything big: staplers, pens, stress balls. Nate thinks she does it because she's trying to get fired. His latest theory is she got pregnant because she finally gave up on being terminated after lifting her boss's iPad without consequence a few months back. She had it listed on eBay before anyone figured out it was gone.

"Should someone pregnant really be drinking?" I ask.

"Depends on whether you believe she's actually pregnant."

I laugh. Nate likes pretty much everyone, which is why, against all odds, he likes Karen. "Sure," I say.

"We can go for dinner afterwards. That Thai place we like is near where we're going."

"Okay," I say, rubbing the back of my neck, the skin warm and feverish under my hand.

Nate smiles at me as he parks the car, and the two of us go inside and make our way upstairs, his arm still looped under mine, his body solid and reliable beside me. Then we lie down in bed together, his face in my hair, my lips against his forehead.

"I love you," I say to his ear, and then he squeezes my hand while he smiles. It's a nice end to a bad day, which is about as good as it gets around here these days. And so maybe that's why I let him fall asleep, leaning on me, giving him the tiniest bit of comfort for once instead of telling him about my impending not-really-a-vacation. I think about how loving Nate is, how he takes care of me, how he never complains. When we got married they should have just said: Viive will get all the better and Nate will get all the worse, because that's what's happened.

Nate is a saint, if you think about it. Sometimes the idea of it makes me smile–an urban saint working in the downtown core, wearing khakis, obsessed with computers, his hero Tesla instead of Superman. But I definitely don't want to be married to a saint, and Nate definitely doesn't want to be one.

So you can see how that complicates things.

2 – UNEXPECTEDLY ROMANTIC DATA SYSTEMS

Yesterday's migraine is full-out this morning, every inch of my brain squeezed to the brim with it, the tug at my left frontal lobe punctuating every heartbeat with a wave of pain, like there's a weather system inside me. I roll over to snuggle with Nate, but his side of the bed is cold and empty, and then I remember he was paged at five a.m. and had to go in to work, even though this is a Saturday. I try to get back to sleep, but it's impossible to stifle the worry that the pain from last night has stirred up inside me. How much longer will this one last? How bad will it get?

I shuffle downstairs to make some tea and find a note in the kitchen scrawled in Nate's handwriting that says *Bite me!* I'm a little amazed that Nate would make breakfast so early in the morning, but he does have a long history of leaving me tasty snacks with intriguing suggestions. Underneath the note is a small plate of bacon, the pan soaking in the sink. I love it when Nate cooks, but have to admit that every time he pours the bacon fat down the drain it makes my stomach clench a little. In the house I grew up in, our socks were darned, our Ziplocs were reused, the bacon fat was conserved, and I had the same lunch box for six years. Sesame Street, duct tape on two of the corners. We were solidly middle-class, and if you looked around there was enough, food on the table, a roof over our heads. But, always, there was a little voice asking: *Are you sure? Are you really sure there's enough?* Our chest freezer was packed to the brim, *just in case*, my mother would say. And then she'd add something else, Tetris in an extra meatloaf like only an engineer could.

I pick up the three pieces of bacon and my pot of tea and pad to the living room, still in my bathrobe, before washing down two yellows with the Earl Grey, a combo that'll hopefully crush the ache in my head. *Only two yellows left now.* Then I turn on the television, the sound on low. In the background, the next-door neighbour's dog barks himself demented. I try to focus on the TV but the figures on the screen are all small and bleary. Smudged. I close my eyes and then open them, trying to focus, but everything stays misty, like the living room has been relocated to the Scottish moors.

Luckily my stomach is fine this morning, so I can eat the bacon, the saltiness making me swoon, probably the only bright spot in what's going to be another shitty day. After a bit, I open my laptop and check on work, reading through an email from Manjit, about an issue that happened overnight with one of our customers. I can barely see my computer screen or think straight enough to make any kind of sense of it. *God, I can't do anything right.* Eventually I muddle through the problem and text him, telling him to run some diagnostics on the client's database and email me back.

My stomach growls, like the bacon never happened, and so I go to the kitchen to forage through the fridge; there are two no-name colas, a clump of wilted greens, and some science-fair-like leftovers I can't deal with emotionally right now. *Shit.* I shuffle back to the couch, my eyes falling on the abandoned laundry basket I've been meaning to take upstairs for the last week, a fortuitous bit of laziness on my part. All I need to do is rummage through it and find some clothes, put them on, and walk to the corner to get something to eat for lunch. *Easy. You can do it.* I sit for a minute, corralling my strength. Finally, I pull on a pair of jeans, slowly so I can keep my heart rate controlled, and then I assemble an unattractive but functional ensemble. I waver after the final zipper is pulled; the store suddenly seems so far away, like the half a block is a flattened-out, Everest-sized trek. *Stop whining and just do it,* I tell myself, like I'm in a Nike ad for underachievers.

When I finally gather enough strength to head out the door, I make my way slowly, like a shut-in who hasn't been out in years, while my headache clangs inside me, punctuating every step. *You can do this, walk to the corner, buy a sandwich. Millions do it every day.* The store is really a gas station with an attached Tim Horton's, a Canadian institution devoted to the worship of sugary baked goods. Inside, the shelves all showcase food that's making me fatter just by looking at it; buying a house around the corner from a twenty-four-hour convenience store really has ruined me.

I shuffle over to the cash, which is manned by a teenage girl who's blonde, bubbly, and loud. Her green eyes are wide and friendly, her ponytail sprouting out of the top of her head like an exuberant fountain. The racks are stacked with pastries and donuts, the displays made of a metal so shiny it hurts my eyes. It's warm in the store, and the air is sugary sweet. Nothing really feels real, though, like I'm trapped inside the world's worst virtual reality game.

The cashier smiles at me before asking what I want, and I reply with a noise that sounds like, "Ieughg." I shake my head and try to ignore the confused expression on her face and the sharp pinch of embarrassment in my gut that follows it. I try to loosen my jaw so I'll stop slurring my words like a drunkard. My ears are getting hot. *Focus.* "Sorry. I'll have..." Now that I'm so close, all of the options look even more enticing. "One cinnamon bun...okay, make that two, and a medium coffee double double, please."

"Anything else?" she asks.

"Chicken noodle soup?"

"Sure," she says, ringing up the sale. "Have a nice day!"

"You too," I say, trying to smile while I collect my food. All I want to do is go home and eat, but the shoemaker is the next store over and I was supposed to pick up a pair of boots weeks ago. I stand there for a minute, so long that people start to brush past me, all of them on the way somewhere interesting. *It'll only take a second,* I pep-talk myself as I head there. The door jingles when I open it.

I can do this.

"Hi Viive," the owner says from behind the counter. He's Greek and stooped, skinny like a rake. His smile is tired but friendly, like always.

I focus on speaking clearly. "Aleksander. How are you?" The store's pungent leather perfume is more magnified than usual today, and it makes my nose start to run. And here I thought I couldn't get any less sexy.

Out of nowhere my right knee buckles and I have to put my hand on the counter to steady myself. It's hard to look nonchalant about it, but Aleksander, thankfully, pretends not to notice. "Can't complain," he says, taking the call ticket from my hands. He searches the shelves, finally getting on a small stool so he can go through the upper racks.

Both my hands are on the counter now. After only a minute or so it feels like I've been standing there for hours, and all the shoes on all the shelves have started to blur into a soupy shoe goulash.

Maybe this wasn't such a good idea.

Aleksander smiles again when he finally places my boots on the counter in front of me. "We replaced the zipper, here," he says, zinging it up and down with a flourish. "Is okay now."

That tiny action flutters in front of me, sending ripples through the air. I try to blink it away. "How much?"

"For you? Eight dollars."

"Thanks." I count the money out, smile at him, and turn to leave. The quiet but deliberate sound of him clearing his throat stops me. "Something wrong, Aleksander?"

He's thumbing the money in his hand, a collection of coins. "Is okay, Viive. No problem."

I try to concentrate on his palm, and after it finally slides into focus, a blush sears my cheeks. I open my wallet and take out two more dollars. "I'm so sorry, Aleksander, I'm not feeling well."

"It's okay." He smiles. "Go home and rest, you'll feel better tomorrow."

I nod at him before leaving, my cheeks still burning, and when I get home I collapse on the couch, exhausted. It seems impossible that so few steps have wiped me out, that every ounce of energy I had is gone, but my back is dotted with sweat and my heart is pounding in my chest and echoing in my head. The trip was a success but I still feel like a failure; normal people get up and go to the store all the time. It's not something you should have to plan for or recover from or write to Dear Abby about. It's only half a block away, for Christ's sake. I feel like bursting into tears, but I can't let myself. Crying with a migraine is excruciating.

I try to calm my heartbeat while I turn my attention to my computer. Manjit has followed up on the problem from this morning with an email saying, *"That problem from earlier is fixed."* I reply to him with a thank you, and after a minute I take a small, tentative bite of the cinnamon bun. The pastry sticks to the roof of my mouth before making its way into my stomach, and after a few minutes I can feel it, the hum of sugar in my veins. Food really is the only thing that makes me feel good while I have a headache (if my stomach is calm enough, that is), especially sugar, or salt or fat or all three together. I sigh, momentarily content.

After a while I eat the soup and tuck the other bun away for Nate, a miniscule act that makes me feel good inside. It seems like forever since I did anything nice for him. On the way back to the living room I grab an icepack out of the freezer, and when I lie down on the couch I position it under my temple. The cold biting into my skin is a new kind of pain, but I have to endure it so that numbness can try to freeze out my headache. And then I'm unconscious, dozing on and off, the headache taffy-pulling itself around my skull every time I come to. I finally wake up fully when my phone buzzes with a text from Nate, late in the afternoon: "We're changing the venue for Klepto Karen's thing, it's now at Roncy and Dundas."

I rub my temples before moving around a little, taking my senses for a test drive. The TV is still on but muted, the screen a motley jumble of colours. The ping pong tournament in my head is better than this morning, but something's still rattling around in there, a pain that's dull but determined. Waiting.

My phone buzzes again, with another text, "Let me know you got this–I don't want you to go to the wrong place. Love you."

I pick up my cell. I don't want to cancel but I just can't do it, face small talk in a noisy, crowded bar. I can barely manage shoes and soup today. And I won't be good company. Hell, I can barely stand to be around myself. I don't want to embarrass Nate in front of the people he works with when I slur my words or wobble on my feet, and I definitely don't want to short-change someone else like I did with Aleksander. Nate won't care–there'll be a ton of people there. I type out a response: "Gonna pass, if it's okay. Not feeling so hot."

After a few minutes, my cell rings. "Is everything alright?" I ask. Nate almost never phones me.

"I'm fine," he says. "Why aren't you coming tonight?"

"I'm sorry."

"What's wrong?"

"I have a bit of a headache," I say. It comes out: ihafbitofheadaghe.

Nate sighs; not a deep, annoyed sigh, but a familiar sound that reminds me of all the other times I've cancelled on him, all those disappointments. "Are you sure? My new boss is going to be there and I really want him to meet you."

"I'm sorry, Nate," I say, my breath catching in my throat.

"It's all right, Vee. Do you want me to come home instead?"

After a beat, I say, "No, honey. It's okay. I'll be fine. Love you."

"I won't stay late." After Nate says an Iloveyoutoo and hangs up I sit there for a while, looking at the TV without really seeing what's going on. *I'll go next time. I'll be better next time. I'll make it up to him next time.* When the TV flashes a Tim Horton's commercial I think about that second pastry. *It'll probably be stale by the time Nate comes home*, I lie to myself. I get up and retrieve the sticky bun from the pantry, and pull off a tiny flake of sugar, sucking on my finger until it's gone. Something surges in my brain.

Eventually, I doze, a fitful sleep full of nightmares. At one a.m. I wake up and Nate's still not home, the TV buzzing, the room dark. Before going to bed I take all the wrappers from my food, the telltale bags the donuts come in, and push them down in the garbage can, putting a few plastic grocery bags on top. It doesn't escape me that I've eaten the only nice thing I've done for Nate in months, a thought that turns my gut oily with guilt.

It's harder than usual to get out of bed the next morning. I burrow myself deeper into the covers and roll over. Nate is already gone, his side of the bed cold. Nate has always gotten up first, ever since we got together in the halcyon days of the Internet. If I close my eyes I can see it all like it was yesterday: we had his-and-hers engineering degrees–mine computing, his mechanical–and we spent all our time in a small, sweaty office. Every day started with a jumble of avant-garde ideas and ended with most of the office having dinner while the cleaning staff vacuumed around us. I moved closer to work so I wouldn't waste time commuting, and in a neat bit of efficiency, Nate and I started having sleep-overs. At that point, there was no time to spare; we were burning sixteen-hour days at work, more on bad days, otherwise known as weekends.

On the other hand, the office was exactly where we wanted to be. Young, dumb, energetic—we were a workforce ready to be squeezed. That was years ago, before the Internet industry busted wide open and left us with stock options good for nothing but drying our tears.

As soon as we realized we had a hankering to see each other naked, and considering the fact that our start-up was merrily going bankrupt, Nate left for a more stable international company, and I went to another start-up, which designed websites for hospitals and promptly entered Chapter 7. Nate and I kept bouncing from job to job, both of us picking up more technical certifications: MCSE, CCNA, NCIE. Our relationship is alphabet-soup awesome.

A few years ago Nate and I found enough time to think about moving out of that shitty basement apartment and getting married. Neither one of us wanted a big pouffy wedding, so we spent a Friday afternoon at City Hall with a small group of friends and family before going for dinner at the Ruth's Chris Steak House afterwards. We decided it would be brilliant to spend all the money we'd saved on a house. Too much money, I'd argued, but Nate overruled me with good humour and promises of happily ever after, which is why we're now house-poor. (*Almost* house-poor, actually, because I've socked a few dollars away in an account Nate doesn't know about.) East end, on the Danforth. We bought a fixer-upper with promise, in an "emerging" neighbourhood near Pape called "The Pocket," a charming area of winding streets and happy couples. The Danforth is the Greek area of Toronto; within a ten minute walk from my house I can see belly dancing, eat *briám,* and stop off at Baskin Robbins on the way home. The houses are circa late 1800s, the neighbourhoods are a cosy mix of post-war bungalows, stereotypical Toronto semis, and Victorians.

We ended up in a semi-detached handyman's dream. Unfortunately, neither of us knew we had no talent for spackle or that Nate was allergic to drywall dust. I insisted on moving in during the winter because it was cheaper, a moronic decision that led to no small amount of misery that Nate has never once complained about. Our house is a narrow 976 square feet that I round up to 1000 when people ask how big it is. Other than the wankers who steal our Halloween decorations, our neighbours are delightful, and for the most part we're all pretty quiet and mind our own business, except for the dog in the attached house next door, which barks at every conceivable hour of the day and night.

Eventually Nate and I abandoned the renovations (we agreed to live with mediocrity rather than spend any more weekends covered in spackle), and tried to shore up our careers and figure out what we wanted to do with the rest of our lives. About two years ago we decided we wanted to be our own start-up. We've been quietly putting things into place ever since, but at least one of us needs an executive title before we make the jump, or we'll never get investors. My father is a finance guy and he says we have a better chance of getting funding if the principals are a little more established, career-wise. Just in case. Last year at my review, Elliot laid out the future as he sees it, me promoted to director of technology, with him stepping back to focus on developing code. The only issue has been timing, or so he's been telling me.

But that was before all this.

Eventually I get up, slide out of the sheets, and face the morning. I find Nate sitting on the couch, reading something on his tablet, and he looks up when I come in. "Hi there," he says, smiling his trademark grin.

"Hi yourself," I answer, flopping down on the couch and leaning into him as he puts his arm around me and kisses the top of my head. He smells fantastic, as usual, a unique smell of soap, shampoo, and Nate. I prop myself up on him while he reads, my head on his shoulder. Eventually hunger nudges me to get up and grab a bag of chips from the pantry. I put most of the bag of zesty ketchup into a bowl, and join Nate back on the sofa. Then I reach over to my side of the couch, to the bottle of painkillers I always keep there, and shake out two whites and take them. Nate reaches over and grabs a handful of chips.

"Not feeling well?"

"I'm fine," I say, before massaging my ankles, try to rub some of the stiffness out of them. "Nate?"

"Mmmhmm?" he says, still engrossed in his tablet.

I wonder, briefly, if I can somehow hide the fact that I'm not going to be in the office for the next two weeks. I don't want to disappoint Nate any more than I already have, but I don't want that kind of life either. I take a deep breath. "I have something to tell you."

"What?"

"It's important," I say softly.

Nate puts the tablet to the side and reaches out to pull my hand into his. "Everything okay?"

"Well…I have good news and bad news."

"What's the good news?"

"We're going to be able to spend a lot more time together from now on."

"What's the bad news?"

"Well…" I exhale and tuck my feet under me, trying to ignore the clench in my stomach. "I kind of might be getting fired from work."

"Jesus Christ. What happened?"

I pull a pillow onto my lap and hug it. "Elliot and Sid pulled me into a meeting this week and told me I don't seem like my usual self and they're making me take a leave of absence to rest up and all that like a medical leave but using my own vacation time and then they said someone told them I've been lying down in the nurse's office a lot and that morale on my team is down." All of this bursts out in a rush of words, the last part little more than a strangled cough.

Nate makes a pissed-off noise, deep in his throat. "Morale is down on everyone's team because your company works the staff like it's a galley ship. And who would have told them you're lying down all the time if you're not?"

I run my fingers through my hair. "I have no clue. Nothing like this has ever happened before."

"What about that new guy–the one you told me about? Joe?"

I think about Joe and his penchant of sitting opposite me in the management meetings, his somewhat creepy staring at me, and his pushy attempts to have coffee with me and Otis. "I barely even know the guy."

"How long is this 'leave' for, anyway?"

"Two weeks."

"Well, that's not so bad." He exhales heavily.

I look away from Nate and rub my fingers over my forehead, before saying, "They say my headaches are out of control."

"Did Avery send you the number for that neurologist?"

"Yeah… I haven't called yet."

A shadow of disappointment flickers over Nate's face. He looks away and then back at me. I hate that I caused that look, that I've let Nate down again. I pluck at the corner of the pillow I'm holding.

"Maybe Sid and Elliot just want you to get better."

I give Nate a look.

"Well, I'm just saying."

"I don't trust Sid," I say. "I could never trust someone with a power colour."

Nate nods.

"It could mean they're setting me up to get fired, so that they have a history of problems with my performance, because, you know, they opened the conversation with 'You're definitely not fired.' It would have been, 'We love you so much we want you to take some time off and visit

Tahiti!' if it was really about a vacation. Sid probably wouldn't have been there, and the two of them wouldn't have been so…serious about everything. And they definitely wouldn't have asked for a goddamn doctor's note." I exhale a shaky breath. "I'll have to be perfect after this."

"I think you're perfect." Nate smiles.

I reach over to kiss him, take his hand in mine. The two of us are quiet for a while after that. Normally Nate and I are good at being quiet together, but this feels different, and not in a good way. I try to stifle the worry in my stomach; I don't want Nate to think of me as a failure, too.

"It'll be okay, Vee," he says, finally, pulling me into a hug.

"Promise?" I ask.

"I promise. And look on the bright side, you could take some time to catch up on all the things you haven't done. Like your taxes," he says, with a smile in his voice. He kisses the top of my head before releasing me and picking up his tablet computer again. After a minute, he says, "You should call the neurologist. It can't hurt, can it?"

It makes my stomach ache when he says things like this. I love Nate more than anything, but he's careless with life in a way I just can't be. And it's not just his enthusiasm for being house-poor or the bacon fat down the kitchen sink. What Nate doesn't understand is there *is* no magic pill for what I have, that the treatments for migraine can actually make things worse, that letting yourself hope for something different is nothing but heartbreak waiting to happen. I don't want to revisit the crushing years after the last time I tried to trick myself out of migraine disease, the crazy pain clinic, the constant push and pull of depression and failure. I don't want to talk about all the things I've lost along the way, what I've given up, or the thread of knowledge, running through me, that everything can be lost, at any moment. There's almost nothing standing between any of us and a chronic illness or injury—some misbehaving genes have their way with each other, a simple wrong turn becomes a car accident, a kid in the hockey rink pushes an opponent just a little too hard. So many ways for your life to change in an instant. Every plan Nate and I make for the future is built on quicksand, and we're not the only ones. Life is precarious, every single minute of it.

I come from a family of survivors, stubbornness a part of our very DNA. I know I can survive anything. It's Nate I'm not so sure about. Nate's world follows rules: *Do your best and everything will be okay. Try hard and things will work out fine.* My world has always revolved around *maybe*. And a part of me has always tried to protect him from what I know, because his untarnished optimism and his perpetual good humour are irresistibly charming, bundled up inside him. I've always taken after the Scandinavian side of my family: pale, morose, sauna-loving. I like the fact that Nate is my opposite.

I look over at him, his face partly in shadows while he taps away on his tablet. The truth is he's survived a lot already, but it would be nice for Nate to actually enjoy our life together for once, instead of just enduring it. It would also be nice to never see that disappointed look on his face again. I suddenly have an image of the two of us out for dinner, artisanal appetizers plated in front of us, white wine and candlelight on the table, me wearing a dress and lipstick, Nate in a suit. Navy pinstripes, maybe. If you looked around the restaurant, the two of us would seem exactly like all the other couples having a nice dinner on a Friday night. Boring, almost. And then I think: don't I owe it to Nate to at least try seeing a new neurologist?

So I say, "Maybe you're right," the *maybe* coming out of my mouth tinged with a doubt he doesn't notice.

"Good," he says, looking relieved, like everything is settled.

Later, when Nate pops out to the store to pick up more chips, I call my general practitioner–a nervous stick of a woman in her sixties, frazzled from years of toiling in one of North America's largest cities–and leave a message asking for a referral to Avery's friend's super-awesome neurologist.

Later, Nate and I lie together on the couch, our limbs entwined while we watch a bad rom-com, and only one of us is worried about what's going to happen next. To distract myself from the weight of that worry I think about one of my favourite memories of Nate: it was the second or third time we'd met, and we were having a lunch meeting about a project we were both working on (Nate likes to say we fell in love because of NetApp, a vendor of large-scale and unexpectedly romantic data systems). When we left the restaurant, I didn't notice that the latch hadn't caught behind me. Nate moved me to the side with a casual ease, put his hand around the door knob, and pulled it closed with a soft click. It didn't take long–just a few seconds–but it was the way he did it, quietly thoughtful, oddly attractive. And I thought: *I could watch that man close doors for the rest of my life.*

The only problem is that this is not how the rest of my life was supposed to go.

3 – We Have Angered The Squirrels

Sixteen hours of sleep leaves me dazed and buries the headache somewhere in the corner of my brain, thankfully. When I finally get up and settle in the living room with a pot of tea, I notice the vase perched on the mantle, full of tulips, purple ones. My favourite. This means Nate went out this morning, bought them, brought them back, and then put them in a vase, all before leaving for work. And Nate is no morning person. The smile on my face fades after a minute; if I don't do something nice for Nate soon I'm going to forget how.

I pour some tea and debate the week ahead. Mid-sip the phone rings, an almost startling noise in the small room, and a small puddle of tea spills out of my mug, barely missing my laptop.

"Hello?"

"Vieyvi McBroom?"

"Speaking?" I'm not sure why my words come out as a question, but the truth is I'm not capable of much coherence right after waking up.

The receptionist's voice is clipped and efficient, the perfect counterpoint to mine. "This is Dr. Throckmorton's office calling. I have your referral fax here. We have a cancellation for this afternoon. Can you make it here for twelve?"

I blink. I haven't taken a shower. I'm barely caffeinated. "I'm not sure–"

"Well," she says, "if you can't make it today, I don't have another opening for three months."

"Three months?" A minute or so passes while the two of us hold the line, and I think about Nate, and then the note I need so I can go back to work, and then Nate again.

"Okay," she says. "So should I put you in for twelve?"

"Yes, please."

"We're in Thornhill," she says. "Steeles and Dufferin." She might as well have said *far* and *incredibly far*.

"Thanks," I say, before the two of us hang up, and I peel my ass off the couch before aiming myself for the shower. By the time I'm done brushing my hair I realize a half hour has evaporated. If I'm going to get up there for noon, I have to leave five minutes ago.

It's crisp outside, with a sharp wind, and I have to go back into the house and find a coat, which I can't, so I have to finally settle on a sweater and hope for the best. The car doesn't start the first five or six times I try to turn it over, so I have to wait until it feels like behaving. Waiting is not my forte, but Nate and I can't afford to get a new car right now, not since his last gambling spree. Nate is convinced he's on the brink of figuring out some new system for playing online poker. He has such a great memory, he says, knows all the odds. It'll happen eventually, he says; I just have to be optimistic, he says.

This is why optimism is a mistake, my mother and I agree. I can remember when I was younger, and my mom would show me research studies about the perils of optimism, how people with positive outlooks have a less accurate perception of reality than pessimists. "Grounded," she would say. "Realistic. Dependable." All I ever wanted could be mine, with the right dose of pessimism and a really good slide rule, she'd say.

Finally, the car starts. I pull onto the street and head north while shaking out a box of M&Ms onto a Kleenex on the passenger seat. Every few blocks I pop one into my mouth. I finally find the office with the aid of my trusty GPS and a bit of non-denominational prayer.

The building is shiny and new, and according to the directory, Dr. Throckmorton is on the eighteenth. Naturally someone gets on or off the elevator at every single floor, and while I inch up the building I try to ignore the flutter of pain emerging at the back of my head. It's just a tension headache, a nothing sort of spasm, the kind I barely notice anymore.

When the elevator finally gets to eighteen, I step out, seven minutes late. There's no handy sign telling me which way to go, and after going right, and then left, and then right again, I finally find the office: *Dr. Lola Throckmorton*, the sign says, and I open the door in a rush. The reception area is all Art Deco, and tastefully expensive in a minimalist sort of a way. It looks much nicer than most doctors' offices, and for a second I feel a spark of hope. There's one other person waiting in reception, a woman who's sitting quietly in the corner. She looks dreadful, like she's going to pass out in her seat or throw up on my shoes. I smile at her a little as she meets my eyes and a quick look passes between the two of us, one that tells me I'm in the right place.

"I'm Viive McBroom," I say to the receptionist. "I have an appointment–"

"Yes, you do," she says, looking at me over the top of her thick black-framed glasses. She's twenty-something, her blonde hair is in a cranky little bun, her shoulders are bunched into a tweed jacket, and her face is screwed into a scowl. "We're running a little late today, which is good, or else–" She leaves the rest of her comment dangling there dramatically, as if waiting for me to break into self-flagellation.

Which, after a brief internal battle, I do. "I'm sorry," I say. "I didn't have quite enough–"

"Here's a checklist for you to complete. Please fill it out as quickly as possible." She thunks it into my hands, a thick sheaf of papers on a clipboard. I flip through it, counting twelve pages.

Question 1:

Have you missed any personal commitments in the last three months due to migraine? Family, work, etc.?

Question 2:

Do your headaches interfere with your ability to live a normal life?

There are little squares to check off, places for you to enumerate your migraine angst, true and false and multiple choice. After filling out the twelve pages, my hand is cramped and I'm wracked with depression; seeing all that dysfunction in black and white has a way of bringing things into an unpleasant sort of focus.

When I'm done I hand the checklist back to the receptionist, noticing the nameplate on the desk that's stamped *Shirl.* "Thank you," she says, giving me a small, hard smile that wrinkles her nose. If I had to pick one word to describe Shirl it would be *scrunched.*

Back in my chair, I pull out my phone and check my work email. Eventually, I hear, "Vyeve?"

"Viive," I say.

"Viyeveh," Shirl says. "Doctor will see you now."

We walk around the corner to a small office where I take a seat in a chair so comfortable each of my vertebrae feel like they're being individually massaged. The room is cosy, inviting, comforting: muted lights, hardwood floor, stylish window treatments. Baby blue. After a few minutes a woman comes in, shuts the door behind her, and then puts her hand out to shake mine. "Hello," she says. She's about my age, brunette hair pulled back in a messy-but-funky updo, black turtleneck, chequered pencil skirt, Fluevog shoes. She looks like the kind of person I'd like to be–hip, savvy, professional. That's all it takes for me to become intimidated by Dr. Throckmorton: *Hello.*

"Viive McBroom," I say as I shake her hand. She even smells better than I do.

"Why don't you run me through your history?" she asks with a practiced smile, flipping through my paperwork. I think about my migraine diagnosis at five, my hellishly painful adolescence, and the clinic I ended up at in my early twenties with a fist full of prescriptions for pills, most of which had horrifying side effects and didn't really work anyway; the daily beta blockers, the ergotamine chasers. I think about how I got sick to death of the endless stream of medications. One day I sat down and counted out all the pills I was taking every day: 23. That's when I gave up.

I give Dr. Throckmorton a sanitized, Coles Notes version. When she asks about triggers I tell her: some scents, hormones, alcohol, not eating, not enough sleep, too much sleep, life itself.

"So, there are a number of approaches we can take," she says, after I'm finished. "There's a new class of preventative medications–anticonvulsants–we're having some luck with. And no one's using ergotamine anymore. We're all about the triptans these days. More effective, less problems with rebound. You know what rebound is, of course?" Even though I nod, she continues, "Rebound occurs when headaches become chronic or daily. Traditional pain meds for migraine actually cause headache cycles if they're used for…oh, more than three times a week. The ergotamine family is particularly bad for this, so I'm not surprised you're having problems. We need to break the cycle you're in. Have you tried the new triptans?"

"I've read about them, but I wasn't sure…"

She raises an eyebrow and flips through the checklist. "Nothing is without side effects, or risk. Even crossing the street can be dangerous." She smiles, her teeth perfect. "But what you've written here shows that you satisfy the requirements for chronic migraine." She cocks her head, looks at me.

All I can think is: it's such a funny phrase, *satisfy the requirements…*

And then I fidget in my chair. *It's not really chronic, is it?* I try to think of the last day when nothing hurt, and I can't. Maybe it just became another part of my routine, the tug on my frontal lobe, the squeeze behind my ears, the perpetual three-ring circus in my head. Sort of like an old friend who wanted to crash on your couch for a few weeks but never left. It's funny, the things you can get used to. But it's not really that bad, is it?

I look up and see Dr. Throckmorton watching me quietly. "Well okay then," she says as if I'd agreed with her, which I haven't. While she scribbles on a prescription pad, part of my brain is churning with the thought that what she's saying can't be true if I haven't sided with her, but she keeps writing anyway. "Number one, stop taking the over-the-counter painkillers, they're making things worse. I've written you a prescription for a daily anticonvulsant-based preventative, and a triptan for acute migraine attacks. And here's a bunch of literature about lifestyle and diet work you can do on your own. I've also included a pamphlet about a local group for people with migraine. Have you ever been in a support group before?"

I almost snort. People in my family don't go out in public and complain about their lives. My family fled the communists, survived two years in a refugee camp, and then set up shop in a new country when they couldn't speak a word of the language, all without a single complaint. All without talking about it much at all, really. God only knows how they learned English.

"Um, no," I say.

Dr. Throckmorton raises an eyebrow. "It's an interesting bunch. You might want to check it out."

"Okay, thanks. When should I come back?"

"Three months." She smiles, stands up and pulls some brochures out from her desk, holds them out to me. "Nice to meet you, Viive. And good luck."

I look down, at the pile of paper that's suddenly in my hand, the helpful pamphlets, the prescriptions that'll more than likely bring a new crop of problematic side effects. There's more I want to say, but Dr. Throckmorton has already gone on to the next head case and I'm alone in the room. I close my eyes and remember the last time I went on a preventative, the cloying side effects, the dizziness, the perpetual nausea, the never knowing what was going to happen next.

I get up and go back down eighteen floors, heading home. I stop off at the pharmacy near my place, emerging with a paper sack of pills and a hopeful lump in my throat. After that, I go to a drive-through to get my favourite meal: a burger with large fries and a chocolate shake. As I chew, I try not to think of how hard it was to get these jeans on this morning.

Back on the couch, I take the bottle of preventatives, small cherry-red orbs, out of the reassuring paper sack, and then open it up and empty the bottle out on the coffee table in front of me. There aren't that many. Only a month's worth can be dispensed at a time; neurologists are always mindful of migraineurs' penchants for melancholy. I look at the pile a long time. I don't want to go down this road again, detailing all the crippling side effects from all the different drugs, the constant vigilance over every piece of food I put in my mouth, the months of pointless cheese deprivation. I've read all the literature, tried all the tricks. I know it all, I really do. And there's no reason to think this time will be any different. Optimism is Nate's bailiwick. Or my dad's, now that I think about it; the same optimism that told him to pick up and move to England for a year to work on a big project with a company none of us has ever heard of. I love my father, but this is one trait of his I don't want to acquire. I prefer two feet on the ground, good planning, hard work, the right results, just like my mom. So I have no plans to become an optimist. Unless I really have to.

But then I think: maybe it's better to make someone else decide. Maybe I should let someone else be in charge for once. Everything is in this little pile of red pills—my future, my job, my marriage. And that's why, after another long moment, I take my first one.

Nate gets home after eight and promptly flops on the couch beside me, pulling me into his arms in one smooth movement. He looks worn out, circles under his eyes, his hair more eccentric than usual. I lean into him, my head resting on his chest, and the two of us sit there like this for a while, watching but not really paying attention to the images on the TV screen. I don't think I even really know what show this is. Something violent and depressing. Eventually he says, "I need to take a conference call in my office. Can you get a pizza?"

"Sounds perfect," I say. He dislodges himself after giving me a kiss, and hands me the phone before heading upstairs. After I order the usual–Hawaiian with triple pineapple for him, pepperoni for me–I pick up my laptop and start working. Manjit has emailed about some odd entries in the security files for one of our web servers, and the two of us start parsing logs, trying to get to the bottom of it. After twenty minutes or so, I get an email from Nate saying, *"Can you come up here?"*

Yes, Nate and I email each other when we're both at home.

I go upstairs; Nate has left on the light in the bathroom, and I flick it off, telling myself not to nag at him about it. Our second bedroom, which doubles as Nate's office, is at the front of the house, over the porch. I knock gently on the door and then go in.

Nate swivels in his chair. "I think the squirrels are back."

The squirrels were here when we moved in, romping in the tiny crawlspace over the porch. When they really got going it sounded like a scratchy little rodent disco. Eventually we called an efficiently good-natured animal expert named Roy, who showed up with a truck sporting the slogan: TORONTO WE TAME YOUR WILDLIFE, which he parked right in front of our house, making the neighbours look at me suspiciously for weeks afterwards.

When Roy showed up, he assured me that his squirrel solution would work, and when I expressed some doubts, memorably promised to sleep on my roof until they were gone. After I expressed reservations, he assured me I'd never even know he was there. Roy is part of what I love about Toronto: the fierce, quirky entrepreneurship, even of the wildlife-extracting variety.

"Roy would never allow such a thing," I say to Nate now.

"I'll prove it."

I kiss the top of his head. "What are you working on?"

"Architecture schematics for the new email platform in New York."

"I love New York. Can we go?"

"Well, anything's possible. It's probability that's the–" He stops. "Listen."

After a few minutes of the two of us standing there like Parisian mimes I say, "I don't hear anything, Nate. I think you're making it all up."

"Listening," Nate says with a grin, "normally involves not talking."

"I see your point there."

The two of us wait while I put my arms around his shoulders and rest my chin on the top of his head. As he loops his hand over my wrist absently I look at his computer screen. He has an architecture application open, showing a multicoloured collage of electronic ebb and flow. There is a chat window minimized in one corner and countless tabs open on his browser just like always. I try not to look for signs that an online poker game is going on. Nate has promised to stop gambling so much and I've promised to believe him, so I try to ignore the pressure at the back of my neck that says, *check the tabs*. I close my eyes against the thought. I can hear it then, the small, angry chewing.

"Oh, crap," I say. "We must have angered the squirrels."

"Time to call Roy," Nate says. He squeezes my hand again before releasing it and going back to his keyboard.

"Is your call over?"

"Yup."

"Come downstairs," I say, and he does. When he gets to the living room, he picks up his laptop and syncs his diagram from the upstairs machine with a few well-placed words on a command line, and then keeps working. I sit sideways on the couch, my feet bumped up against Nate's legs, nudging him every once in a while, just to tell him I'm here. A little later, he puts his hand over my toes and squeezes gently in response. I love watching Nate work, his lips slightly pursed, his head cocked as he runs through a problem, the finger aerobics he does over his keyboard, like he's getting ready to play a baby grand piano. The two of us sit together and work like this all the time; quiet, but not really silent. I nudge him again. He keeps his eyes on his computer, but starts to smile. I love the way he smiles, slowly, like he's working on making it his best smile yet. Like he's working on a masterpiece.

Eventually the pizza comes and Nate pays for it at the doorstep, making small talk with Allan, our regular delivery guy. The pizza fumes waft over me while Nate burps softly on his side of the couch and the two of us try to puzzle through our work problems. Later, Nate reads through some of Dr. Throckmorton's pamphlets, a thoughtful look on his face. At some point I realize I forgot to ask the doctor for a note so I can go back to work.

Later we go to sleep, folded into each other like bloated bookends, all those carbs coursing through our veins. Nate snores softly while I lie on my back, staring at the ceiling. Nate and I both like to cook, but making an elaborate meal at ten at night after a long day's work is too exhausting to even think about, even if there was any food in the house, which there isn't. And anyways, takeout is our drug of choice, some solace after a hard day at the office. We deserve a treat after working so hard. The only problem is I didn't actually go to work today, and all this fast food is draining our bank accounts and ruining my girlish figure. I don't think we should have more than one vice at a time, and ours are Nate's gambling and my headaches. So there's no room for takeout and this much heartburn, I tell myself, trying to be quiet beside Nate's sleeping body.

There's not a lot of Thanksgiving joy in our car, which is currently pointed towards my parents' house, probably because it's not actually Thanksgiving. Canadian Thanksgiving happens in early October, but Avery asked my mom to make it even earlier this year, on a Tuesday, because Avery and Patrick are going to his parents' place up north this weekend to celebrate with their side of the family. My younger brother, Martin, is also coming. He'll likely be alone.

Nate is driving our car, which seems more tortured than usual, the heater generating only the suggestion of warmth. We're aimed towards North York, where my parents live in a neighbourhood of generously-sized front lawns and speed bumps. It isn't the house my brother and I grew up in; when we were little we lived in a small town a few hours outside of Toronto, where all the girls were named Jane and Jennifer and Julie. When my brother and I were teenagers we moved into our first Toronto house, in Leaside; my parents eventually moved to North York after Martin and I left home. It was my father who wanted to move into the city, my father who never asked for anything. My mom preferred her long commute to being hemmed in by neighbours, but as soon as we moved she realized everyone here was ethnic too, that no one cared our family came from an unheard-of tiny country halfway across the world. Raw fish! Lumpy sandwiches! Foreign beers! Toronto is one of the most multicultural cities in the world, and everyone here has some variation in their own family tree. My mother's world view has always been simple and direct: work very very very hard, be a good Canadian, appreciate everything that we have, but every once in a while, look over your shoulder. Just in case. She was thrilled to find a community of people from all over the world who believe the exact same thing. We went from being oddities to fitting right in in a single day.

Nate stops the car in my parents' driveway, jiggling the parking brake until it catches, and then kisses my nose as he helps me out of the car, not because he's chivalrous, but because he knows I need it, although maybe that's its own kind of chivalry. "You ready?"

I run my fingers through his hair, straighten it out a little before I kiss him back. I have to blink a few times to bring him into focus. I woke up today with a full-out migraine, a good eight out of ten on the pain scale. I don't know if last week's headache has sparked itself back up, or if this is a new one. It's probably a new one; it felt fresh and angry and a little different this morning, more rat-tat-tat than usual. I took one of the new migraine pain meds–triptans–that Dr. Throckmorton prescribed for me at lunch, and then I spent the rest of the day in bed. I took another before we left home, and the pain is muted now, a hum behind my ears. Everything else is wobbly, my feet on the concrete, my legs, my brain. Right now I feel terrible, but in a new kind of way; more impaired than agonized, more confused than in pain.

But we can't just not show up, because I refuse to ruin Thanksgiving, especially since my mom has taken the day off to get ready. So here we are.

When Nate opens the front door to the house, the warm air hits us, pungent, inviting, festive, and oddly depressing. "Hi everyone," Nate calls. His voice, so close to my ear, clangs like a bell.

Breathe, I tell myself as I sit down on the chair in the entranceway and start unlacing my shoes. *Smile. Look happy. Do not ruin Thanksgiving.*

When I glance up, my mom is standing in the hallway, leaned against the wall. She makes a small, sympathetic noise in her throat.

"Tere, Ema." *Hi, Mom.*

"Tere, Viive. What's wrong?"

"Everything's fine."

"Tere, Anne," Nate says to my mom as he kisses her cheek, pronouncing her name in the Estonian way; Ah-neh.

"What's wrong with Viive?" she asks Nate.

"I'm fine, Mom," I repeat, before getting up to hug her.

"Headache?"

"No," I say, trying to be as convincing as possible so no one will make a fuss. "I'll be okay. Everything smells great. What did you make?"

"Do you want to lie down?" she asks, still suspicious, and I shake my head, no.

Avery comes out from the kitchen, gives me a dry peck on the cheek before giving Nate a slightly more robust hug, and steps back so her husband, Patrick, can shake Nate's hand in the manly way men do. Patrick then shakes my hand so hard it basketballs my brain around my skull. I smile weakly.

"Dinner isn't quite ready," my mom says. "Why don't you guys settle yourselves in the living room? Avery and I can finish up."

"I'll help, Ema," I say.

She squeezes my arm and says, in Estonian, "We've got it all under control, you should go sit down."

It stings, for a minute, to be excluded from all the kitchen camaraderie, but she's right that I need to take a load off, because all this moving around has added a dash of momentum to the dizziness thudding in my head, and I'm suddenly exhausted, even though the only thing I've done all day is lie in bed. You'd think it would be relaxing, all that nothing. But migraine sleep isn't authentic, REM-packed rest. It's more like being unconscious; coma lite. All this was punctuated with worry about work (there's a piece of network infrastructure going in today, and I didn't get an update from Brian until Nate and I were halfway out the door). I blink a few times before nodding. When my mom turns to join Avery in the kitchen, a hard, short thought flashes in my brain: *Useless.* That's how I've felt ever since Sid ousted me from work, and this small domestic failure hardens that thought into something even uglier: *Even useless at holidays.*

Patrick, Nate, and I all settle ourselves in the living room. My parents' house is spacious and comfortable, two bedrooms, two bathrooms, a nice-sized living and dining room, muted colours and pillowy easy chairs. My parents seem to like it here, and it's nice, in a weird kind of a way, to see them so at home in a place I never lived in. I wish my dad was here.

"So, guys," Patrick says, smiling. "When are you going to replace that old clunker? I could hear the muffler from up here."

I like Patrick well enough–more than Avery, actually–but the two of them seem to find a way to position themselves to compete with Nate and me all the time. Who has the bigger house (them), who has the newer car (them, for goddamn sure), who makes the most money (us, except for the fact I'm probably about to get fired). I'm not that eager to tell them they're now winning in all categories.

Nate smiles. "We've got our fingers crossed she'll last through winter."

"Driii-iinks," Avery singsongs, entering the room with a tray and giving what's probably a scotch and water to Patrick, a glass of red wine to Nate, and some white wine for me. When she sees my face she says, "I would have given you red, but you know...*your problem.*"

I brush past Avery and make my way to the kitchen. I can hear her behind me, saying, "What's wrong with her?" and the sounds of Nate shushing her.

"Mis sa tahad?" my mother asks: *What do you want?*

"Water," I answer, going through the cabinets until I find a glass. When my mom tries to fill it from her purifier, I wave her off and turn on the tap. I take a sip from my cup and brace myself before making my way back to the living room. Mom has laid out crackers, cheese, and some herring-topped eggs, fishy Estonian delicacies that only she and Martin eat. Avery passes the plate, her nose wrinkling when she gets a whiff of it. Everyone politely declines the fish and helps themselves to everything else.

"So, what's new?" Patrick asks.

"Not much," I say. "Where's Martin?"

"What about Martin?" my mom calls from the kitchen.

"Kus on Martin, Ema?" I call back: *Where's Martin?*

"English please," Avery singsongs.

My mom steps out of the kitchen and leans against the doorframe. "I'm sorry, Avery," she says, before looking at me. "He's working a little late, but he texted me a half hour ago to say he was on his way."

"Is he bringing anyone for dinner?" I ask, trying to ignore the fact that the living room is starting to gyrate a little, like it wants to boogie. I blink a few times.

"No."

"How's work going, Viive?" Patrick asks as he rolls his scotch around in his glass.

"Well, you know," I say, and even I can hear the catch in my voice, "work's work. How about you?"

"My last trip was very successful," he says, straightening his tie. Patrick is in his early thirties–I forget how old he is exactly–but he already looks like a mature, responsible grown-up. Nate and I will never look like that. I glance over at Nate now—he's wearing tan cargo pants and a short-sleeved white dress shirt over his favourite Tesla t-shirt, which you can kind of see the outline of, and the overall effect is one of overgrown high schooler instead of serious thirty-something professional—and for my part, I'm just happy I managed to get myself into pants today.

There's a frenzied banging on the front door that echoes throughout the house, followed by a shouted, "Lemme in!"

"Martin," Nate and I say at the same time. Neither one of us gets up, because we know Martin loves to do this, make a scene on the front porch and try to convince my parents' neighbours we're a bad family. It drives my mother crazy.

Bang bang bang.

"I'm going to kill this boy," my mom mutters, heading for the entranceway.

Martin bounces into the house. "Mommy!" he yells, aimed mostly at the next-door neighbours. "I thought you weren't going to let me in, like last year."

My mom's face is Scandinavian sombre, the face she uses when she wants everyone to just calm the hell down. Her arms are crossed, and her spotless white apron is starched to a Victorian level of domestic efficiency.

"I've missed you so!" Martin cries.

This is what Martin is like *before* he drinks.

My mom finally cracks a smile as Martin puts something down–a floral centerpiece he's spent the last three days on, no doubt–and hugs her before shaking her like the spin cycle in a washing machine and then noisily kissing her. Martin is taller than my mother, and his kisses land on the top of her head. He's wearing a blue sweater that matches his eyes, over a collared shirt, with designer jeans. He looks a million times more together than I do; blonder, fitter, happier.

"Oi, Martin," my mom says, "please be quieter."

"I'm sorry, Ema," Martin says, "I'm incapable. You only get one quiet kid, and that person's name is Viive."

"I've always been sad each of my children got completely opposite character traits," my mother says. "Can't you be more like Viive?"

"Well, Ema," Martin says, his arm around her, "if I were more like Viive–if everyone was more like Viive–we'd all be Viive, wouldn't we?"

"You say that like it's a bad thing," I say.

"Oh, it speaks!" Martin says, crossing the living room with his arms out. "Vee, how nice to see you in your usual funeral black. And you're looking even paler than usual today. Vampiric, almost. What a delight." He reaches over to hug me, and I tickle him on his ribs, just like I've done ever since we were little. I can feel myself smiling. Martin has always been like this, sunshine and smiles and lightness.

He releases me before clapping his hands. "Attention everybody, do you want to hear what I'm thankful for? Of course you do. Come, Avery," he calls to the kitchen.

Avery bangs a few pots before joining us in the living room.

"Now that our ragtag little family is together I wanted to announce–"

"Oi," my mom says.

"Oi indeed, Ema," Martin agrees. "I wanted to say that I'm thankful my shipment of calla lilies was not late, so I could make this beautiful arrangement for my delightful family."

"Isn't it kind of big?" Avery asks.

"Darling Avery," Martin says. "There are some things in life that simply cannot be too big. Flowers, and–"

"We get the picture, Martin," Avery says.

"Paycheques," he finishes with a smile.

"You know," Nate says, turning to me, "your brother really is the most…outgoing Estonian I've ever met."

"He takes after the Canadian side of the family," I say.

Martin takes his vase to the kitchen and comes back out with a drink in his hand, something likely vodka-laced, a twist of orange peel floating in the clear juices. "So how are we all doing, hmm?"

Nate clinks his empty wine glass against Martin's. "We're good, how about you?"

"Fabulous as always," Martin answers. "Patrick, how are you?"

"Good," Patrick says, leaning forward and tenting his fingers. "In fact, we have something–"

"Marvellous," Martin says, "can't wait to hear it. Look, I have to know, is crazy Aunt Florence coming for dinner?" Aunty Florence is a relative on our father's side who's been known to unexpectedly show up with a tuna noodle casserole and a spare lamp in tow.

"Ei!" my mother yells from the kitchen.

"So, mom votes no," Martin says. "Viive, what's your take?"

"Could go either way," I say.

"You are *so* Switzerland, Vee," Martin says. "So what are you up to, my dear sister? How is your sweatshop job doing? Anyone get clogged up in the machines lately?"

God, I miss Martin. "Only five or six. How's the flower business treating you? Any fallout from your hostile takeover?"

"Hostile…moi? All I did was expand into the space next door. They wanted to retire anyway. And they love me, naturally." He grins.

"Everyone loves you," I say.

"Well, I *am* adorable. But enough about the wondrousness of me, how are you doing, dear big sister? Are they working you to the bone? Because I'd like to go to see The Angry Bridesmaids next week, and I'd love for you to come with me."

The Angry Bridesmaids are an eclectic jazz-ish band Martin has been following for ages. They're funky and a lot of fun and I like them almost as much as he does. "Sure."

Martin's just taken a deep breath to lead in to his normal convincing tactics (whining, pleading, blackmail), when he registers my answer. "What?"

"Sure, I'll go." Next week feels foggy and far away, and who knows what might happen?

He swirls the orange peel around his glass suspiciously. "You don't even know what day."

"What day?"

"Wednesday," Martin says triumphantly. He knows my team and I do a lot of our late-night client maintenance on Tuesdays; I can almost never do anything the next day.

"That's fine."

Martin's eyes narrow. "Fine, hmmm?"

"Yes, but if you keep making such a big deal about it, I'll change my mind."

Martin raises his hands. "No need, I know a victory when I see one." He looks around. "Anyone else want to go?"

"No thanks," Nate says, and Patrick nods agreement.

"Supper!" Avery calls from the kitchen. She and my mom start moving serving dishes to the buffet in the dining room.

"Viive, can you put out the place settings?" Avery asks.

I walk toward the dining room, noticing the unsteadiness in my legs. If I tell them I can't set the table, it'll be tantamount to me admitting I have a headache, and then the whole night will be derailed, because everyone will focus on that. But if I drop one of the plates–plates Martin and I bought for our parents at William Sonoma a few years ago–my mom will freak out, even though there are two spares in the cupboard that I picked up at the same time, just in case.

Nate sees my struggle and gently squeezes my arm before he starts setting the table, centering each plate carefully before adding the silverware. I watch him, even though he's a little blurry, and try to remember the last time I did something with such care and precision. Nate sees me looking at him and smiles, as Avery and my mom bring the serving bowls into the dining room. My mother usually likes to seat everyone, but as I'm standing behind one of the chairs I feel my left leg give out. I recover, hoping no one saw me, and then I pull out the chair and sit down in it, everything inside me feeling cumbersome and heavy. Avery squints at me when the chair creaks.

"Sit, please," my mom says, before taking a seat to my right, at the head of the table. Nate sits on my left, reaching to hold my hand. Avery,

Patrick, and Martin are all on the other side of the table. Martin is opposite me, like usual. Easier for him to kick me.

My mom fusses with the vase Martin brought for her, moving it a little to the left and then to the right. Martin's design is calla lilies arranged in a graceful swoon, the throats of the lilies a dark purple fading to white tips, their long stems elegantly entangled with each other in a gorgeous cut-glass vase, tiny violet peppers anchoring the stalks. It's a variation on my mother's favourite arrangement, and it's beautiful. I see my mom smile as she finds the perfect spot for it.

She says, quietly, as she tweaks the placement, "Hea laps." *Good boy.* Martin's face breaks into a wide smile.

The table is covered with traditional Thanksgiving dishes: turkey, gravy, green beans, and white bread. But my mom has seeded some Estonian goodies too: *rosolia* (a beet salad that normally has herring, which she's left out tonight) and *kurgisalat* (a soupy cucumber salad in sour cream which everyone will probably end up fighting over). Dill as far as the eye can see.

Avery says, "And while we're eating, let's think of what we're thankful for." She clears her throat before looking at the rest of us expectantly. "I'm thankful a new yoga studio opened up near my work. They do fitness classes and personal training, too. I've signed up for the next six months."

Martin spoons some potatoes onto his dish and passes the serving plate to his right with a wicked smile. "That sounds wonderful, Avery. Where is it?"

"Gerrard and Coxwell."

"Why, isn't that close to you, Viive?" Martin asks, unrolling his napkin with a neat snap.

"Hmm," I say, nodding. I kick Martin under the table, a pre-emptive strike.

"Oh my God!" Martin says, his head tilted to the side, his expression shameless. "I have the best possible idea in the whole world."

"Martin…" I mutter.

"Viive should come to yoga with you!" Martin says, turning to me. "You could get in touch with your inner feelings."

"I don't have any inner feelings," I say.

Nate, who's normally on my side during times of angst like this, puts his fork down, his face thoughtful.

"What?" I ask.

"Did I say anything?" Nate asks, with a small smile.

"I know that face."

"Well, you do have some time on your hands," Nate says.

"What?" my mother asks.

"Nothing," I say, trying not to let my voice waver. "Pass the gravy please."

Martin picks it up, his expression turning suspicious. When I try to take the gravy from him, he refuses to relinquish it.

"Martin, just give it to me."

"Not until you tell me what's going on."

"Nothing," I say.

"Oh, I know when something's going on," Martin says. "I am the king of something going on!"

"Mom," I say. "Remember how Martin came out to you?"

Martin was the president of his civil engineering class at U of T and worked for my mom's firm for exactly three years before sitting my parents down and telling them he was going to abandon engineering to open a flower shop. After they freaked out he said, "Just kidding guys, I'm only gay!" The thing about that was this: Martin had already come out when he was in junior high, making him the only person I've ever known who tried to come out twice. In any case, now Martin runs a business called Floral Engineering and his arrangements are quirky little masterpieces. He specialises in designs that incorporate engineering principles with an artistic flair; fulcrums, off-beat containers, and when it's my mom's birthday, tiny bridges. Technical and earthy all at the same time. He does set decorations for a few local TV shows, and even though he doesn't talk about it much, he's very successful. And happy.

"Good one," Martin says to me with a cheerful grin.

"Not so fast," my mom says. "What's going on, Viive?"

"Can you please pass the turkey?" I ask Nate.

Martin watches my face as Nate hands the plate to me.

"What are you thankful for, Viive?" Martin asks.

"Oh, you first."

"I'm thankful for Skype," my mother says. My mom has been thankful for Skype every Thanksgiving since it launched in 2003, the brainchild of three nerdy Estonian boys who made good. Every once in a while I see her looking at me with what I call her Skype face, and I know she's thinking: *When will Viive invent the next Skype?*

"I'm thankful my business is doing so well," Martin says.

"We're very proud of you," my mom says.

"Also, I'm thankful my new FedEx delivery man is so adorably cute."

"Congratulations, Martin," my mom says. "That's very nice. Nate, what are you–"

"And finally," Martin says, "I'm happy my sister will be getting into shape by going to the gym with Avery."

"I really–" I say.

"That sounds like an excellent idea," Avery says. "There's a booty boot camp class I want to take. It's before work, at six-thirty. You should come, Viive."

"As much as getting up at the crack of dawn appeals to me," I say, even though the thought of Avery and I doing anything booty-related together is horrifying, "I don't–"

"I think it's a fabulous idea," Martin says.

"I don't really have the money–"

"Oh, Christmas is coming," Martin says. "I'd love to get this for you as a present. I'd be delighted."

"I just bet you would," I say darkly.

"I'll send you a link," Avery says, as Nate passes me the carrots. I spoon them so quickly they slide on my plate in a gush of orange.

Nate leans forward a little. "Maybe it's not such a bad idea."

A zing of disquiet runs through me.

"What was that?" Avery says.

"Nothing," I answer.

"I'm sure I heard–"

"It's fine, Avery," Nate says.

"Right," I say, too quickly.

Nate squints at me. "Well, maybe it's not fine," he says.

Traitor.

"You know what I'd be thankful for?" Nate is piling his plate with food, enough to make my mother pleased. Nate was super-skinny when he was younger, but now he's starting to get a little bit of a tummy. I should remind him of this when we're alone again. Nate continues, "I'd be thankful if my wife would work somewhere normal."

"Nate–"

"What do you mean, normal?" my mom says.

"Viive's boss has put her on medical leave," Nate says, and his voice is getting more terse as he continues. "Leave that's actually her vacation time, which probably isn't even legal. Without any notice, or discussion, or anything."

"Can they do that?" Martin says, his grin fading.

"It's not a big deal," I say. "And it's not medical leave. I'm just off for a little while."

"Why?" my mother asks.

"They want me to rest up," I say. "So, you know. No big deal."

My mom's forehead is a mishmash of worry lines. She reaches out and rests her hand on my arm, her fingers clenched in a maternal squeeze.

"Maybe it's not such a bad thing," Nate says again. "Maybe you can do some meditating or yoga, or whatever with Avery."

"Six-thirty a.m.," Avery says. "Booty boot camp. You'll love it."

"Thanks, but I'm not going to go to yoga or a six a.m. booty anything," I say, my voice sharp.

"Why not?" she asks. "It's not like you'll be doing anything else."

"Oh, I'll be doing something else," I say.

"What?" Avery asks.

"Sleeping."

Martin snickers.

"Then what's the plan, Viive?" Patrick asks.

"How long has this been going on?" my mom asks.

"I just found out–"

"When?" my mom says.

I look down in my lap and back up before answering. "Last week."

She exhales, and all of a sudden she looks old and worn out. "Maybe Nate is right, it is for the best. Maybe there are new therapies you can try. When's the last time you saw a neurologist?"

"Well–"

"You were twenty-one," Martin says. Martin remembers this because he's the one who forced me to go, with his relentless Canadian-side-of-the-family optimism and energy.

"Aitab, Martin," I say. *Enough.* I've lost my appetite, but I shovel potatoes in my mouth anyway.

"Maybe you could make an appointment," my mom says.

I point at my stuffed mouth and shrug.

"Didn't the referral work out?" Avery asks.

I swallow. "Yes," I say. "I saw her on Monday and she seems excellent, thank you, Avery."

She beams and then the conversation blessedly moves to other topics, and I withdraw, worn out from it all, looking around the room while I pick at my dinner. Like the rest of the house, the dining room is spare, dotted with antiques and quietly comfortable. What visitors don't know is that everything in the room used to belong to someone else's family. Estonians who fled during the war–and this is no euphemism–generally got out with nothing but the clothes on their backs, and my dad's working-class Canadian family were strictly Formica. So the dining room table we're sitting at, the chairs, the buffet, are all part of a history we've appropriated from someone else's family. And even though we've had it for a long time, for some reason it's never really seemed to fit us.

My eyes rest on the corner of the buffet, on the one toy my mother was able to smuggle with her when they left. It's a small cloth figurine with a tiny stone in its belly. It used to be red, but now it's faded to a dull rusty colour. If you put it on a slope–anything will work, a book, a cutting board, whatever's handy–it will do somersaults. When Martin and I were young and acting bratty, wanted more candy, more toys, just...*more*, my mom would take out the one toy, balance it at the top of an impromptu incline and let it roll down the miniature hill she'd erected.

After it was done she'd turn to us and say, "Any questions?"

We never had any. And sometimes I think maybe that's why Martin and I both turned to other, bigger questions, ones with answers: How does this work? Why can't we do it like this? Questions that make you want to build something, fix things.

I guess you could say it's the family business, figuring things out, which is part of the reason I don't ever tell everyone how bad things really are for me. It's a fragile sort of camouflage, making work my only success. But up until recently, it worked like a charm.

I turn away from the buffet and try to think about what I'm thankful for. I'm thankful my family is in Canada. I'm thankful for Nate. Mostly, I'm thankful everyone is ignoring the fact that I'm not quite here right now.

4 – I Was Told There Would be Pancakes

My whole world is sweat and sunlight.

I blink, my eyes fluttering against the blanket, my brain a blurry patchwork of thoughts. Could it be Monday? That sounds right. No, no…it's Thursday. Fake Thanksgiving was two days ago. I glance at the clock on the DVR; one p.m. *It's Thursday at one p.m.* I take stock of the rest of me. My feet are slicked with perspiration and I'm roasting under the quilt-fort I've built on the couch, a fort so well engineered it would make my mom proud. After a minute I kick the blankets off, sit up, and snatch up the water glass from the coffee table. I start with just one sip but suddenly I'm gulping hard and fast and my stomach is a ball of water. I blink again before my eyes sweep the room, all shimmering corners and hazy detail.

Knock.

I start. There's nothing I'm expecting to get delivered. No one knows I'm here.

Knock knock knock.

I get up, my feet wobbly under me, the room tilted at a jaunty angle. I'm used to wacky visual problems but if I'm honest, I have to admit that the floor isn't usually *quite* so aggressively angled, and the thirst thing has never happened to me before. I try not to think about the shiny new red pills I've been swallowing every morning, the ever-present migraine preventative Dr. Throckmorton has me on, and all those new side effects, just waiting to happen.

I take a few steps before peering around the living room doorway, my hand on the wall to steady myself. There's a tiny multicoloured blur in the window, stamping a foot and reaching a hand to pound on the door again.

Ruby Flumenbaum. I met Ruby at university in a class I can't remember now, and after a half semester of sitting two seats away from each other we finally decided to swap notes over drinks one night. She's in the home stretch of getting her PhD in library science, and works at Robart's library at U of T. She's a tiny whirling dervish of overachievement.

I step back, away from the hallway, away from where she can see me. I love Ruby, but I still haven't RSVPed for her birthday party this weekend, and I just got a whiff of how I smell.

"I see you Viive McBroom!" she calls from the front porch. Her yelling wakes up the dog next door, who starts to bay like something out of a Farley Mowat saga.

I close my eyes and count to three before heading towards the front door. The scant distance wears me out and I have to lean on the wall to steady myself. "Ruby," I say, after opening the door.

"Nice to see you too," she says.

Ruby is minuscule; one hundred pounds soaking wet, a smidge under five feet. Her hair, hoisted up in her trademark schoolmarm bun, adds about three inches to her height. Her outfit today is a sweater set in Kermit the Frog green over an ankle-length black skirt, and her coat is a sixties kaleidoscope. After a minute she exhales an exasperated breath and pushes past me. "I have smoked meat from Caplansky's," she says. Ruby was so happy a deli went up near Kensington Market a few years ago that she made a vow to go there at least once a week, a promise she's fulfilled admirably. If I had to think of three words to describe Ruby they would be: *smoked meat desperado.*

"It's good to see you too, Ruby Tuesday." And it is, but I don't know if I can face food right now. Right on cue, something turns over in my stomach, but Ruby's already in the kitchen unpacking the food, not commenting on the lack of counter-top real estate, all the takeout cartons and dishes already there. When Ruby's eyes run over the mess I feel like a hillbilly.

"Of course it is," she says, putting my smoked-meat sandwich on a plate and cutting the pickle into smaller pieces just the way I like it. The coleslaw gets spooned onto the side. Then she ushers the two of us into the living room, settling herself on one of the armchairs while I sit on the couch. All of her movement and hurry is overwhelming, a punch to my nervous system. I pour myself a Coke so I can wend some caffeine into my bloodstream and try to keep up.

"So I talked to Nate," she says.

"Hmm?" I say, chewing on a tiny mouthful of pickle.

"I phoned him."

Neither Nate nor Ruby are phone-call types of people, but I nod, so I can seem like I'm keeping up.

"I phoned him because lately all my calls to you have gone to voice mail."

I don't want to tell her I've been ousted from my job like an

Eastern European coup d'etat, so I try to come up with something brilliant. When that fails, I say, "Sorry, Ruby. I've been off…uh, sick."

"Oy," Ruby says decisively.

"Oi," I agree.

"Why?"

Oh, Ruby. She's so close to defending her dissertation that she's practicing on everyone. "It's a leave of absence, I guess."

"You guess? How long have you worked there again?" she asks, nibbling on her sandwich. I notice the mustard cascading over the lip of her bread and hand her a napkin, which she ignores. Her bites are so dainty she barely needs one anyway. I wish I could be that delicate instead of being so perpetually oversized, Viking-like, clumsy.

"Four years."

"I keep telling you to quit," Ruby says, swallowing. "No one should work those kinds of hours. What are you going to do?"

I drain my Coke but I'm still thirsty, so I go get some water. *God, my mouth is the Sahara.* I fill a pitcher from the kitchen tap and bring it to the living room, but the liquid is flat and tepid and doesn't quench my thirst at all. *Ice?* I roll the thought around in my head, and it takes way more effort than it should to hoist myself off the couch again and open the freezer door. Two packages fly out, one clipping my left foot, the other smashing into the dishwasher with a jaunty *ping.*

"Everything okay?"

"Never better," I say, sitting back down. My sandwich is radiating meaty pheromones and normally I'd love to just dig in–Ruby is right that Caplansky's is fabulous–but at this moment it's nothing but a lump of something I don't want to eat. I feel a flare of guilt spark inside me. I can't enjoy even this small thing, yet more evidence I can't do anything right. After a beat I pick up a sliver of pickle. The sandwich isn't the only thing that smells; every movement I make is unleashing something fetid from under my arms. I look down. There's a stain down the front of my shirt I've just noticed–and can't identify–and when I scratch at my ear, a snowflake of skin lodges under my fingernail. Maybe I am a hillbilly, after all.

"What's wrong?" Ruby asks.

"Nothing." I tuck my feet under me and rub the pain out of my ankles for a few minutes before picking up my sandwich to show her I'm eating it. God help me if I waste a deli delectable like this; wars have started over less.

Ruby's eyes narrow.

I chew, even though the meat feels slimy and lukewarm and unwanted against my tongue. I chew even after the pieces are a pulpy mush in my mouth.

"Nate said you were having some problems," Ruby says.

I have another sip of water. I finally swallow.

"Viive," she says sharply.

"Sorry, Ruby. I was enjoying this sandwich so much," I say, my cheeks frozen into a forced smile. My brain used to be bigger than this. I used to multitask like a mother of octuplets. I used to meet deadlines and charm customers. Well, I used to meet deadlines, anyway, the charm part is probably a little overstated. In any case, I used to be responsible for a team of twenty and a multi-million dollar budget and now I'm barely responsible for putting on pants, a thought that does little to help improve my mood.

"Is it Nate's gambling?"

"What? No, of course not."

"Why of course not? The last time I talked to you he had lost over two grand in a weekend. Where was he again? Rama?"

"It was a bachelor party thing. He was just letting off some steam." I decide not to tell her this particular debacle still festers inside me on nights I can't sleep.

Ruby gives me a look.

"What do you want me to say? At what point between my never-ending migraines do you want me to bring up his gambling? I mean, he needs something to get his mind off the fact that he has to take care of me all the time and I'm basically cheating on him with an icepack."

"It's just–"

"I wish he had a cheaper hobby, but it's a hobby, Ruby. That's it."

"I thought you were going to ask him to stop?"

I remember the last time when Ruby and I talked about all this, about a year ago. I was feeling particularly well at the time and Nate's gambling loomed larger than usual. "I just couldn't do it. We have basically a perfect marriage." I don't say that Ruby knows nothing about keeping a marriage going, about honouring vows. Ruby is a serial dater with an eye for unsuitable younger men. And by unsuitable I mean atheist, which is why she can't take any of them home to her parents, both devout rabbis.

"You know, I love Nate and I think he's fantastic, but two grand in a weekend is crazy pants."

I shrug in a way that says it's not really a big deal, a not-so-easy-to-pull-off task.

"And you never even brought it up?"

If I was Ruby I'd probably say the same thing, so I don't blame her for persistence. Ruby is, after all, a great devotee of persistence. Two grand *is* crazy pants, which is why I can't tell her it's actually a lot closer to three.

But what about what Nate has to put up with? After this migraine is over it's not like I'm going to jump up and run a marathon; nothing will go back to Ruby's version of normal. It'll just be a different kind of bad time in my marriage, the chapter when we reboot our eternal vigil for the next headache.

Ruby still looks suspicious but sighs with trademark panache: tiny shoulders raised and then dropped, a hangdog look that the world is against her. "All right, I wanted to come by and talk to you about my birthday plans."

I wrack my brain to try to think of how old I am and how old that'll make her. "Love to hear it," I say. *Thirty. She's going to be thirty.*

"I don't know if you read the invitation, but we're going to have a couple's dinner party thing at Luma. Twenty of us."

"Fancy. Who's the other half of your couple?"

"Intriguing question," she says, polishing off her sandwich. "I might drag along one of the teaching assistants. He's a transfer from down east and hasn't made his way around campus yet."

"Get 'em while they're young and fresh," I say.

"Indeed," she agrees, forking coleslaw onto her plate. Caplansky's does it with a vinegary bite, which we both love. Usually. "So, what's going on with you, my unwashed waif?"

"I smell that bad?"

"Why do you think I'm sitting over here?"

"Touché."

Her face is puckered, a little from the vinegar, a little from her disappointment in me. Ruby is a maestro of Jewish guilt. The good part of that is for years she's been trying to teach me how to use this skill on others; the bad part is that sometimes she turns her superpowers on me. Right on schedule, a cold weight settles on my chest. "I'm sorry I've been so out of commission. It's been a tough fall."

"Nate said you went to see a neurologist."

"Yep," I say. "She's up in Thornhill. Good shoes, interesting hair. She has me on a new medication regimen. There are some new drugs out, we're giving them a whirl."

"So, new drugs," she says, like she's saying, *new shoes*? "That's great, isn't it?"

"Probably not. Actually, there are very few medications that are actually designed for migraineurs. We get the cast-offs from all the sexy diseases."

"And what disease does yours hail from?"

"The preventative is an anticonvulsant. For epileptics."

"Same brain patterns?"

"Who knows." I shrug. One more bite and this sandwich will look almost eaten. *One more bite.* "And, awesomely, I can have a seizure if I miss doses."

"Charming. Is it working?"

"It can take weeks, or months, or whatever, to kick in, so I can't tell yet."

"What are the side effects?" she asks.

"Flop sweat, upset stomach, brain fog."

"Sounds intriguing. What's brain fog?"

"Problems..." The TV is flickering in the background, full of sandy beaches and bouncy twenty-somethings.

"Problems..." Ruby prompts.

I turn off the TV with a little laugh. "Problems focusing. Problems with word finding."

"That'll be fantastic at work when the network's down and Sid's screaming at you," she says, with a smile. "How will you cope?"

I try not to think about Sid or Elliot or what's waiting for me when I finally get back to the office. "I'm sure it'll be fine," is all I manage to say.

"Enough about you, more about me," she says with a grin. "So, are you coming out for my birthday or what?"

Of course, one of the very worst things about migraine is that it makes the future a complete unknown. I can't even see far enough to this weekend to promise I'm going to Ruby's birthday dinner, which is why I never sent that RSVP. The real problem is this: a migraine isn't just a headache, it's a nerve storm that can last for days, and even when it's over, it isn't *really* over. That's because it's book-ended by two nasty phases. The quirky symptoms I get before an attack (vision problems, balance problems, projectile vomiting) are the *prodrome*, but there's also an ugly post-migraine backlash called the *postdrome*. At that juncture it feels like someone's taken my brain out of my body, shaken it, and then put it back in my head. I spend this time not moving around a lot, meaning *at all.* So knowing what I'm going to do next isn't really my area of expertise.

"Iris will be there," Ruby continues. "You haven't seen her in forever." Ruby and I used to be members of a group of friends at university–not a large group, but still. She keeps in touch with them and lets me know about baby showers, weddings, and birthday parties. If I'm invited and I can't make it, Ruby sends along the presents I buy, as well as my regrets. I try not to dwell on how those conversations go.

"I'm not sure," I say, wishing for the millionth time that I could say yes and mean it.

Hurt sparks in her eyes. "It's just dinner, Vee. It's just three courses and out the door. Can't you try?"

"I'm sorry, Ruby. I'll try. I will."

She smiles and nods, and gathers her stuff up. "Love you, kiddo," she says. "*Shalom*."

It's quiet after she's gone, too quiet as I stare out the living room window, the sky outside a slab of icy grey. I don't know how to look forward to the rest of today, since there's really nothing to look forward to. Maybe I'll re-organize the freezer so no more frozen food tries to maim me. Maybe I'll do my taxes. Maybe I'll call Roy and take care of those squirrels, finally. Maybe I'll pop in the new hard drive I've been meaning to put into my laptop, the one that's been sitting on my side of the couch so long there's dust on it. Of course, there's dust on everything in the house.

I wonder if I should dust.

Then I wonder how things are going at work, and I log on to my computer to find out. Manjit needs approvals on a whack of purchases, which I dizzily review and send. I'm glad he's so trustworthy because I immediately can't remember any of it, if I've signed off on a new build for a client, or if I've approved monkey bars in the office. After that colossal piece of workplace success I idly flip through a never-ending series of TV channels, trying to pretend I'm a normal person having a normal, if couch-potato-ish, day. Our channel purchasing has increased over the last few years, new networks blooming in our house like some sort of virus, even though we almost never actually pay attention to the television when it's on. Nate and I eat in front of the TV, work in front of the TV, sometimes we even have sex in front of the TV, which I definitely don't tell people when they come over and sit on the couch.

Eventually, my thoughts wander to Ruby. It feels like she and I are heading to the end of the road too, just like what happened between me and Avery. But Avery and I are trapped together in the same family, in the same fake Thanksgivings, and I'll never really be free of her. But if I lose one of my last friends, what will happen then?

Ruby helped me through university, delivered meals to my doorstep every once in a while when I had a migraine. For some reason my disease wasn't so virulent when I was younger, and when I first met her things were pretty good for me. But time has been my enemy; every year I get worse at life while all the people my age (or younger, like Ruby) get better. They accumulate wisdom, friends, skills at racquetball or robot-building or croquet or language or travel, while I accumulate empty pill bottles and quietly moulder in a dark room in my house. While other people are perfecting the art of guerilla gardening, I'm working at becoming proficient at not moving around and making noise. *Viive McBroom: expert at sitting quietly.*

I love Ruby, and God knows I can use all the *shalom* I can get, but she always reminds me of what could have been. If everything had stayed the way it was when we met at twenty my life would have been completely different, my *what-if* life. It would have been perfect: Friday dinners with Nate at Canoe, weekends in New York City, skiing at Tremblant. If I was still only that sick, then at the end of the day there would be energy left over for a whole other life, one where I made Nate happy.

After I get up the next morning, I try to concentrate on the weekly reporting for work, a grinding task I struggle at until being blessedly interrupted by my phone, my mom proposing a Friday afternoon lunch date in a tone of voice that makes it more a summons than a suggestion. When I get to the restaurant, a café downtown near her office, she's tapping her spoon against the side of her coffee cup in a way that shows she's most displeased. Something is obviously on her mind, but I know it's best to let her express the reason for her angst in her own time. My mother is not a woman to be rushed.

After she hugs me and I seat myself the tapping starts up again. "Martin is thinking about opening a second shop," she says finally.

"That's good, no?" I pour some more tea into my mug and then add some sugar. It takes me a few seconds to realize I'm tapping my spoon in the exact same way as my mom. I put it down.

"And I'm worried about his expansion. I don't want him to get overextended."

"Ema, he's doing a great job. We should be proud of him."

When Martin and I were little, my mom had dreams of the two of us designing bridges and transit systems, things that would quietly help shape our city, like a pair of urban-planning superheroes. She was thrilled with the engineering degrees both Martin and I got, especially since Martin's is civil, just like Mom. But she was a partner in her firm by the time she was twenty-nine and I'm not even a director yet, and when Martin abandoned conventional engineering it must have dashed her hopes one of us will ever invent the next Skype. Which doesn't stop her Skype face from popping up every once in a while, like it is now. Maybe in her own way, my mom is an optimist after all.

Her head lolls to the side. "Of course I'm proud. I just worry, you know." The stirring starts up again.

"Mis on viga, Ema?" *What's wrong?* I ask, and my voice is sharper than I meant it to be.

"Viga ei ole," she says: *I don't have a problem.* "I just want my children to be successful and happy, is that so wrong?"

I sigh. My mom's immigrant hopes were transmitted to us via lectures about the necessity of working hard and being dependable, from her perpetually anxious parental advice, via osmosis itself. She doesn't seem to be able to connect her behaviour with her children's untidy adult outcomes, or to realize worry has always clung to her like an expensive perfume.

"Ema, it's fine. Martin will be fine. And everyone works long hours. Everybody everywhere. It's a hell of a lot easier for me to sit at a desk than it is for people to work construction in the cold."

"Mmmm."

"Mmmm."

"Martin will never settle down with a nice boy if he's working all these hours. I want some grandchildren, you know," she says quietly. "And you, you're getting sicker."

I pick up my teacup, trying to hide the expression on my face. "I'm okay."

"Hmmm."

"Ema, I was told there would be pancakes, not a lecture."

"I worry," she says flatly. "And there will still be pancakes." She wriggles around in her seat for a minute. "This is a very poorly designed chair."

"Ema…" I think about saying the words, *You're right, Mom, I am getting sicker.* I think of what her face will look like after that, the worry, the disappointment that will etch themselves into frown lines that'll never really go away. And then, for some reason, my thoughts fall on Dr. Throckmorton and her pitch for the migraine support group. I can't help but think that being exiled from work has put me at a crossroads I'm going to have to deal with one way or another. Would it be so wrong to talk about being sick? What if it could help? I don't want to let my mom down, but I don't want to let Nate down either. A small part of me aches to tell my mom how bad things really are, but my desire not to disappoint her is bigger than the truth. It always has been.

"What?"

"I'm…" I take a sip, trying to hide the tears in my eyes. "I'm looking forward to the pancakes."

She smiles. "So, what did you do this week?"

"Caught up on some reading, got some new drugs. The usual."

The server comes over and asks us what we want, and my mother closes her menu with a snap and orders pancakes for the two of us, with a side of bacon, just like always. My stomach is back to normal today, and the food on my plate disappears in a wink. After we finish eating my mom arranges her silverware on her plate at four o'clock, and then we chat about what my dad is doing. I haven't talked to him in forever, and she gently reminds me to call him. Before we get up to leave, she unfolds one of the napkins on the table and drapes it over the two buns still left in the bread basket. In one smooth moment she tucks the rolls into her purse.

When she sees me looking she murmurs, "Igaks juhuks." *Just in case.*

Today is Ruby's birthday, which means dinner downtown in the entertainment district, a throbbing pulse of an area, one that's perpetually, noisily drunk. God, I can't wait to get out of this house, step out of this skin, leave it all behind. But first, breakfast. I get out of bed, go downstairs and then shuffle into the kitchen, ground zero for a mess that's getting easier to ignore. The counters are still piled with dirty dishes and the scent in the room is vaguely fishy, an ominous sign since Nate and I never actually eat fish. *Nate.* Where is he again? I search my memory until I remember that he's out with Avery today.

I can't find a spot to put a cereal bowl down, so I have to balance one in the crook of one arm while I try to fill it with the milk I'm holding in the other. It's a tricky business, what with me wobbling so much, each small movement sparking a twinge of pain in my ankles. I empty the milk carton and meander over to the recycling bin, which is overflowing onto the floor. When did that happen? I reach down to pick up an errant plastic carton and put it back on the pile. It promptly falls back over. I lean down to pick it up again and then I have to put my hand against the refrigerator.

I blink.

The floor is colder than I thought it would be, which is probably why I'm shivering. My cereal bowl is on its side a foot or two away, Cheerios gently bobbing in a milky little pond. I don't know how long I've been here, flat on my back and looking at the ceiling.

I think about the carefully folded, litigiously-worded insert from the migraine preventative I'm taking, wondering how the advertising folks come up with the side-effect verbiage. Do they all get into a room, spitballing ideas? Does the warning with the biggest laugh get the win? I wonder. *Possible side effects might include falling on your ass. Ha!*

It's more comfortable on the floor than you'd think, what with it being ceramic and all, but from this angle I'm able to see a disturbing amount of stuff that never hits my radar from my normal vantage point.

There are crumbs, sticky spots, nameless careless droppings.

My God, I need to wash this floor.

I wonder if the crumbs are clinging to my hair, how much of the floor is going to come with me when I get up. I have to wash my hair anyway for the party tonight, which I'm going to go to because everything is fine and I'm going to celebrate something simple; Ruby turning one year older. All over the city–hell, all over the world–people are going out tonight to celebrate a loved one's birthday. It's not too much to want, this small thing. Ruby wants me to go and I want to be there.

But my eyelids are so heavy. *I'll just close them for a minute. Just one minute.*

I turn my head to the right, gazing at the clock on the microwave. It's now 12:13, a prime number my mother would appreciate (growing up I was the only kid in my class with a parent who had favourite prime numbers), but the time itself is a little disconcerting, because it would seem to indicate I've been lying on the floor for a very long while. Electricity pricks up and down my spine when I do the math, and a contraction of fear pulses in my chest. *What is happening to me?*

I slow my breathing, force myself to calm down. Dinner isn't until seven. All I need to do is wash my hair, dry it, and struggle into the outfit I laid out on the chair in the master bedroom last night when I had a spurt of energy. It's just pants and a new blouse I bought on the Internet because it was on sale. Not too complicated. Nothing I can't handle. Granted, it doesn't fit perfectly, but I haven't had time to go clothes shopping in forever, which sounds kind of funny because I've been on vacation for a full week and theoretically I've had a ton of time on my hands. I mean, really, where has the week gone? I'm supposed to be organizing the house and doing my taxes. What *have* I accomplished while I've been off trying to fix my life? Nothing, definitely. I've accomplished a lot of nothing. I can't believe how lazy I've been, how many things are still undusted, how much work is bunching up for me at the office. And if I faint on Elliot, he will definitely, definitely fire me.

Am I dreaming or is it getting hard to breathe?

There's a commotion at the door, the usual bustle of Nate coming home.

I have to get up before Nate sees me.

But it's so pleasant, the floor, as if it's exactly where I'm supposed to be. My eyes close for just one more second. The migraine has finally broken, I realize. My head is full of wool, I'm lying on ceramic tile, but the ache in my head is finally gone.

Well, that's good news.

"Viive!"

Nate is yelling in my ear, his voice frantic. He's shaking me hard, too hard, and it hurts. My head wobbles as he jostles me around. Then he lifts up my shoulders and my head lolls back; it doesn't feel connected to the rest of me and I can't seem to control it. The shaking is uncomfortable and I really wish he'd stop, but he's doing it so hard my teeth are clacking against each other.

"VIIVE!" Nate's voice is edging towards hysteria.

"Nnn…Nate…"

Nate pulls me to his chest. He's trembling and I can hear the wheeze from his lungs while he tries to control his tears. His chest pulses, one big thump, then another.

But I don't feel anything. I feel preternaturally calm. Like I'm very, very far away.

"What happened?" Nate asks.

"Yeah…" I say. I blink, trying to wake myself up. I feel like a puppet someone else is controlling. "I dunno. I was eating cereal…then, here, on my back."

"Howw llllllg…this?"

I cough. "What?"

Nate is talking but I can't hear anything he's saying. I close my eyes for a minute and he shakes me again. "How long have you been like this?"

"Please stop doing that, Nate."

"Stop going to sleep," he snaps.

"Can we get me up?" I say. "I'm cold."

"What's wrong? Is it the medication?"

I close my eyes again. I don't really feel like chatting, and I definitely don't have the energy for twenty questions. How the hell should I know what's going on? I'm the one on the floor.

Nate helps me to my feet–not so easy, that task–and then up the stairs. "Should we go to the hospital?" he asks.

I think about what it would be like under the grim fluorescent lighting in the waiting room, the hellish trip to get there, the noise, the smells, the interminable wait, the way they'll roll their eyes when they hear the word *migraine.* "It's okay, Nate," I say. The bed is so very soft and inviting, the sheets exquisitely delicate against my skin. It's so warm. So much nicer than the kitchen floor. My eyes close again, even though I'm trying to keep them open.

I'll just shut them for a minute.

It's dark when I wake up again. I blink a few times. The blob sitting beside the bed turns into Nate.

"What time is it?" I feel like I have five hangovers, like I've been hit with ten trucks. The inside of me feels numb and hollow and ruined.

"Nine," he says.

I exhale and then take a deep breath, forcing myself to sit up. "Ruby's goingggh," I say, my words a jumble in my throat. I try again, "Ruby's gonna kill me."

"It's fine," Nate says, as he reaches forward to kiss me. "I called her. She's fine."

"Kill…me." I start to cry. It was just a pair of pants and a blouse, the entertainment district and some steak and wishing someone I love happy birthday. It wasn't too much to want.

Nate reaches over and hugs me. "It's okay, Vee," he says over and over, his hand stroking my hair, his voice a lullaby.

After I finally cry myself out I take a shuddering breath, and say, "Can you get into bed with me?"

"Sure." He kisses my forehead, my face, my cheeks before pulling back the covers and lying down beside me. I put my head on his chest and listen to his heartbeat: young, strong, and alive. I try not to be jealous of Nate while his pulse sings for me, because it's not fair; it's not fair he's wasting his life taking care of me, but it's also not fair that I'm sick and Nate is so healthy.

"What do you think happened?" he asks again, later.

"It must be a reaction to the preventatives," I say.

"Did you take any today?"

"Yup, when I got up." I've been taking them every day for almost a week now, every morning at the same time.

"No more," he says, his voice firm.

"If I stop taking them, I might have a seizure."

"You might have had a seizure in the kitchen."

I close my eyes. "Maybe."

"I'll call the doctor on Monday."

I don't want to think about this Monday or next Monday or any Monday. I don't want to think about how shitty I'm going to feel when I get back to work after my hiatus. And I definitely don't want to think about what will happen if my migraine comes with me when I do. "I'll do it, Nate. You have to work."

He rubs my shoulder with his fingers, strums them against me in a calming rhythm. "Make sure you call them first thing, okay?"

"Okay. I love you, honey," I say, before rearranging the pillow under my head a little. I think of saying more, but I don't actually want to tell Nate that the next medication might be even worse, that I still don't believe there's a pill out there that will make everything better, because I'm too broken to fix. I remember the wavering pitch in his voice this afternoon, a keening tone I've never heard him make before. He's been through enough today.

Beside me, Nate snores. He looks young and untroubled in his sleep. I want him to look like this all the time, free and happy, but what's really happening is this—that expression is getting wiped off his face, one day at a time. It's hard to swallow, that just me being alive is the worst thing that's ever happened to Nate. If it was just one bad night we could find a way to live with it, but when you string all these failures together it becomes a ruined life. A ruined marriage. And a not-so-small part of me dreads the day Nate figures it all out.

5 – The Migraine Mafia

The hold music for Dr. Throckmorton's office is appalling–an instrumental mash-up of a Pearl Jam song that was hip when I was younger but has since been awkwardly transitioned into the world of elevator music. When the receptionist, Shirl, finally picks up the phone she says, "Doctor is busy all day." Shirl sounds even more scrunched than the last time I saw her.

"No problem," I say, rearranging myself a little on the couch. "Can I get an appointment for later this week?"

She makes a noise that could only be described as a snort. A delicate snort, but still. "We're booked for the next three months. I can give you something in January." After the silence stretches she clarifies, "Of next year."

"Okay," I say, pressing my hand against my chest. "I have a problem. I think I might have had a seizure on the weekend, and I'm not sure what to do about this medication she's got me on. Can I just stop taking it?"

"Hold, please."

I look down at my knees, both of them covered with bruises I can't remember getting. I put my thumb on the purple Rorschach of my left knee and watch the colour change. If I was going to take stock of the rest of me I'd be forced to admit I ache with the echoes of my weekend tumble to the tile, the sore elbow, the gimpy ankle, the dent in my pride.

"Hallo?" The voice on the other end of the line is forcefully Eastern European, sort of Bond-villain lite.

"Hello?"

"Yes, hallo, vat I can do for you?"

"I'm not sure," I say. "Because I don't know who you are."

A heavy sigh. "I am nurse practitioner."

"I think maybe you've picked up the wrong line?" I say.

More elevator music rumbles through the phone, a tortured disco tune this time, and I guzzle a glass of water while I wait. My thirst is still sharply intense, worse than I've ever experienced before, and I've had my share of saunas, hot days, and overly enthusiastic sporting events. It's starting to worry me. New prescriptions always make me feel like I'm going through puberty again, and I'm already sick of the constant lab-rat questions I have to ask myself when I'm medicated: is this thirst, dizziness, fatigue, flop sweat normal or is it the new meds? Am I just parched or is the need for water really a sign of something more ominous? I'd much rather focus on things like, how much chocolate am I going to be able to eat today?

To distract myself, I examine the bruise on my other leg. From the right angle it looks a little like Australia. I've always wanted to go–

"Hello?"

"This is Viive Mc–"

"Why are you back at reception?"

"Someone else picked up the–"

"Hold please."

"Hello?" another voice says after a few minutes, a whole new woman.

"I'm Viive McBroom," I say, trying not to sound irritated. "I'm taking an anticonvulsant medication and I think I might have had a seizure this weekend–"

"I doubt that," the voice says drily. "What are you on?"

"Zunosoe, 100 milligrams a day. It's listed as a side effect."

There's a pause, then the sound of keys clicking on a keyboard. "It's highly unlikely. You've only been taking it for a week."

"Right, but it *is* listed as a side effect, and if you Google–"

"Please don't Google," the voice says. "Please don't try to practice medicine. That's our job."

A beat passes, during which I tell myself, *Don't make trouble.* "Anyway, I passed out this weekend, on the kitchen floor. Maybe I fainted, maybe it was a seizure, but–"

"For how long?"

"A few hours."

"Well, it's probably not a seizure." More keyboard clacking. "I have your file here. Just in case, I mean…if you really want, I'll call in a prescription for a different type of preventative."

"Still an anticonvulsant or something different? Because I feel–"

"Something in the same family, but with less side effects. What's the number for your pharmacy?"

"One sec."

"I'll put you on hold." Instead, she wraps her hand over the phone and starts chatting to someone. I can't hear them all that well, but it sounds like they're discussing where to have lunch. A loud string of muffled conversation is punctuated by someone yelling, "Purple monkey underpants," and then laughter. "Pharmacy number," the voice says, a few moments later.

"You know, I'd feel a lot better if I could come in–"

"Doctor is booked for the next few months. I'm her intern, I've reviewed your file, and this is standard procedure. Do you have your pharmacy number?"

"Yes," I say, before rattling off the digits.

"I'll call this in now. Have a nice day."

"Should I–"

"Everything will be fine, Mrs. McBroom," she says, just exactly as if she's speaking to a child. "It often takes several iterations before we find a medication that works. And we can't help you if you don't follow our protocol. I mean, how could we?" And then this nameless, faceless person on the other side of the line sighs exasperation into the phone. "Or is it that you don't *want* to follow our protocol?"

I hear the subtext in her voice, and she for goddamn sure knows it. She's mean, this one. I exhale, my heart a quiet thump in my chest. We're now moving into "non-compliant patient" territory, and once they make that assessment, they'll never take anything I say seriously, will never really try to help me. I remember that brief moment when I met Dr. Throckmorton, when she seemed confident and knew what I should do. But she's surrounded herself by scrunched receptionists and angry, nameless interns and I can't help but let it shake whatever confidence I might have had in her. *Shit.* Frustration floods through me, the back of my neck surging with heat, tears in my eyes. The silence between me and the intern is suddenly an ugly thing, something actually menacing.

"No, of course not. But I also–"

"Good," she says crisply. "Good day, Mrs. McBroom."

It takes me forever to sweet-talk myself off the couch and out to the pharmacy, and a few hours later I'm pumped full of the new medication–Zamaxia, green little pearls–in the same class as the first one, but not really known for causing less side effects. (Oh yes, I Googled.) When Nate gets home and I tell him, he seems satisfied now that I'm off the first medication, but then, Nate thinks this is as bad as it can get. What he doesn't really understand, still, is that we're just getting started.

After dinner I finish up some reporting for work, answer a bunch of emails from Manjit and Brian–everything is okay at the office, thank God–and then try to focus on a whitepaper I needed to read two weeks ago. After a few minutes of my eyes running over the same paragraph again and again I put my laptop down, my gaze drifting over the room. I'm stuffed from dinner, my thirst is finally slaked, and I'm inexplicably tired. My eyes fall on my to-be-read pile beside the couch, and I pick up a bunch of items off the top and flip through them idly. After discarding the flyers and some mail, I come across the pamphlets Dr. Throckmorton gave me. One of them has a neat, hopeful sticker slicked on its face, stamped with information about the migraine support group she told me about. I still don't want to sit in a circle and listen to a bunch of complaining, especially if it's me doing all the complaining, but for a minute I think about going to a place where everyone understands what I'm going through. Where people listen to me. I think about being in a room where I'm the normal one and Nate is the exception. And a not-so-small part of me wonders what would happen then.

My general practitioner isn't a bad person, just one who's at the end of both her career and her wits. I call Tuesday morning for an appointment, and they tell me to show up at one. I have to wait for almost an hour before she comes into the exam room.

The appointment goes like this:

Me: "I need a note which says I can go back to work, please."

Doctor: "Can you go back to work?"

Me: "Yes."

The doctor scrawls something unintelligible on a prescription pad, mumbles a few wistful things about retiring to British Columbia, and then she's gone.

The bedroom floor isn't as cold as the one in the kitchen, or so hard. Thank God this room was carpeted when we bought the house, because we would never have gotten around to putting it in.

I don't know how long I've been lying here–sort of passed out, sort of not–this time, but if I just close my eyes for a minute I know I'll feel better. This is based on no information whatsoever, but it lets me justify closing my eyes. Suddenly I'm in space, I'm in a circus, I'm underwater. I dream other universes, brightly coloured clowns, an Atlantis that's hiding at the bottom of Lake Ontario, with all night BBQs. I dream of head massages and mountain tops. I run until there's no road left under me. There are aliens in the woods, fish in the sky. I try to explain to them that all I want to do is go home. There are creatures with Band-Aids on their heads who only nod in agreement.

I wake up with a start. I can hear the squirrels romping in Nate's office at the front of the house. God they're loud. I really need to call Roy. And how long has there been a crack in the ceiling? And how come I never saw it before? I really would be the worst international spy ever. I'd get killed my first day on the job, an embarrassment to the team they'd never talk about again, except in sentences like, "You really Viive'd that one up, dincha?"

I'm still lying on the carpet, thinking all of this. If Nate comes home now and sees me, he'll have a heart attack. But I'm so tired…

"Vee?"

Shit.

It's Nate, home from…what day is it again?

I don't want to see that expression on Nate's face again. I have to get up. I have to get up right now and get off this goddamn floor.

I struggle to sit up, my breath coming in short gasps, my legs wobbly like Jell-O. I can hear footsteps on the stairs. In another few seconds I've hoisted myself to the bed. Then I'm standing, pulling tangles out of my hair.

"Hi honey," I say, my voice more breathy than I'd like, but at least I'm on my feet.

"Hi gorgeous," he says before kissing me. "What are you up to?"

"Trying to find a book." It's not a big lie. I hate lying to Nate, but this is so small, it can't possibly count.

He puts his arms around me, pressing his forehead against mine. "How was your day?"

"Good," I say before patting down his hair, which is sticking up, just like usual.

"That's great," he says. "I picked up some Greek. Feel like some dinner?"

There's no pang of hunger in my belly, but I say, "Sure," so I can keep up the pretence that everything's hunky-dory.

"Maybe it's time to get dressed, eh?" He grins at me.

When I look down I realize I'm still in my bathrobe, and then a short, awkward minute passes between us. Finally, Nate reaches forward and kisses me before heading back downstairs. I sit down on the bed with a sigh, and then pull on my favourite jeans, struggling to wiggle them past my ass, my zipper protesting a little more than usual. When I finally get the jeans closed, my stomach smooshes over the side in a muffin top. It's not that big, just a mini-muffin, really, but it's there. Ominously. And it's not like these jeans were a size four to begin with, if you know what I mean. I sit there for a minute before I finally get up and go downstairs.

Nate's making a racket in the kitchen as he puts the food onto some dishes. "Here you go," he says, putting a tray down on the coffee table in front of me.

"Thanks, gorgeous."

"How was your day?"

I check the time. The clock on my laptop says eight p.m., which means that I was only passed out for a half an hour this time. I wonder, for a minute, if this is an improvement of some kind. I don't know if my most recent fainting spell is because I still have the old meds in my system, or if the new ones are going to mean more impromptu tumbles are in store for me. If that's the case I definitely need to look into gymnastics classes.

"Vee?"

"Sorry…" God, for a minute I can't remember my husband's name. There was a justice of the peace, some friends and family, and some city officials with clipboards. I know I'm married. "Nate," I say, finally, my voice sounding strangled. "Nate, your name is Nate."

"Last time I checked," Nate says, his eyes narrowing.

"Sorry, babe," I say, sick of me being sorry and Nate being someone I have to be sorry to. "I had a headache, spent most of the day in bed." The lie makes the back of my neck hot, an unwelcome warmth that makes me squirm. I hate lying. But Nate will worry if I tell him about my most recent foray on the floor.

"I'm sorry, Vee."

"It's okay."

"Have you thought more about that support group?" Nate tucks into his dinner, shovelling the food into his mouth like it's his literal last supper. He's always had such an appetite for life. He's always so open to new ideas and activities, to new kinds of fun. I can't remember the last time I focused on anything other than working towards being a director by thirty-five, like I've been blindered by that goal. It feels so far away from me these days. *What will happen once I finally get that promotion? Will I have an appetite for anything else, or will I just spend the whole time playing catch-up, like I do now?*

I poke my gyro with my fork. I love this dish; meat, rice, potato; an overabundance of starch. After cutting the meat into small bites I put one in my mouth, but it tastes like Styrofoam, like old newspaper, and yesterday's socks.

"Can you try this?" I ask Nate, who spears some on his fork, consumes it with gusto, and then gives it the thumbs-up before returning to his meal.

"As much as I adore your ability to dodge a question, my sweet, I mean it. Have you thought about the support group?" he asks.

When I take the fork out of my mouth, it comes away bloody. I dab the small tear on my bottom lip with a tissue before making a noncommittal noise in response to Nate's question, and then we eat dinner while both of us work. After I clear off all of my pressing tasks, I pen an email to Martin, cancelling our plans to see The Angry Bridesmaids tomorrow night, and every word I write feels like a new kind of failure. I can't take the chance that I'll faint in front of Martin, but the unfairness of having to cancel plans twice in less than a week feels like acid in my gut. *Why can't this be the last time I cancel something with him, or with Ruby, or with anyone? Why can't this be the last time I let someone down?*

For some reason I think of my greedy moment with Nate's cinnamon bun the other day, the way I can't do even the smallest nice thing for him anymore, and I feel a dark sort of shame. I might be hiding the things that are going on, but that doesn't mean they didn't happen. And that's probably why I eventually start composing an email to the migraine support group. I mull over how to write about getting help without actually admitting I need any, a not-so-easy task that churns around in my head before I come up with: *I don't really have a problem, I'm doing a research project on support groups.*

After a while I start a second email: *Hi, my name is Viive McBroom. I've fainted twice this week, and my neuro has given me some meds that we all know aren't going to work. I feel like I'm going crazy. Xamaxia sucks. How are you guys doing?*

No, that won't work either. I pull up the support group's website. It's spare and functional, a site belonging to a group who's not looking to sell anything. God, Otis would love to optimize it, even though it would hardly be appropriate. Make migraine sexy? Nonsense. I look up from my laptop and rub my hands over my face. Of course in the end I accidentally send the *Xamaxia sucks* email.

"Yeah," I say. "I sent them an email." Even though the last time we talked about it was hours ago, I know Nate will know exactly what I'm talking about.

"Good," he says, and the smile he gives me is happier than I've seen him in a long while.

The rest of the night is unexceptional, a movie, *dolmades*, dessert, but there's a hum in the room, a pleasant note in the background. Right before bed I check my messages and find:

> *Dear Viive:*
> *Your doctor has probably given you too much Xamaxia to start off, surprise, surprise. Get a pill slicer and cut the tablets into halves, or quarters if you're still having problems. Only titrate up when you have no side effects. You are the patient, it's your body, you set the schedule. Our support*

group, the Migraine Mafia, meets Thursdays at St. Barbara's Hospital, at 7:30, so feel free to bring your gimpy ass down and join us. Please don't wear any perfume or other crazy trigger items like blinking reindeer sweaters or whatever. We sometimes go to the pub around the corner, where we pretend to drink beer afterward.
Cheers,
Paulie

I read the email twice before I realize I'm smiling. I really don't want to have to go to therapy, sitting in a room and talking about my feelings, telling people I have a problem. But I can't deny that ending up sprawled on the floor twice in one week isn't exactly awesome either. And there's another part of me–not so small–that wants to see what a group called the Migraine Mafia is all about. Paulie's email is the first time in a long time I've found anything funny about being sick. And that's not nothing.

The group meets in a building attached to one of Toronto's teaching hospitals, a mangled heap from the sixties that was a mistake from the minute the first brick was laid. Over the years it has graduated from functional but boxy to rundown and soulless. Today it smells sharply of disinfectant and a thousand washed floors.

Room 237 is an elusive little destination, one I've been trying to find for the last twenty minutes. I stop again, pull my phone out, and check the room number for the fifth time. The knot in my stomach is duelling with my lunch, and the back of my neck is dotted with sweat. I glance around one more time, and then I turn to leave.

"Hello there." A few feet away is a little old East Indian woman, her hair a ropey braid down her back, her electric blue sari cheerfully beaded. She's watching me with an expression on her face that's part curiosity, part amusement. "Can I help you?"

I half-turn to her, still aimed for the door. "No, I'm okay."

"Are you sure?" she asks, her voice a sing-songy melody. "I'm Asha."

"I'm Viive," I say, mostly just to be polite.

"Ah, Paulie told me about you. What a lovely name," she says, with a smile so big her eyes close and her shoulders rise a little, like her whole body is smiling. "Come with me, young lady." After a minute, she gestures at me, still smiling. "Come."

I pause for a minute, before giving up and joining her. *I can always leave if I want,* I promise myself, *I'm sure no one will notice.*

As we walk I glance down, see her sneakers, brightly pink and faintly hopeful, shoes that clash with room 237–institutional, fluorescent lighting, sticky tile flooring. The overhead lights are all turned off. A few people are sitting in chairs around a small circular table and a few camping lights.

Asha walks towards the circle and then smiles at everyone. "This is Viive," she says, motioning for me to sit down beside her. It takes a long time to cross the small room, and as I walk, I'm thinking, *There's still time to leave. I can still go.*

It's a ragtag group; a woman in her thirties who's knitting furiously, something complicated and purple and bunched up under her arm. Her skin is toffee-coloured, her hair straightened and in a net bun, her suit tailored but funky. Good shoes. She looks like she's deep in contemplation. Beside her is a guy in his forties who's wearing a suit and tie; a Bay Street refugee. Two chairs over is a young, sullen teen, his blond hair spiky, his body short and rounded, the physique of indulging in too much time on the couch, a lifestyle I think we can all agree I have more than a passing knowledge of. The equally plump brunette sitting beside him–a woman of indeterminate age but who seems quietly worn out–is murmuring to him as he plays with the computer tablet in his hand, ignoring her. I wonder which one is Paulie. Tie guy?

The knitter looks up and smiles. "Welcome," she says, and you can hear the Caribbean in her voice. Jamaica, maybe.

Asha puts her overstuffed purse on the ground and lifts out a pile of her own needlework, which she settles in her lap before looking over at the teenager. "Jaden, can you please shut the door?"

The room is big enough for thirty, at least. Including me, there's only six of us here. The teen sighs and keeps his gaze centred on his tablet, and after a minute the woman beside him says, "I'm sorry Asha, we're having a challenging day." There's another pause before she gets up and closes the door, which makes an institutional-sounding *snick*; exactly the sound the point of no return would make, if it could.

"Thank you Ruth," Asha says. "So, Paulie says you wanted to come and meet us, see what we're all about, is that right Viive?"

I nod, try to smile. My stomach is fluttering a little, more than enough to make me feel on edge.

"So, everyone, we want to make Viive feel welcome, so we should all be on our best behaviour, right Jaden?"

"Well, Asha," Ruth says, leaning forward, as if to shield Jaden from Asha's question, "you know how we've talked about Jaden's difficult days, and how we're going to work together to help him through them? You know, like a village?"

"I certainly do," Asha agrees, and her voice is friendly, but there's steel in her eyes. "Perhaps everyone could introduce themselves."

Tie Guy adjusts his tie before reaching his hand out to me, which I shake. "I'm David," he says. "Cluster headaches, you know, the excruciating one-sided ice pick stabbing kind, ten years now." He smiles, a youthful grin that shows off some great dental work and even better dimples.

"David is often travelling for work, so we don't get to see him as much as we'd like," Asha says, her eyes twinkling. "Where are you off to next, David?"

"Dubai," he answers.

"Gonna go first class?" the sullen teen mutters.

"You betcha," David replies, in a way that says he's used to getting lip from Jaden.

"Oh, David," Ruth says. "You know we've talked about how–"

"Ruth," David says, "if Jaden has something to say, then I think we've all agreed he has to say it himself. Remember rule number one?"

Ruth blinks, opens and closes her mouth a few times before saying, "You're right, David, my apologies. It's just that it's been such a…trying day."

The thirty-something knitter looks up. "I'm Claire," she says. "Migraine with aura–I get the full fireworks kaleidoscope visual experience. Followed by excruciating pain, naturally. Since I was a teenager."

Asha is knitting now too, green wool, but at a more relaxed pace than Claire. It seems like there's some sort of complicated duel going on between the two of them, as if they're competitive knitters. "I'm Asha, we met in the hallway," she smiles. "I have common migraine, no aura. I've had them most of my life, but they're better now." She comes to the end of a row, loops the green wool around her finger. "Menopause," she says succinctly.

Jaden huffs and looks down at his shoes. "Moooooom," he says. "Can we go home now?"

"Oh, sweetie, can't you please try to stay a little longer?" his mother asks. She looks at me and then smiles, a fleeting please-just-ignore-us smile. "I'm Ruth, and this is my son. J-a-y-d-y-n. Jaydyn has migraines with aura, like Claire. Mostly only the aura, actually. For the last year or so."

Everyone turns to me, helpful, pleasant smiles on their faces.

I look from Jaydyn to his mother to Asha and then back again. As I struggle to find the right words, it occurs to me that I have almost no experience telling people how bad things really are. I've made an art of downplaying my migraines and all those lost days and toxic side effects. No one in my family has migraine, so I grew up in a home where everyone tried to help, but no one really understood what I was going through. This is the first time I've ever been in a room where everyone was like me, and for a minute I wonder what comes next, if it's time for me to stop pretending everything is okay.

I clear my throat, twice. "I'm Viive. I have plain old common migraines, too, no aura. Since I was born, as far as we can tell." The tiny admission ratchets up my heartbeat, and suddenly I don't know where to put my hands.

Everyone makes a small, compassionate noise, a quiet support-group chorus.

"I should tell you a little more about us," Asha says. "We're funded by the hospital. We're supposed to have a facilitator, but she knows nothing about migraine and she almost never shows up, so we're trying to get her ousted. Lovely woman, but if she keeps telling me to take an aerobics class I will kill her with my crochet hook," she says with a small smile. "If I try exercise like that, I get terrible migraines."

There's a grunt of sympathy from the group, even from Jaydyn.

"We don't have a set format," Asha says. "We try to share tips and information with each other. The people who are doing well try to help out others when they're in a migraine pattern. We don't preach at each other." She pauses. "Except at Ruth, a little."

Jaydyn sniffs.

"You keep sniffing, young man," Asha says, "I've raised six sons." She starts to knit again, not looking down, her hands like some kind of performance art. "We can help get you to a better neurologist. We can…help." Smile. "The group is about twenty people, but we normally get around six or seven, depending on who's sick and who's in town. I like for all of us to talk about things that have gone well over the last week, or since the last time we've seen them, and what has been difficult."

I nod.

"So, Viive, am I saying that right?" she asks.

"Yes," I say.

"My last name is Balasubramanian," she says, sounding out the impossible name with a smile. "I know all about English and problems with foreign names."

"Wow, I guess I don't really have it all that hard after all."

"Why don't you start with your story, young lady?" Asha asks.

Jaydyn snorts. "Young!"

David pulls a small bubble sheet of meds out of his pocket and pushes one of them through the foil before popping it into his mouth.

"Uh…well…" I say, thinking that I've already shared as much as I'd like. More, actually.

"Viive," Claire says gently, "if you'd just like to watch today, it's okay."

Jaydyn's head whips up. "You never say that to me."

"You do nothing but watch," David says. "You don't contribute, you play video games, you don't help anyone. You don't–"

"Now David," Ruth says, "you know how we–"

"Let's try not to interrupt each other," Asha says.

"Viive," Claire says, and my name sounds like music coming out of her mouth, "just jump in when you feel like it."

"Thanks." I clear my throat. "Uh, I guess…"

Asha, Ruth, and David all lean forward.

"Yes," Claire prompts.

I take a deep breath. "I think I might have fainted this week, but I'm not sure. I'm trying some new meds, and, you know how that goes."

"We do," Asha says, meeting my gaze. And then I realize that she does. It's stupid, almost, to be so surprised, but the truth is that it's the first time I've met someone who's been where I am right now, and there's a quiet dignity in how Asha speaks, a friendly sort of wisdom. Nothing she's done is earth-shattering, except for the fact that when she looks in my eyes, she seems to know me, which is impossible, obviously. But still, there's a peaceful sort of calm about her, something about the way she says things that makes you want to pay attention.

"Which one?" David asks.

"Zunosoe, and then Xamaxia."

"Ah…" everyone says, nodding.

"Did you lose consciousness?" Asha asks.

"Did you convulse?" David asks.

"What did your doctor say?" Ruth asks. "Did you get an EEG?"

"All good questions," I say, wishing I could hold up my hands and call *time*, like I'm in the middle of a sporting event. "My neuro can't take me for the next three months, and her office didn't say much, other than giving me a new med, almost the exact same one. And it never occurred to me to get an EEG, but that's a great idea, thanks."

"Who's your neuro?" David asks.

"Dr. Throckmorton. In Thornhill."

"No," David says. "Go to your GP and get a new referral. Dr. Throckmorton is a quack."

"But my GP referred me. Doesn't that make her a quack?"

"My GP will take you," Claire says, putting her knitting to the side.

"Just like that?" I say. "I've been going to my doctor my whole life. It's my mother's doctor. My mom would be upset if I left."

Jaydyn laughs.

"What's so funny?" I say.

"It's hilarious, dude. You're like a hundred and worrying about what your mom thinks."

"Well, now," Asha says. "I think we're going to have a time out, Jaydyn. If you can't remember that this is a safe place for people to talk about their issues, then I guess you'd rather be somewhere else."

"Thank G-o-d," he says, gets up, and leaves the room.

"I'm so sorry," Ruth says, and her face is pinched but puffy, her left eye drooping. I'd bet my left nut–if I had one–that this woman has a killer headache.

"C'mon Mom," Jaydyn pops his head back in the room. "You have to drive me h-o-o-o-me."

Ruth apologizes again as they leave.

"Well," Claire says. "I think that went well."

"I agree," Asha says. "She seems to be getting a little better."

"Really?" I say. "That's better?"

"I know it's hard to cope with…what's the word I'm looking for?" Asha says.

"Nonsense?" Claire says.

"Bullshit?" David says.

"Something like that," Asha replies. "But because we are federally funded we have to take everyone, even horrible teenagers. And don't forget, we were all his age once."

"I was never his age," David says.

"Should I verify that with your mother?" Asha's eyes are shuttered again with her incredible smile. "My dears, being a teenager is hard enough, but realizing that the bright shiny future all your friends are looking forward to isn't what you're going to get…well, that's especially difficult. My youngest child is the only one of my sons to get migraines, and he had to watch all of his big brothers excel at sports and do all kinds of things which were not possible for him. It's not fair, and it's definitely not easy."

We all sit there for a while after that, the slow strum of Asha's knitting needles the only noise in the room. It's nice, I realize, to sit with people who don't have to speak all the time, who understand me, even though we only met each other a few minutes ago. It would be impossible to explain this to someone healthy, if I had to, especially after all my pre-support group jitters. But if I had to choose two words to describe this experience so far they would be: *not horrible.* Which is a lot better than I was hoping for.

"How's your trial going, Claire?" David asks.

"Good, thanks," Claire says before looking at me. "I'm a lawyer," she says, and then one of the largest law firms in the country rolls off her tongue with a lilt. "And I'm first-chairing the Wilson trial. We're almost finished, probably this week we'll rest, and then it will go to the jury. I haven't had a migraine the full length of the trial, six months. I really think the medication combination I'm on is finally working." She sits back in her seat and picks up her knitting again. Her nails are perfectly manicured, her pale-but-still-interesting suit hangs on her shoulders exactly right, and she's probably my age, give or take a year or two. I recognize the trial she's working on; it's been in the news, corporate tomfoolery and redress. A big deal. A small, sneaky thought blooms in my brain: *See? It can be done. You can have migraine and find the right medicine combination and be successful. You can have your what-if life.*

"I might even stop taking my preventative," Claire says, a small smile on her face.

"Oh God, Claire, don't do that," Asha says, turning to me. "You know what can happen if you stop taking a preventative that works, Viive, yes?"

I nod. A med can fail for you, like, *forever* if you stop and then start taking it again; like it can't quite latch on properly the second time around. Like it's still angry about being rejected in the first place.

"Just joking, Asha!" Claire says, giggling a little. "We love to get Asha's goat."

David joins in laughing and Asha harrumphs a little, but you can tell they're all kidding. Migraine comedians.

We sit there, quiet again. "Where's Paulie?" I ask, out of nowhere.

"Dialysis," David says. "She had to change her routine tonight for some reason."

"She?"

"Oh, yes indeedy. Paulie is all woman."

"David, we're not going to objectify women anymore," Asha says.

"Are you sure?" David answers, a wicked grin on his face. "It's pretty much the only thing I'm good at."

"Lies," Asha says, waving her hand at him as she smiles that smile.

"Hmm," I say as David passes me a business card, seemingly out of nowhere. "Thanks. Do you just carry these around in your wallet?"

"Yes," David says, his head rakishly tilted. He's not bad-looking, David. "You never know when you're going to meet someone who needs a hand."

"We believe in patient advocacy," Asha says. "But we also understand how hard it can be to get out of bed sometimes. So perhaps it's better to say we believe in patient advocacy on your own time. You don't have to do anything to belong here, you don't have to show up every week. Just when you're able."

"This is how we're stuck with Jaydyn." David snorts.

"This is how we're helping a young man come to terms with his illness," Asha says, giving David a look that's stern in a motherly kind of a way. "And David's neuro has a little more…testosterone than I'm personally comfortable with. We have others as well."

"Can you talk like that…testosterone?" David asks. "Aren't you a grandmother?"

She gives him a look.

"Sorry, Asha," David says, and he sounds sincere. His belt vibrates. "That's the call I'm waiting on from Dubai. See you in a few weeks, guys. Nice to meet you, Viive." He gathers his stuff, kisses Asha on the head on his way out.

"He's never going to get rid of his headaches until he slows down," Claire says, shaking her head.

"He'll do it when he's ready," Asha says, nodding. Eventually, she turns to me. "I hope Jaydyn didn't turn you off of our little group. We have lost other members because of him. We don't want this to happen again."

"I'm sure I'll find a way to ignore him, but I'm not sure why he's here–it's his mother who has the real headaches," I say.

Claire snaps her fingers. "You're right. I've been suspicious that she's migraining, and I think she's getting worse. Today her eye was–"

"All puffed up," I finish.

"Exactly," Claire says, with an impressed look.

I smile back, probably prouder of myself than I should be, and Asha and Claire talk about Ruth: is it subterfuge or is she in denial, and so on. While they chat, my attention wanders over the room, a tangle of thoughts nesting in my head. For some reason it feels easy to think here, and I like not having anything to prove or explain. I like being in a room where living with migraine is a normal thing, nothing to be sorry for. And everyone in the group seems to have the same quiet patience, that they know what to do, especially Claire, whose whole persona emanates the type of confidence I've always wanted to portray. I wonder what it means that they're all so similar, what they know that I don't.

And then my thoughts turn to an old snapshot, one taken back in university. It's one of Nate's favourites, even though I've never quite figured out why. I was twenty-one in the picture, taken at a wedding that ended up in the society papers. My hair was done professionally–$100 dollars plus a dress that almost wiped me out financially. My hair is big and I'm almost painfully skinny, my arms like pipe cleaners, even though at the time I already thought of myself as oversized, and I'm hoisting a wine glass for a toast. I was a regular pain clinic attendee at the time, and when the picture was taken, I was riddled with drugs, ebbing on a sea of migraine preventatives and counter-point meds which blunted the edges of the headache treatments. At that time in my life I was always at some point on the medication spectrum: About to take a med, eating something so I could take a med, retrieving my meds before I got ready for bed, lining them up so they'd be ready for me to take first thing in the morning. Once you're in the grip of that kind of medical care (and, oh God, you should see the pain clinic Martin hooked me up with), you have to give yourself over to being ill, and I refused to do it, which is probably part of the reason I've spent the last ten years ignoring being sick and focusing on my job.

Of course, life has a way of going on whether you like it or not.

I look from Claire to Asha and think: *What if there was another way to be sick? Like David with his first-class globetrotting or Claire's public success or Asha's happy family, all outfitted in award-winning knitwear? What if there was a way to live a better kind of life?*

"Young lady," Asha says, interrupting my daydreaming. "I think you're in the right place."

And for a small, hopeful moment, I let myself believe her. Being here feels like standing on the edge of something, being surrounded by newness. If I'm honest with myself I know I'll never get better unless I start over, like a reboot. I do it all the time at work; something fails, and then we start over. It's easy.

Right?

6 – Triage

My alarm has been trying to murder me ever since six this morning, set early because Nate has a meeting with his boss. After I mashed the snooze button the first time the clock fell under the bed. Now to reach it I have to dislocate my shoulder in a twisty yoga move that's almost impossible to complete unless you limber up first. Which I'm in no state to do right now.

I can hear Nate in the bathroom, whistling cheerily while he showers.

I thought I'd be happy to be going back to work, and I am, except for the fact that my arms and legs weigh eight hundred pounds.

There's a chill in the room, a reminder to set the timer on the furnace, that makes me pull the covers around myself a little tighter. Underneath the bed, the alarm bleats. Sitting up–when I finally get my shit together enough to do so–is not pleasant. In the background I hear Nate belting out *Hello Dolly*, a good indication he's his usual chipper morning self. If I could bottle the energy Nate has, squeeze it out of his hypothalamus when he's not looking, I'd seriously consider it. It's probably some kind of spousal abuse, but I'll stack the jury with migraineurs, who will never convict.

I reach under the bed and hit snooze, and as I run my tongue over my teeth I feel the sharp sting of the skin on my lower lip breaking open again. I put my finger up to my mouth; there's blood. Not a lot, but enough, an ugly little smear on my finger. My stomach tightens at the sight, and I have to push down that worry and all the ones underneath it; am I going to faint in the lunchroom, is my migraine really gone? It feels like it, and the weekend was quiet, but you never really know. I close my eyes again and I try to focus on the positive: my exile is over.

Nate gets out of the shower after a big finish for his song, and then starts on his manscaping. Eventually he opens the bedroom door, which he must have closed so he wouldn't wake me up. Nate is like that, considerate, fastidious about things that'll make my life easier. Even if I was magically cured today, I could never make it all up to him; I'll always be playing catch-up.

"Morning babe," he says. He looks boyishly refreshed, his caramel hair as neat as it'll get today, his green eyes sparkling.

"Morning, honey." I try to smile.

He climbs back into bed with me. "Looking forward to work?"

I kiss his neck while he wraps himself around me and we burrow into the covers together. "Can't we just stay home today?" I ask. "Together? You know, play hooky?"

"Weren't you the one who was so pissed off about having to take all that vacation time? And weren't you the one who was so excited to go back to work?"

"Mmmm."

The two of us lie there, lazy and entwined in each other. A perfect fit. He smells like aftershave and shampoo and Nate, and with any luck, he's ignoring my sticky sleep smells.

"Okay, I have to get dressed," he says, too soon. "I have a meeting with my evil corporate overlords."

"F-i-i-i-ne," I say, pretending irritation that's only partly exaggerated. After two weeks I've gone soft. This is terrible. I lie in bed while Nate gets dressed; a light sweater over his favourite Tesla t-shirt, and khakis. He looks like the young corporate nerd he is, but his eyes are particularly mischievous today.

"Why are you so happy?" I ask.

"Because normally in the morning you act like some kind of swamp monster," he says, with a grin, and then continues in an awful falsetto, "Naaaaate, just five more minutes. Naaaaaaate, can you make me lunch? Naaaaate–"

"Oh my God," I say. "That's terrible. I'm sorry."

"It's okay, honey," he says. "I know you're a little slow–"

I lob a pillow, which he neatly sidesteps.

"Slow in the morning," he says. "Only in the morning, babe. The rest of the day you're like Flash Gordon."

"That's it. I need a new husband."

"Sorry," he says, "you're stuck with me."

"Oh, *fine*," I say, trying not to smile.

He reaches down and kisses me, on my forehead, my nose, my lips. Butterfly kisses. "Have a great day, and don't overdo it."

"Me?"

"You heard me." He kisses me again, I run my fingers through his hair to try to neaten it, and then he's gone. The minute he leaves, a shiver runs up my spine and all the thoughts I've been trying to ignore for the past two weeks flood back in. Is today the day Elliot fires me?

I glance at the clock. So early, but I might as well get up, take my medication. I put one foot on the floor tentatively, and then the next. I stand up. After a shower–no singing this time, no reason to torture the neighbours–I put the kettle on before looking through the pantry for the fancy tea Nate and I normally only drink on the weekend. A can of green beans falls out of the overstuffed cupboards and lands on my toe. I hop around for a bit while I find the tea and then try to jam the doors shut. Next I take half the normal dose of the mint-green anticonvulsant and wash it down with some Earl Grey; thanks to Paulie's advice I've reduced my meds and I think that it's making me feel a little better.

While the tea steeps, I grab an apple from the fridge and sit down on the sofa in the living room before logging into my work email and IM accounts to see what's going on today at work. I should be up-to-date on everything–I spent most of the weekend working–but there's always that little voice in my head telling me, *Just in case, check on this one thing too, look at this log, avoid that mess, squash this problem.*

The news is on in the background, the stories about traffic (bad, as usual), the weather (gearing up for winter, I still need to find my jacket), and a special musical guest who's playing a sitar and looks a tiny bit like a lunatic. Sitting there, with my good tea and my crisp apple, the thud of my headache just a memory, another pesky worry sneaks under my radar: *What, exactly, is waiting for me at work?*

On the way to the office I grab a ginormous tea and a chocolate croissant–still warm, also enormous. For reasons I don't quite understand I've always hated eating breakfast. I've remained mystified over the years by the relentless propaganda about breakfast being the most important meal of the day. This morning, though, I know I'll need sustenance.

Our receptionist, Hattie, is a perpetually happy ex-retiree who always sneaks extra cookies to me if she's ordering food for meetings I'm in. This morning she's wearing a red dress with white trim that's most likely an original from the sixties, modish and back in fashion, her grey hair in a neat silver bob, her shrewd hazel eyes seeing me immediately, even though she's bustling around the reception area, juggling three couriers, a visitor, and someone on the phone.

"Hello young lady," she calls to me. "Don't move a muscle."

Hattie is no one to be trifled with, so I plop into a chair and look around. Everything looks the same, which should make the butterflies in my stomach disappear, but doesn't. I try to look casual while I sip my tea, even after I spill some on my lap.

Hattie dispatches the crowd in a few minutes and then comes over to me, sits down. "You horrible girl," she says.

"What?"

"You never said goodbye to me before your big vacation," she says, her mouth twisted in ersatz pique. "I was going to take you out for tea first, but I never saw you."

I exhale. "Oh, shit, sorry. I looked for you and you weren't there. You were probably off on one of your dates." Hattie's husband ran off with another woman last year and ever since she's been throwing herself into the online dating world.

"That's true," she says. "I am highly in demand. Buy me a tea this afternoon and all is forgiven."

"Done," I say, giving her a little squeeze.

"Did you have fun?"

"I did, thanks."

"Where did you go?"

"I had a staycation," I say, as she hands me my mail.

"You know that new guy, what's his name…?"

"God, Hattie, we hire new people like every five minutes." I smile, even though the back of my neck has started to tingle.

"Joe, that's it. It was the strangest thing," she says. "This is…a week ago maybe? I stepped away for a minute to get something to eat, and when I came back, he was where the mailboxes are. And I could swear he was going through your mail."

"Are you sure?"

"I had just put a letter for you in your mailbox and I had pushed it all the way in. I remember, because it hit the wall when I did it. But when I came back, it was hanging out."

"Thanks Hattie," I say, searching through my mail. There's nothing unsettling in the pile, bills, marketing fluff. My stomach flutters briefly, anyway.

"No problem, dear."

"Hey, did you order lunch for the management meeting?" I ask, casting out for a change in subject. This particular meeting is every Monday, generally a three-hour ordeal that starts at noon, and Elliot almost never orders in lunch. Elliot seems to be able to go forever without eating–like a camel–but usually on Mondays what ends up happening is I don't eat anything at all until three and I'm ready to faint. Dr. Throckmorton's trusty pamphlets proselytize about not letting yourself get too hungry. So today, I'm smug and eating and on top of everything.

"Elliot had to leave town, late last night," she says, giving my arm a little squeeze. "Your management meeting is moved to Thursday." She sighs, patting my hand happily, before the CEO appears, standing beside her desk, pointedly looking at a wristwatch that Nate covets–I can never remember what kind it is–so I leave reception and walk upstairs to my office. I was worried that Sid would have told everyone I'd cracked up, but it looks like he's kept the reason for my exile to himself. Hattie knows *and* tells me everything, so if she doesn't know, then no one does. There's a fast exhale of breath that accompanies this realization, that maybe things are a little less precarious than I thought, that the worried nagging ideas at the back of my head ever since the sit-down with Sid and Elliot two weeks were maybe all for nothing.

Although probably not.

On my way upstairs, I stop by a few people's desks to say hi. By the time I get to my office, it's almost a half an hour later. I drop my bags in the doorway before checking my voicemail–there's a two a.m. message from Elliot, asking me to go to the executive sit-down for him, which has been moved to ten this morning. I love attending these meetings when Elliot is out of town or otherwise occupied. I smile and then go next door, to Otis's office, where I plop myself in one of his chairs.

"My God, I've missed you," Otis says. "Everything has been pants since you left. When are we going out for drinks? Immediately?" He's wearing his usual, a crisp white dress shirt with suspenders and black trousers. The only thing that ever really changes is the pattern on his suspenders.

"Dice today?"

He grins and snaps the suspenders, the smile lines around his brown eyes crinkling like usual, before running his hand through his sandy blond hair. It goes back into place like it always does, a neat realignment that's just a little bit creepy. "Yes."

"New suspenders?" I pull the top off my tea and dump in a few more sugars.

"I've had these for years."

"I must be going senile."

"Probably already halfway there."

I shrug a little, in a way that says, *probably*.

"What's going on, McBroom?" He leans forward, raises an eyebrow. "Did you get the doctor's note?"

I nod.

"I dropped by your place, you know. Last week. I was hoping we could grab a drink."

"Must have been out," I say, even though I was probably flat on my back, tracing out the cracks in the ceiling when he came by, a little detail I decide to keep to myself.

"Viive?"

I look up. My two team leads, Manjit and Brian, are both hovering at my doorway. "Hey."

"Busy?" Brian asks.

"Nope." I get up and go to my office, the two of them on my heels. They sit down in the chairs in front of my desk, which looks just like I left it. My heart makes an excited little jump at the sight of it.

"Hey boss lady," Brian says, his smile wide, mischievous. "I am so glad you're here."

"Good to see you," Manjit says, a little less stiffly than usual, which is about as wild as he gets.

"Really glad you're back," Brian repeats. "Don't go away again, okay? I haven't slept since you left."

"You guys did a great job," I say. "I really appreciate all your hard work."

"I had to cancel a date," Brian says. "A date with a *woman.*"

"Need a hug?"

"Probably," he says, holding out his arms, both of them sleeved with tattoos; gothic tats mixed in with cartoon characters that somehow look good together.

"Maybe later," I say, and smile. "Anything I should know that I don't already?" I pull up the landing page for the monitoring system, the pulse of our environment. I have three screens at my desk, and the monitoring cluster floods all of them with a simple colour-coded system. Machines running smoothly are a cheery green, ones with minor issues are amber, and the ones that are screwed are red.

"We have some boxes that're flapping," Brian says. "And we're not sure why."

I frown.

"Pull up the Tatooine cluster," Manjit says, and I jump to that page; twenty physical machines, at least that many virtual. As the three of us watch, two squares turn from green to red and start to pulse.

"Whoa," I say, my attention elevating. "How long has this been going on?" Next, the two boxes blink grey before turning green again. "That's bad. What's the impact to the customer?"

"Started at about midnight last night," Manjit says. "We have enough automated recovery steps in place so it hasn't caused any impact yet."

"Anything changed in the environment recently?" I ask.

"The last code release for these guys was a few weeks ago," Manjit says.

"Hardware's okay? Any patches or changes to the operating systems?"

"Yes, and then no," Brian says.

I tap my pen against my chin, careful to avoid the ruined skin on my bottom lip. "Is it all the machines? Virtual or physical?"

"Both," Brian says. "And it's affected about half the web servers."

"*Half*?"

The two of them nod.

"What does your gut say?" I ask.

Brian looks at Manjit, and then at me. "It doesn't make a lot of sense."

The second he says this, my monitoring screens blink once and then explode red, all the servers lit up like they're on fire. The three of us sit there, our attention rapt on the sight, barely breathing. We wait for a count of ten, and then twenty, to make sure there's no change. And there's not; the customer is now completely down. Websites completely down mean cancelled contracts, agonizing post-mortems with the exec team, our company name in a snarky newspaper article. In an instant the three of us are on our feet.

"Get everyone," I say, "Get your laptops and get in here. Now."

In less than three minutes half the team's in my office, and I distribute investigative tasks to everyone there: checking out hardware, logs, applications, virus status, unusual network activity, running diagnostics, and then I swing my rubber chicken, for luck.

"Earl," I say, "run point on communications, if you get any hassle, text me. I'll send out the initial word to Elliot and Sid." Earl nods once, a tight, stiff movement. Being in charge of information during a customer outage is a nightmare because you have to deal with a ton of pissed-off people. But Earl is a natural charmer, perpetually calm, and just a tiny bit physically intimidating, what with him being six-foot-five, muscled in places I didn't even know you could get muscles, and all, which is why he always gets stuck with it.

Susie, who thankfully isn't sporting any pink taffeta today, pulls three desks into my tiny office and then closes the door, standard operation procedure in cases like this. We can't concentrate if people are asking for updates every three minutes. Ten people mash themselves into chairs.

I text Elliot, Sid, and the salesperson for the customer, telling them that the client is down and that Earl will be updating every fifteen minutes, also standard operating procedure for these types of situations. I try not to think about the weather report I looked at this morning. Rain coming: headache weather. It's all just triage and adrenaline now, getting the customer back up, figuring out what the hell is going on.

Oh, it's good to be back.

"Alright," I say to Brian and Manjit, who are huddled around my desk. If I looked in the mirror right now I know I'd see a smile on my face. I clear my throat and focus. "Brian, are the web servers running in a contiguous address space?"

"Yes."

"Manjit, take them out of rotation on the firewall. Brian, shut the machines down. We're going to run virtual. I'll put up a clean operating system and grab a known-good copy of the code." If we can get back up in less than a half hour, there won't be any business penalties because of the outage, and no outrage from Elliot and the rest of the execs. We're now at thirteen minutes and we're all breathing hard and fast, focused and quiet. Everything outside my doors just falls away.

"Is there any database stuff I need to worry about with a roll-back?" I ask Manjit.

He reviews his testing notes before shaking his head. "No changes for a long time with these guys."

Pushing out a clean virtual server takes me four minutes, my heart buffeting against my ribs the whole time. All I need now is the website code, so I try to find the latest iteration in the code vault. There's the copy that Manjit promoted a few weeks ago, a bunch of older code, and then a folder date-stamped last night. It's odd to have so many code versions–it's like rearranging your furniture twice a day, especially since this client is in financial services; they're traditional, conservative, and don't like to change or pay for anything. And there's no reason for there to be code from last night on an Internet-facing box, but I push that thought to the side and then find the right version and promote it to the single web server, watch the files explode on the hard drive, tweak the config, and the customer is officially back up. I filter all the downed servers out of the monitoring screen so all we watch is the new fledgling machine with its fresh IP address hold up the weight of all the customer's web traffic.

The screen blinks green.

My heart gives a lusty thump at the sight of it, and I can feel myself smiling. "Hit the site from an external source," I say to Brian, and then add, "please." There's no time for social niceties when a customer is hard down, just questions and responses, orders and actions. Now that we're back up, it's time to resume being polite to each other.

Brian smiles at me, a thank you for the *please*. "I'm on my BSD machine at home, site's up."

I check my watch. "Okay, that's down for…twenty-three minutes.

I'll roll a second server in," I say, as I text Sid, Earl, Elliot and the rest of the critical notification list. After I finish, I prep the operating systems for ten more machines.

It wasn't a particularly complicated problem, but there's a warm glow of success in my belly anyway, endorphins fired up and buzzing around my brain, my heartbeat still banging away in my chest. "Good work, guys."

"Well, I am wonderful," Brian says, reaching around to pat himself on the back.

I laugh and reach for my tea, which I realize I've left in Otis's office. I head to the break room for some water; Otis has probably turned my tea into some kind of pop art exhibit in the lobby by now. As I fill my cup I massage the back of my neck, which is clammy with sweat. I drain my glass twice before heading back to my office.

Joe, the new guy, the snail-mail molester, is there, standing over my desk, his voice raised as he grills Brian and Manjit. Manjit tends to withdraw from conflict, and he's sitting in his seat, his face thoughtful. Brian is on his feet and arguing with Joe.

"What's going on?" I ask.

Joe turns to me. "You guys took down my code without telling me."

I smile and turn to Brian and Manjit. "Brian, the new virtual machines should be ready. Can you bring them in? I'll be back in a sec."

Brian's jaw clenches, but he nods and sits back down. Then I walk Joe out, to his office and away from the work that's still going on. After we get there I shut the door after myself. "So, you're new here," I say as we both take a seat. "We should probably run through how we do things." Joe makes himself comfortable in his chair, a chair that seems newer and shinier than mine. There are some kitschy knick-knacks on his desk, some framed posters on his walls; extreme motorcycling and race cars. Joe looks like he's making himself right at home here. He also looks much more calm than he did in my office. I hate that, people who yell at my staff but are pleasant to me. My post-crisis endorphin rush starts to sour in my veins.

"Please," he says.

"When we're running a problem, we need to work undisturbed," I say. "We can't focus if we have to update people every few minutes, especially if we have less than a half hour to figure out what's going on and get back up and running. You should be on the incident list. Did you not get Earl's email?"

"Well, with all due respect, Viive," he says, smiling an unpleasant sort of grin, "I'm not just 'people.' I'm the head of development."

Yes, but everyone always thinks they're not just "people." I stifle a sigh. "I understand. Did you get Earl's email?"

"I have no idea, Viive. I can't check my email every five minutes."

"Hmmm." I sip my water.

"I can't be in a situation where I don't know what's going on. That's why I paged Elliot."

The back of my neck twinges, a quiet *ping*. "What?"

"I was on the site and noticed it was offline. You pulled all your staff into your room, how was I supposed to know what was going on?"

"Well, you could have knocked on my door."

The two of us sit there, a heat in the small room. Not only do you not berate someone else's staff, you definitely don't go over a manager's head to complain about them, not in the middle of an incident. It just isn't done.

"I need to be texted," Joe says.

"Okay," I say. "I'll add you to that list. And I'll ask you, instead of escalating issues, to speak to me from now on."

"You weren't there."

After a beat, I say, "You're welcome to text me, if you can't find me. Okay?"

The "okay" hangs in the air between us, an invitation for him to push his point. Finally he says, with an oily smile, "I guess that's alright."

"Thanks Joe," I say, giving him my calm-and-professional smile in return. "We appreciate it when we can all work together for a good outcome." I stand and nod at him before going back to my office, which has emptied out in my absence, except for my leads. I shut the door behind me. "Where are we at?" I ask Brian.

"I've put three more servers in with that code version and they're all solid so far, they're good," Brian says.

"Pull up one of the servers that had the old code," I say. "Make sure it's out of rotation."

Manjit boots one of the old servers and logs on.

"What's the date of the active website code?"

He drops down to command line and types for a few minutes. "They're timestamped." He looks at me. "Last night."

"I thought so," I say.

Brian looks at me, realization dawning. "It was never even tested. It never hit QA."

"So someone's been sneaking unauthorized code onto those servers," I say, tapping my pen against my chin.

"It looks like it, yes," Manjit says. "It never cleared testing, and my team never promoted it. I'm sorry I didn't check the code version earlier, Viive."

"You wouldn't have had any reason to," I say.

"It's got to be Joe," Brian says. "Or someone on his team."

I nod. "Okay, I'll deal with it. Thanks guys."

The two of them collect their gear and get up. "Viive?" Brian says, stopped at the door.

"Mmm?"

"It's good to have you back," he says, grinning.

"Yeah, yeah," I say, waving him away with a smile.

After they're gone I finally have time to unpack my bag and get ready for the day. When I pull open my desk drawer to put my new meds with my migraine stash, the drawer is empty. I open the other three. Same.

Otis.

I deposit the bottle of pills in the empty drawer and check the time. It's nine fifty-eight; two minutes to get to the executive meeting. I'm out of breath by the time I reach the main boardroom–the one only the execs are allowed to book. The room is an oasis of calm after the morning that I've had so far, and there are gourmet muffins, pastries, and fruit, along with coffee and tea. I get up and take a chocolate croissant and a cup of Earl Grey before settling myself in a plush leather chair as far away from the CEO as possible; he's a mouth breather and it always gives me the giggles. The room is full of c-level execs: the chief executive officer, Lyle, the chief financial officer, Aadi, the chief technical officer, Sid, the vice-president of marketing, Rhonda, the vice-president of HR, Violet, a few other execs, and a few assistants, who will take minutes (Elliot tells me that sometimes the minutes don't match and then the execs fight about it later, which I've always found hilarious). There's an abundance of tailored suits and flashy ties in the room. I'm wearing my only suit, navy, with a white blouse, with stylish, painful heels Avery bought for me for Christmas last year. If I compare myself to Rhonda and Violet, I think I look okay. Rhonda has thick ankles and dresses like it's still the eighties–aggressive shoulder pads and colour choices smacking of neon. Violet is petite and elegant, wearing a taupe suit with a long, slitted skirt. I'd like to squish myself between the two of them, find out what they talk about when it's just them.

I want to belong in this room.

The meeting is a jumble of timelines, budgets, strategy, and leveraging our market position. When it's time for my update, I manage to deliver my status without screwing up or falling out of my chair, so I file it under success. I should know what I'm talking about, after all–I'm the one who puts this report together every week, not Elliot. Sid asks about the outage this morning and I give him an update, which he replies to with a nod and a brief, "Good."

The meeting passes over to someone else, while I try to seem like I belong.

I try not to twirl in my seat.

While I'm sitting there, trying not to twirl, I think about why I want this so badly. It's not the money–this is a small company and will never pay what a director or VP could command at a larger corporation. Maybe it's that I think it would be the ultimate marker of success. And since I've spent a good portion of the last few years lying in a dark room with an icepack over my eyes, well…there haven't been a lot of successes. Not to mention that I want my mother's Skype face to go away, eventually. I also want to choose the technology I implement, and I want to do it the right way, not seat-of-the-pants hacks, but proper, reasoned technology solutions at my own company.

As I watch Sid pull on his bowtie–the demure, striped, grey number that's his go-to for exec meeting days–and listen to Lyle droning on about EBITDA, I know one thing for sure: the timelines they're presenting will never happen. The deliverables simply can't be met unless I, and every other manager, pushes the people actually doing the work even harder. And there's not a lot of room to push, these days.

But the meeting goes on anyway, as these kinds of meetings do, and when it finally breaks up, it's all smiles and handshakes, mentions of golfing on the weekend, and who went to what restaurant. I lean in a little, listen to the conversations, try to look like I know what I'm talking about.

Later, I eat dinner at my desk–Thai–with Brian, Manjit, Earl, and Susie, who's still there, hovering. Everyone catches me up on the gossip; I sit back and let them fill me in (the head of finance was spotted out at dinner with a woman not his wife, the mouth-breathing CEO ordered a big screen TV but had it delivered to his home instead of his office, Sid's assistant, Bethie, stapled her finger to a document and demanded to be driven to the ER), and some speculation on whether we're going to get some gear we're waiting on released from customs this week (yes, I'll take care of it), and if we're all going to die from overwork (probably, but not today, we all agree). After everyone finally takes off at ten, I pull up the monitoring system again, flood all of my screens with it. I'm so happy looking at it that the small burst of emotion exhausts me. It's a good kind of tired, watching the hum of the monitoring cluster, a patchy in-house job, a labour of love the last development manager built for me before he quit the biz and headed to Tahiti. All those green lights promise that everything is okay. I wish the rest of my life could be like that, with log files showing me what was wrong, status updates promising that everything is going to turn out all right.

This is the very worst part of migraine, the good days, the what-if days, the ones where I pass for normal. It gives all the bad days a hazy glow that says: *This isn't your real life. This isn't the way it really is.* It's the good days that always make the focus in my life on tomorrow, because things might be better then. It's the good days that make the bad ones bearable, because I know they'll come again. They always do.

It's dark outside, and most of the city went home hours ago, but it's still the very best kind of a what-if day, the kind where I barely look up from my computer, barely know that time is ticking, where my weekend sickness falls away and I'm good at something. A day of saving the world one customer at a time, pastry with the executives, the knowledge, firm like an apple, that everything is going to be okay. With all that green, how could it not?

7 – THE LAYAWAY PLAN

Since I'm still not sure if I've been having seizures or if I'm actually just about to explode, I call my GP's office to organize the EEG. To prep for the test, I'm not allowed caffeine or styling aids, so today, not only am I stimulant-deprived, I have really bad hair. Right now I'm on my lunch hour, and my friendly cab driver, who's utterly convinced we're in the Indy 500, is driving us to the clinic while I check my work email for the last time and try to ignore the uneasy buzz in my stomach. I hate being unreachable.

When I get to the clinic, a squat, unwelcoming building, I fill out the requisite phone book of forms before sitting down to wait. I try to shake off the chill in the air while I take out my eReader, registering a pang of regret when I remember it was a gift from Ruby. Things I am failing at so far today: *Calling Ruby. And let's not even think about those squirrels.*

After a half an hour of waiting, I hear, "Viev McBroom? This way please." The clinician is short, her walk a brisk waddle, and her eyes are hard and flat, grey-blue marbles in a tired and jowly face. If I had to think of two words to describe her they would be: *pissed off.* If I was pressed about it, I'd probably add *and slightly scary.*

I don't trust my head in her angry, tired hands, and for a minute I think about bolting, but we're suddenly at the room and it's too late to formulate an escape plan. "Sit," she says, and then proceeds to attach so many nodules to my scalp that I start feeling bionic. As she works, she moves my head back and forth in rough, jerky patterns. At the end I get a terse explanation: some parts of the test will be with my eyes closed, others open, before a bunch of other stuff I can't remember because my throat is all of a sudden tight and dry and it's hard to swallow. And then I'm alone. The room is very cold, and all I can think is how much I want my sweater, hanging on a hook too far away for me to reach.

The test starts, and I sit there quietly for a while, trying not to think about anything. The machine chugs away in the cold room while the clock on the wall ticks. The anxiety starts slowly, with a nibble on my left foot. I try to ignore it and think of something happy, but the electrodes and the sterile environment all scream *seizure!* and the panic has my foot now, like a dog with a bone. Suddenly a chill zips up my left leg and then my right before ratcheting up my spine, and I'm trying not to break out in ragged, desperate breathing. I look around to see if there's anything positive in the room I can focus on, but there's nothing but plain white walls, the hum of machinery, and the unrelenting cold. *What if I keep fainting? What if this is my new normal?* I think about the machine probing into the ruined landscape of my brain, sniffing out the residue of a maybe-seizure, and I want to rip the nodes off my head. I want to cry.

Breathe.

My blood pounds in my ears.

Look at the door. I force the thought into my consciousness. It's just a normal room, a normal door. Nothing bad is happening here.

Breathe.

I didn't even know I was worried about the test until now, so all the panic is a shock as it runs through me. All I can think is: *I can't have seizures. I can't have a new problem.*

It's not a good moment, me and my bad hair and any number of worse possible futures. I close my eyes and try to focus on a time in my life when I had something to look forward to. Ruby flashes in my mind, with her oversized bun and her yen for the perfect sandwich. I wonder what it would be like to have a meal make your whole day, to know when you got up that you were going to be able to go to a restaurant, your favourite place, 365 days a year, if you wanted, and order anything off the menu. So many choices, ones you could rely on. The decadence of it all makes my hands feel numb.

Breathe.

Since English isn't working I decide to try Estonian: *Hingata!* And when that doesn't work either, I try a multicultural combination: *Breathe! Hingata! Breathe! Hingata!*

Eventually the technician interrupts my self-pity and separates me from the nest of medical machinery. She doesn't bother to say anything to me, and I don't bother to thank her before I leave, plunging my arms into my sweater sleeves as I go. With every step away from that room I feel better, warmer, more whole inside.

After I flag a cab I text the finance manager to let him know I'm running late for the budget meeting I'm supposed to be in right now, and when I get back to the office I take the stairs two at a time, because the elevator is out again. I make an appearance at the meeting, hoping everyone will ignore my sweatiness, while we review our budgets for the year. I've kept mine in the black, and there's even a little bit of padding in the numbers. (Thanks, Mom.) I promise to bring donuts to the next meeting, to make up for being late, and all is forgiven.

When I finally make it back to my office, Otis is sitting at my desk with two coffees and a smile on his face.

"Thanks!" I say, reaching forward and taking one. "How'd you know I'd be back now?"

"I like to sit in your office when you're not here."

"Creepy."

"I asked Brian."

"Sneaky *and* creepy," I say.

Otis smiles like I've just given him a compliment.

I pull the top off the coffee and sniff it before taking a sip. It's hazelnut, with cream and just the right amount of sugar, and it helps smooth out the leftover ragged feelings from the EEG. "This is perfect, thanks." I try to think of the last time I picked up coffee for Otis. *Tomorrow*, I promise myself, *I will do something nice for Otis tomorrow. I will be a good friend tomorrow.*

"So, I didn't get a chance to talk to you about Joe," Otis says, snapping off the lid of his drink and hanging his nose–a good, patrician nose–over it, inhaling the scent. Unlike mine, his coffee isn't sweetened or flavoured, it's dingy and dark-roasted, with so much caffeine it'd make me stay awake for the next three days. He fancies himself a connoisseur.

"Should we shut the door?" I ask.

Otis looks up at the open ceiling above us and gives me a look that says, *really?*

"Just asking, slick," I say, grinning. "So what's the deal?"

"What do you know about this guy, Joe?"

"Not much, he's never worked with anyone I know," I say, wary. "He's only been here a month or two."

"Yeah, I know. But he's a complete tosser. You should have seen the kind of stuff he pulled while you were gone. He's been pushing himself into situations that have nothing to do with him, and trying to tell everyone what to do. Denise from HR even told me he's been trying to get them to change the bonus structure. I never told you that, by the way."

"Course not."

"Anyway, he missed a deadline for some website code, and then tried to tell Elliot it was my fault, which is bullshit. We had a meeting about the requirements. It was in the minutes, for Christ's sake."

"What did Elliot say?"

"Well that's the thing. I tried to get Elliot to read the minutes, but you know how he is, can barely sit still for five seconds–"

"Sure."

"Elliot didn't really seem to believe me. And we've always gotten along pretty well. Not as good as the two of you, but still."

I raise an eyebrow. "If Elliot was so fond of me, none of this would have happened. I mean, I've never gotten a bad performance review in my career, and it has to be in front of the CTO?"

"Over-achiever," he says. "Hey, didn't you tell me you were up for some sort of promotion?"

I sigh, trying to ignore the warmth collecting at the back of my neck. "Right, Elliot has been saying for the last year that they're going to split the tech group into two; he's going to lead up one team, the developer side. And he's basically told me the operations part will be mine. And I want that job. No offence."

"I wouldn't take it if you put a gun to my head," Otis says. "I have my hands full, thanks. I'll wager Joe's got his eye on it though."

"You've got to be kidding. He just got here. He wouldn't even know about it. And he doesn't do ops work."

"I'll bet you, right here, right now, fifty bucks that's exactly what he's doing. Remember how you were saying someone was complaining about you using the nurse's room? Was Joe ever around when you did?"

I blink. "Yes. You know that big build we released back in September? It was about nine o'clock on a Friday and I still had a ton of work to do, so I took some meds and lay down for an hour or so. And Joe was walking by when I went to lie down."

"Well, there you go."

There's a growing tightness in my stomach that makes me shift in my seat. "Aren't you supposed to be trying to cheer me up?"

"I never received the specifications for that, I'm sorry. Anyway, I'm not quite sure what his problem is yet, but I bet it's hard to pronounce."

I smile.

"No laugh, huh? Want to grab drinks after work on Friday? That'll cheer you up."

"Maybe."

"I will take your maybe as a yes," Otis says, and then gets up to leave.

"Can I have my stuff back?"

"What stuff is that, Viive?"

"From my desk, Otis. You know."

He stops at the door, with a smile. "I have a meeting now. I'll bring it back later." With that, he drops his coffee cup into my recycling with a wet thump and goes.

My thoughts turn sour. There's always a lot of competition in technology environments, smart people who work long hours and sometimes skimp on social skills. That doesn't bother me, and this Joe guy seems like a chump. But as I try to focus on my work, Otis's words stay with me anyway. There are one hundred and three new emails since this morning and I work through them until the nagging rumble in my gut makes me stop. Normally I'd keep going, but today, day three of my first week back, I am still afire with my one resolution: *Eat more often.* I go down to the lunchroom to buy a cookie out of the vending machine, which I bring back to my desk.

When I look up again, it's almost eight p.m. *Enough*, I think.

I feel much better than I usually do after a long day at work, especially considering my unpleasant lunchtime rendezvous with the cranky EEG technician, so on the way home I stop off at the market on Pape and find something nice to make for dinner. I pick out shallots, two marbled rib steaks, cheese, cream, the mixings for potatoes au gratin, a whack of thin green beans, and fresh crab cakes for an appetiser. I get two pieces of chocolate cake for dessert. Nate has had to deal with all of my craziness over the last month; I want to do something nice to make it up to him, finally.

When I get home I rub the steaks with some kosher salt, cracked pepper, and the shallots, and let them sit while I make the scalloped potatoes and clean the kitchen, dismantling the leaning-tower-of-Pisa piles on the counters as cheerily as possible. When Nate gets home, he kisses me, pours himself a beer, backs himself out of the kitchen, and sits on the couch with a small smile. I'd be lying if I said I didn't peek into the living room once or twice to make sure the smile was still in place, which it is. Making your spouse happy should be a trivial task, this far into a marriage, but I've failed at it so badly and so often that it's hard to tear myself away from the sight of this small success.

I feel restless, but I'm not quite sure why. Eventually it occurs to me that it might just be that today is a good day–I'm so out of practice I've almost forgotten what normal feels like. I'm tired and hungry and my ankles are killing me, but there's no real headache, no thumping hard-rock marathon in my head. It *is* a good day, I decide, and I'm going to end it with a nice dinner with my husband. Nothing unreasonable, nothing that's too much to ask for. And later, I'm going to tuck Nate into bed and enjoy those few sleepy minutes at the end of the day when we're bundled together under the covers. The thought makes me smile.

After dinner–decadent, delicious, perfect–Nate and I watch a movie, curled up on the couch together. Even though I want to check my email, I force myself not to look at it until later, right before bed. There's a thread bouncing between Elliot and Joe that I've been cc'd on. The conversation starts with Joe claiming there are issues with the testbed Brian runs. And then he says:

> *Vivian, I notice you're using Windows servers for the company's large-scale web hosting. I'm sure you know Linux is far superior at caching and scalability, so I'm wondering why this hasn't been implemented yet? I did mention this to you. If this change had been made, we would never be seeing these types of problems.*

I look at my screen, thinking about my conversation with Otis today. *Oh, Joe, what are you up to?* Anyone who actually understands systems would know Joe has no clue what he's talking about, but unfortunately, Elliot's background is also in constructing code and he doesn't really understand infrastructure. He thinks he does, but he doesn't, which is a tricky business to navigate with your boss. Especially these days.

Nate goes up to bed alone while I pen a quick response:

> *Joe, as I said in my email to you a few weeks ago, those servers are all Linux, and always have been. Can you please send me your specific issues with the environment, and I'll take a look at them?*
> *--Viive*

When I get back to bed, Nate is asleep, the covers tucked in around him, his face smooshed into a pillow, his chest rising and falling with each snore.

Goddammit.

"I need to make sure I have lunch for the meeting." I say, sipping the coffee I picked up on the way into the office this morning. On Otis's desk in front of him is the über-caffeinated drek I bought for him. Things I am succeeding at today: *coffee.*

"Why didn't you *bring* a lunch for the meeting, like me?" Otis pulls a little cooler out from underneath his desk, unzipping it with a flourish. There's a small thermos latched to one side with a miniature bungee cord, surrounded by little stacks of cut vegetables, a yogurt, two sandwiches, a Ziploc with three chocolate chip cookies, and a little insulated Tupperware container. Everything snaps together, in a NASA-worthy design. Otis's wife is domestic at a Martha Stewart level and works nine-to-five in North York (I can never remember doing what, something with money). I adore her.

"What's in the Tupperware?"

"Chicken noodle soup."

I put my head down on his desk. "Homemade?" When he doesn't answer I lift up enough to see him; he's wearing a smirk big enough–I swear to God–to be seen from space.

I pick up my tea. "I need a wife. Specifically, I need *your* wife."

"She is a delight, yes. Look, McBroom, are you all right?"

"I'm okay," I say.

"Are you sure, because–"

"Otis?"

"Yeah?"

"I'm fine."

"All righty, then. Let's get you some lunch."

"I just got here."

"I know, but you're almost an hour earlier than usual."

I squint at my watch: 8:30. "Yet somehow I'm already behind."

Before I know it, Otis is steering me out of the office and down the five floors and out to the street, to a small salad shop I've never noticed, even though I walk by it every single day. I get a large, one with all of those dark, angry greens that are actually good for you, and two boiled eggs. It feels a little unseemly to be so smug over a single healthy meal, but this does not stop me.

A little before noon, a knock interrupts my attempts to detangle a payment issue with two of our vendors. "Hi there," Elliot says, sticking his head through the doorway. "Got a minute?"

My stomach clenches. "Sure."

He runs his hands over the top of the chair in front of my desk before taking a seat. "I thought I'd walk you to the management meeting."

"Sure," I say, looking down, my palms suddenly moist. Elliot and I always used to get along so well and I don't want to be angry at him, but there's something new between us now, something that's hard to find a word for. Before, if you'd asked me to describe Elliot in one word I would have said, *polished,* or *accomplished.* It feels like it's time for a new word for him now, but I can't quite figure out what it is yet.

"Sure?" he mimics, his face pursed.

"Sure," I repeat, trying to inject a little more enthusiasm into my words.

"How was your vacation?"

I rearrange the two folders of invoices on my desk, the paper tacky against my palms. "Good, thanks. How've you been?"

He sighs. "Viive, I understand if you're upset with me. But we felt we needed to take some steps."

"I'm not upset," I say, still looking away from him, a soft murmur in my ears saying: *Be careful.* "And I appreciate it. I feel much better now. All ready to go." I stand up.

"Well that's good," he says. "I'm glad it all worked out. It's just business, Viive. Christmas will be here in a few months and we need everyone to be at a hundred percent. It's not personal."

It was personal to me.

"Right?" he says. He's still sitting, his arms crossed lazily over his chest, drawing the focus away from his eyes, which are glinting in a way I can't remember seeing before.

Be smart, Viive. Don't be dumb.

But then, like an idiot, I hear myself talking anyway. "I wish you'd told me there was a problem. I mean, we have weekly status meetings, isn't that what they're for?" The words are still hanging in the air, and I'm already cursing my big mouth. I look down at my desk to try to seem busy, to minimize the moment. I pick up my lunch.

Elliot gets to his feet, and after a pause says, "Aren't you forgetting something?"

"Hmm?"

"The note, Viive."

I rifle through my bag until I find it, hand it over.

"Great," Elliot says, not looking at it before he puts it in his pocket. "Let's go."

"Sure."

"And Viive?"

"I don't want us to get to this point again," he says, and his words are not quiet in the small, ceiling-less, room, floating over the side so that Otis has most certainly heard them.

The two of us don't say a lot on the short walk to the meeting room downstairs, and by not a lot, I mean nothing. Normally when I talk to Elliot I try to seem professional, competent. In charge. A lot of times, I try to channel my mother. But not today. And maybe it's his dismissal of my feelings (which he's done before, I have to admit) or maybe it's the muscle that flashed in his jaw when he said it: *just business*. Like I'm a stranger. Like I'm nobody. I don't even want to think about his last words, the soft threat in his voice. I might not be fired (yet), but this does not bode well for my promotion.

When we get to the meeting room I sit down in my usual seat, and a few minutes later, Otis plops down beside me. We talk about nothing much until Joe walks in, seating himself opposite me. Otis and I fall silent. For the first time I notice how Joe's eyes stick out so far that he looks bug-like, that his hair is in an angry crew cut, that his fingers are fat, that his beard is just a shade past stubble. His suit is wrinkled, his tie a dingy greenish-beige.

A few other people have brought lunches to the meeting, something I guess I never really noticed before. I've always thought–my mom always told me–it's unprofessional to eat in a business meeting. Well, if they can eat, I decide, so can I. I open up my salad, smugly, and pour the dressing over it. I put the first bite in my mouth, and within seconds I'm coughing.

"What's wrong?" Otis whispers.

"This salad tastes like farts," I whisper back, and watch while he tries to muffle his laughter. I push the salad away and cut into one of the eggs. They're cold and slippery and radiating those strong egg-smell fumes that eggs sometimes do.

Elliot starts the meeting, running through updates from all the managers. The meeting goes on forever and after beating the Christmas schedule to death, Elliot turns to me. "Are you up to speed on the gear that's stuck at customs?"

Joe leans forward in his chair. "I can pick that up. I have a ton of contacts over there. I know everything about it." He smiles a little, like *aw shucks*. "I'm surprised this problem's been going on so long–it's such an easy fix."

"It'll be delivered this week," I say.

"It's no problem, Vivian," Joe says. "I'm sure you're swamped with–"

"My name is Viive," I say. "And it's been resolved, Joe. I talked to them yesterday."

"Well, I'm just trying to help," he says. "You seem so under water."

"So it's coming. Good," Elliot says, and then consults his tablet for the next item. "What was the root cause of the outage on Monday?"

"It appears to be untested code in the production environment," I say, trying to keep my voice flat and neutral, even though inside I'm *really* looking forward to this.

Joe leans forward, tenting his fat fingers. "On Friday, I authorized some code to go up."

"You might have signed off, but the only department that promotes code into production is my team," I say. "And the last launch we did was weeks ago. I don't know how Friday's software got on those servers, but the code was unauthorized and unstable, and it caused the outage."

"You don't know that," Joe says.

"I know that because when we rolled back, the site came back up," I retort.

Otis reaches out and pokes me on my leg, and I bite my tongue. There's a thick silence in the room, while everyone waits to see what Elliot will do. I try not to smile; I know Elliot will kill Joe. He's fired people for less.

"We used a much better system for promoting code at the last place I worked," Joe says smoothly, his expression not changing even slightly. "I can teach you about it if you want."

"Well, right now, all deployments go through Viive's team." Elliot looks down at this tablet. "But we certainly don't want to get complacent if there's a better way to do it," he says. "Let's take this offline, guys."

I blink a few times, looking at Elliot, and then Joe, whose face is almost completely blank except for a small, shit-eating grin that, if I'm being honest about it, he's not trying to hide at all. Meanwhile, I feel like I've just fallen off a bridge. I cannot believe Elliot has let Joe get away with causing a customer outage with bad code. It's like building a house and then scattering it with a wrecking ball. It's like…if we're just going to screw everything up, if that's the new standard we're going to use, what are we all doing here? Elliot moves on to other things, and my head buzzes with all these thoughts, my chest uncomfortably warm and tight.

After the meeting breaks, Otis and I walk back to our offices together, him loping calmly, and me taking tiny angry steps beside him. We're silent until Otis breaks it with, "What's the problem with Joe releasing code?"

"I own the production environment, and I'm responsible for all the changes and any problems that happen there," I say, my throat strained. "*Everything.*"

My words come out harsher than I intended, and after a beat Otis gives me a playful shove on my shoulder. "Doesn't Joe seem like the kind of guy who'd steal your lawnmower?" he says, his voice a pretend whisper.

"I don't even know what that means, Otis."

"He's a tosser."

"A wanker," I say.

"A plonker."

"Are you sure you're even speaking English?"

"Oh come on, Vee. If you don't at least smile, I'm going to move into your office and officially drive you crazy. Remember the time I put the Pomeranian in your desk drawer?"

I smile, even though I don't really feel like it. "Speaking of my drawers, can I have my stuff back, you plonker?"

"Your wish is my command," he says. But when he brings my stuff back in, he brings himself too, sitting on the other side of my desk and working on whatever it is he works on while I debug one of the monitors we use to measure website performance. It's good to throw myself into a technical problem, one with finite boundaries and a solution just waiting to be found. It's the very best antidote for thinking about things that aren't quite so clear.

At about five, Asha sends a gently reminding email about tonight's meeting, and asks if I'm coming. When I don't answer, she sends another one a half hour later, saying, *"We'd really like to see you."*

I think about all the work in front of me that's still left to do, but there's something compelling about people actually wanting to see me, especially after a day like this. *Yes*, I finally email her back. I can finish up my work at home afterwards. At seven I leave the office with a fairly significant amount of subterfuge (I don't want Elliot to see me leave before eight, although he's probably already gone) before flagging a cab to St. Barbara's, since I'm already running late. I'm able to navigate the institutional corridors without the aid of a GPS, and when I show up, I'm the first one there. After plunking myself down in a seat, I pull out my phone to check on email from the office, just in case something has happened since I left. I try to ignore the hospital smells: chemical and caustic, smelling of sickness and the half-hearted attempts to cover it up.

A while later, there's an over-exaggerated clearing of the throat. When I glance up, I see a woman who's probably in her forties, very thin, petite but not in a delicate kind of a way. Her hair is frosted, short and blonde, and she's wearing jeans and a jean jacket, a red sweater poking out at the neck. She has no makeup on and three earrings in both of her ears. She looks like she's been around the block a few times, and she's chewing gum with a faint *snap*. If I was going to use two words to describe her, they'd be *tough broad*.

"You must be Vivi," she says, her smile lopsided, her teeth just a little bit crooked, but the result is oddly charming.

I laugh. "Veev-eh." I lean forward and we shake hands.

"Ah, like *Viva Las Vegas*, huh?" She smiles.

I return her smile. "Close."

"Nice to meet you," she says. "I'm Paulie. David is overseas, Asha is on her way, Ian and Bela are having an affair they think no one knows about and tonight is the only night they can see each other. And with any luck Ruth and the monster won't be coming. And for the record, I refuse to remember his name. Asha says we have to be inclusive and let everyone in, but all he does is distract from what we're trying to do here."

I wonder, for a minute, what exactly I'm trying to do here.

"Good evening, ladies," Asha calls from the door. Her sari today is festively green and she's wearing the pink sneakers again. She smiles at both of us warmly.

"What's wrong?" I ask, when I see she's favouring her right arm.

"It's an old knitting injury," she says. "I'll be fine."

"Is the monster coming?" Paulie asks.

Asha sighs. "Please stop calling him that, Paulie. But no, and in fact, it's just us three tonight."

"Yeess!" Paulie says.

"I'm surprised it's so few people," I say. "I mean, Toronto is so large. I'd expected a lot more."

Asha smiles. "That's true. But not many people know about us, and we're always more focused on helping our existing members than going out and recruiting, so to speak. I wish we had a facilitator who was healthy but understood migraine. Then we'd be able to accomplish more." She pauses. "Viive, since you haven't met Paulie before, and because you're new, why don't you talk a little bit more about yourself, and how migraine affects your life." She smiles her trademark smile as she sits down.

"I'm not quite sure what to tell you," I say, after a moment. The back of my neck is tight with tension and my stomach is fluttering. "I'm not really very good at this."

"It's okay," Asha says. "It can seem overwhelming, at first, to speak to strangers about things we probably don't talk to anybody else about. Please don't worry about how you sound or what you're not supposed to say. This is a safe place." She reaches over and puts her hand on my arm, squeezes gently.

To be honest, I've always thought that if I didn't complain out loud I wasn't really a complainer, that if I didn't tell anyone, then all those sad, weak, whiney feelings inside me weren't a weakness after all. And how do you tell people who've always looked forward to a new day that all you really want to do is take to your bed? I come from a family that's lived through so much; complaining about a few headaches has always seemed ridiculous.

"Well…" I take a deep breath. Maybe I could just say a few words, nothing too much. Nothing that'll give away all my secrets. Maybe that would be all right. I came all the way here, after all. I try to smile. "Uh… I'm the senior manager of technology at a medium-sized Toronto start-up, and I guess I've always had migraines; it's my first memory, actually. I learned to speak very early, and I guess I learned how to bitch about things pretty much immediately, so that's how I was diagnosed. Uh, anyway, when I was little, they weren't so great, I guess, but after I hit my teens they got worse." I pause and take a sip from my water bottle. "And I started getting a new kind of headache in my twenties–tension type ones, annoying but not on the same scale as the migraines. But the last two years or so both kinds of headaches…well, I guess. You know. It's not good."

Paulie and Asha glance at each other.

"Anything else you want to tell us?" Asha asks, and the lines beside her eyes deepen as she smiles, just a little. I glance from Asha to Paulie and then back again, and the two of them suddenly look like people I could say anything to; people who are just like me. I swallow, my throat sandpapery. I've never met people I could say anything to before, and it makes me uneasy and unsettled, and suddenly all my old rules don't feel like they're wrapped quite as tightly around me anymore, like something has eased. And then my heart is thumping and I'm thinking: *Why am I here if I'm not going to say anything?* Would it really be so bad if I stopped worrying about how it sounds, would it be so bad if I just told the truth, for once? And how horrible can it be, really, talking to two people in a room somewhere? Who will I disappoint if nobody knows what I've done?

It feels like I'm about to plunge into something dangerous, my hands are clammy with it. And that's when my mouth opens, like it's acting on its own. "But I'm in this vicious circle where I get migraines, usually on the weekend–usually all weekend–and when I'm better, I rush around to do everything I couldn't do when I was sick, but what usually ends up happening is we're ordering in takeout all the time and it costs like a million dollars, I haven't cleaned the house since the nineties, and I'm always exhausted, and my husband has to take care of me and the housework never ends up getting finished. And my work just made me take two weeks of vacation because they thought–well, I'm not actually sure what they thought, but it wasn't anything good. Anyway, almost anything can throw me off–hormones, noise, not eating, the weather, sunshine. You know…life. It's so pathetic. *I'm* so pathetic. I never know when it's coming, and so I live in fear of the next migraine, the next day I'm going to lose, the next failure. And if I look back at the last few years that's all I can really see. Not to mention my husband, who's a saint." I glance around, not at Paulie, not at Asha, but looking for something to focus on, my hands in two tight fists. "I mean, I know it probably sounds melodramatic, the fear thing." I'm out of breath, my heartbeat's thudding in my ears, and there's a stream of fear running through me that I can't pull away from. Like it's let loose inside me now. I feel alive and scared and lost.

"It sounds fine," Paulie says. "What steps are you taking to manage your disease?" Her voice is matter-of-fact, she's not even mildly horrified at what I've just blurted out, and that's when I decide I like Paulie.

"I've started taking preventatives again." I close my eyes for a minute and then slowly unclench my fists, first my right, then my left. "Xamaxia. And I'm trying to eat more often. I made steaks last night. I mean, I actually cooked."

"That's wonderful," Asha says, her face disappearing into her trademark smile.

"I know what you need," Paulie says.

"What do I need?" I ask.

"Migraine boot camp. Start out with some diet stuff, get your food sensitivities checked. Get your back cracked, see a naturopath, work on your sleep hygiene," Paulie says.

Asha nods.

"Sounds expensive," I say.

"You're a hotshot executive. I'm sure you can find the money."

"I'm not a hotshot anything," I say.

"I bet you are," Paulie says, before smiling that lopsided smile, in a take-it-easy-we're-all-on-your-side kind of a way. "Hey, if you're in a situation where your work is forcing you to take vacation, and you and your husband's idea of a good time is putting two steaks under the broiler, then I'd say you might want to think about revisiting how you're doing things."

I rub my forehead. "Part of me feels…this is how it is, you know? Thinking that things can be different… Trying to change is just fooling ourselves. And I got the EEG," I say. "Isn't that enough?"

When Paulie looks confused, Asha leans forward and says, softly, "Viive fainted, or had a seizure, last week."

Paulie nods briskly, before saying, "I don't know, is it enough?" Her arms are flung out in an exaggerated shrug. "I understand you don't know what to do, and that hope is scary. But things can get better. Sometimes you need a little faith. That's why you're here, isn't it?"

I don't know how to answer that. "It's been a long time since I thought about faith," I say, finally.

After a minute Asha saves me. "How did the EEG go, Viive?"

"I don't have the results yet, but it was okay," I say, skipping the part about my not-quite panic attack.

"Good," Paulie says. "You know what? I have a dialysis appointment that got moved to tomorrow night and now I can't make an appointment with my naturopath. Why don't you take it?" She scrawls something on a notepad, rips it out, and before I know it, it's in my hand. Then she leans over and drops two one-dollar coins–loonies–into a small jar on the chair beside Asha.

"What's that?" I ask, the paper still in my hand.

"The swear jar," Paulie answers with a grin.

"But you haven't said anything bad yet."

"It's pre-emptive," she says. "Eventually, there will be swearing. I'm on the layaway plan."

And then I'm thinking about how I'm living my life on a layaway plan: work now for something good that's coming later. How Nate is always waiting for things to get better, for him to get his way for once. How all of my energy is focused on tomorrow. I put the piece of paper in my pocket, and Paulie smiles at me.

"And one's for you," she says.

"Why?"

"You said bitch."

"Oh, sorry," I say.

"It's no problem," Asha says, leaning forward with a smile, her hand on my arm. "You can say anything you want. We just don't want every other word to be a curse word. Plus, we use the money to get snacks."

After that Paulie runs through her back story–her migraines seem to be related to her kidney disease, and Asha jokes that the reason she had so many children is because she never got migraines while she was pregnant–and then the three of us converse about nothing much. Both of them have had good weeks, and I definitely don't want to talk about myself anymore. It seems ridiculous, for someone like me to be in a support group. If anyone could fail at therapy, it would be me. But it feels strange, too, to be with people who understand me, without me having to explain myself. To be myself, without having to downplay how bad I feel. It's a moment without apology, one of the first I've had in a very long time. And it makes me wonder what's going to happen next.

8 – So Many Bagpipes

A not-so-small part of me is wondering if Paulie made up her story about a dialysis snafu–I mean, who gets dialysis at nine on a Friday, anyway?–because I'd definitely rather be out for drinks right now with Otis, who was less than thrilled I had to ditch our plans for an appointment with a hippie in an office on the Danforth, a tiny space with a faintly bitter smell I can't quite identify.

The receptionist (young, three holes in her left eyebrow, purple hair, shy smile) makes me fill out another insanely long medical history, pages upon pages of depressing minutiae about my life. As I write I have to grudgingly admit that the waiting room is cosy and welcoming, the decorations running to the macramé side of things, which isn't so bad, except for the fact that I don't want to be here. Right on cue, my temples squeeze together, reminding me how I got wrangled into all this in the first place.

After a few more minutes, I look up to see two women coming down the hallway, their voices calm and pleasant. The taller one, a satisfied-looking woman of indeterminate age, pays and then leaves. The other woman is very petite, Asian, and is wearing an electric blue tie-dyed shirtdress with clogs on her tiny feet, and if you think that sounds crazy to wear on the cusp of a Canadian winter, you'd probably be right.

"I'm not even going to try to pronounce your name," the clog-wearer says, turning to me with a smile.

"I'm Viive," I say, standing up and shaking her hand. "Hi."

"Fantastic," she says, taking the clipboard from me. "I'm Dr. Tess Bompaine. Paulie called me about you. Let's go into my office and chat for a bit."

Both of us walk down the hallway and then settle ourselves in two chairs in a small room. The odour is stronger here. It's not particularly unpleasant, but concern niggles at me anyway. It's a quick, hurried worry, one that's always lurking; which trigger will erupt next? Which smell, sound, drink, is going to spark up a headache? Sometimes I feel like I'm going to run out of adrenaline any minute, like I've used my quota up.

"I just smudged," Dr. Tess says. "It'll go away shortly."

"Sorry?"

"I burned some sage to purify the space. It shouldn't cause a headache, but let me know if you're having a problem."

Oh my.

She smiles when she sees my reaction. "So, I'm not sure if you know or not, but I'm not taking on any new patients right now. But Paulie can be…very persuasive." She starts flipping through my medical history. "Can you give me an overview of what you're hoping to accomplish by seeking alternative therapies?"

It's such an unexpected question that a startled laugh pops out of me, one sounding more than a little like a snort. I cough a few times to cover it up.

"What?" She doesn't seem upset at my reaction, just mildly curious.

"Sorry. It's…the first time a medical professional has asked me what I want. It's…it's a little hard to think of my sickness in terms of goals."

"That's okay, Viive. We do things kind of differently here."

It's the thought of doing things differently, the thought of *being sick differently*, that makes me close my eyes for a minute. As long as I'm here, I might as well be honest, at least inside my own head. What I want is my other self, the one I see when I think about my life. I try not to daydream, because I have the absolutely most boring daydreams in the history of the universe, but sometimes it happens anyway. I imagine myself in shape, healthy, and *out.* Outside. Doing things. Being spontaneous. Going out for dinner. Walking somewhere instead of driving. Not needing a strategy session every time I have to leave the house.

I want my other life, my *what-if* life, and I want it right now. I want a miracle that'll solve all of this, and I don't want it to come out of a pill or an injection or a doctor's office. I want to wake up and jump out of bed, instead of dreading everything that's going to come next after I open my eyes. I want to watch a movie in the theatre instead of six months later when it's out on Netflix. I want dinner and drinks and dancing. I want the salty-sweet first days of romance again. I want to say I'm going to do something, and then I want to actually do it, even if it's just something stupid and simple. I don't want Nate to have to hide his disappointment–in me, in our life–yet again. I want to forget about being sick, to lose track of all the logistics and details and pills and all that worry.

I want my life back.

When I look up, Dr. Tess is looking at me, her face kind and confident, like she knows exactly what I'm thinking. "It might help to think of some small goals to focus on right now," she says. "Sometimes it can get overwhelming if you try to fix everything all at once. This isn't a sprint, and we can go as slowly as you want."

I fidget in my chair, trying to think about something small and simple. I suddenly notice how bulky I am, how much of the chair my oversized Viking body is taking up. It makes me feel hot with shame. I don't know how I got this big, or when these pants got so small. I haven't worn them in forever and the pinch at my waist is aggressively strong. A small seed of disappointment takes root inside me; disappointment in myself, in my pants.

"Would you like some tea?" Dr. Tess asks.

"Please," I say, not bothering to ask what she's making. It'll probably be full of twigs.

She leaves me alone in the room. There are photographs up on the walls, most of them full of life and colour. There are some children's finger paintings as well. Dr. Tess must have kids. In a few minutes she's back, with two hand-thrown, steaming mugs, and as she passes one to me I sniff it as surreptitiously as I can. Mint. It smells delicious, not a twig in sight.

Dr. Tess smiles patiently at me while I blow on my tea and search for the right words. Finally I say, "I'm an engineer, and I went to university on scholarship, I was made a senior manager by the time I was thirty-two in a technical, male-dominated field. I'm in line to be a director, which I want more than anything, but lately my boss is unhappy with my work, so that sucks. For the last couple of years it seems like I'm always in pain. So I started seeing a neurologist again, and I'm taking an anticonvulsant as a preventative."

"So you want to be a director?" Dr. Tess asks, like she's talking to herself. "Okay. Tell me something, what do you…you're married, yes?" She shuffles some papers. "Yes. You and your husband, what do you do on the weekends?"

"What do you mean?"

"For fun."

There's a pause while I look around the room, at the textile wall hangings, the cheery childhood artwork. "I…I don't know. I mean, we both work a lot. He's in the business too, more on the security side of things these days. We do family stuff. It's tough because the weekend is when I have my worst headaches."

"It's not unusual to have let-down migraines. What do you do at night when you come home from work?"

"Most nights we get home at nine or ten. We order in dinner. We both work, so we can be ready for the morning. We watch some television.

And then we go to sleep."

"What do you watch on TV?"

This all seems like an odd narrative for a medical appointment, but I try to find an answer anyway. "I don't know…whatever's on, I guess. We're working or reading at the same time, so I don't always pay that much attention."

"Why don't you turn it off, then?"

"What?"

"Why don't you listen to music or do something else?"

"I don't really know," I say, while I run my finger over the rim of the mug. "It's just a bad habit, I guess." I never thought about it before, but Nate and I only really half-watch TV. And lately everything feels like that; half done, never quite right.

"So what's your pain level?" she asks, but she's talking to herself again as she flips through pages. We sit in silence while she skims my history, and then she runs through some tests, her hands gentle, looking at my tongue, taking my blood pressure, palpating me to within an inch of my life. When she's done making notes, she sits back in her chair, her arms crossed over her chest, humming a song that's tuneless, but oddly charming. Dr. Tess couldn't be more different from Dr. Throckmorton, and it's funny to think about what's missing; I'm not intimidated by Dr. Tess. My Canadian grandmother was a macramé superstar, and sold her wares all over the country. I have a soft spot for wall hangings.

She stands up and then pulls a medical book off the shelf over her desk and starts leafing through it. "All righty," she says. "We have to do something about your activity levels, your nutrition, and your habits." Then she flips through the brief food diary I've written down for her. "Ms. McBroom, just a heads-up, ketchup is not a vegetable." She grins. "Look, we need to get you stabilized so your headaches are under better control. Diet plays a huge role in health, and we need to improve your eating habits, and lower your overall level of inflammation."

"What kind…of diet changes? Because I'm pretty attached to how I eat."

She smiles. "Nutrition is the cornerstone of health, and if you're not eating properly you're not going to get well. Food is also medicine, you know."

"Uhh…"

She takes in the expression on my face. "Okay, let's look at it like this. We can tell each other lies, if you want, and then you can pay me and you'll never get better. But I'll take your money. And when you see my new car, you'll be all like, *How can you possibly have a new car when I still feel so shitty*?

And then you'll key my car."

I laugh, I can't help myself. "Uh-huh. And what kind of car do you drive?"

"A bicycle. But you get my point." She smiles. "Viive, the WHO says migraine is the fourth most debilitating disease. Like, in the world. I've never had a migraine, but I have other patients who do–other patients I've been able to help, by the way–and this is how we do it. Living with migraine is basically like getting the shit kicked out of your nervous system all the time. You guys are fighting a serious disease. That makes your choices different than other peoples'."

"I know. I understand." And I do. It's just that change always feels so…dangerous. It's impossible to figure out how to plan for it, to make sure your *just in case* is accounted for.

"So the question is, do you want to get started, or do you just want to talk about getting started? Because we have a therapist who works in this office too." She grins again, in a way that can only be described as endearing. *Goddammit.* There's something so calming about her it's positively maddening.

"I'm not sure."

"Okay, tell me something…do you feel in control of your disease?"

"I used to," I say.

"Is that a no?" She smiles.

"Well, what I do know is I'm much worse than I used to be. And if I think about the future, is this all I have to look forward to? Another year like this one? Because how much more of this is Nate supposed endure? He takes care of me all the time, he basically has no life, and every single time we make plans I have to cancel. Or, I force myself to go to whatever anyway, and then I have a terrible time, which he figures out, which then makes him miserable, and then we leave early anyway so what was the point of going out in the first place?"

Dr. Tess scrawls on her notepad after that, and all I can think is: *My God, when did I become so verbally promiscuous?* "It's tricky, navigating a marriage when one of the partners is chronically ill. The divorce rate is close to 75%."

Jesus. Nate is probably starting divorce proceedings as we speak.

"Are you okay?" Her eyes are kind.

"I've never thought about myself like this. I've just always thought I had to survive, keep going, make it happen. But I had two weeks off and all I did was sleep. I accomplished nothing."

"Nothing?" she echoes.

"Well, I worked a little." It takes everything I have not to check my phone, which is vibrating in my bag beside me. The two of us sit there, listening to the electronic hum. Finally, it stops.

"All right," she says. "Part of healing yourself holistically comes from your ability to accept your current circumstances and then make small changes which support your entire being so you can get better."

For a minute I think about acceptance and change and the Migraine Mafia.

Dr. Tess is still talking. "…you eat a little better, sleep a little better, are a little more active. You're never going to be like everyone else, but we can find a way for you to exist without this level of pain and illness. And that's empowering."

I nod.

"But some of it will ultimately be up to you. No one is going to watch you when you're alone and eating cheesecake out of the freezer. No one is going to see if you take the elevator instead of the stairs. Actually, that's not true." She reaches behind her and pulls out a small, square object. "Pedometer," she says. "Let's see how many steps you're taking daily and work with that. So, other than the pedometer, no one will be watching you. Oh, and except this too." She pulls out a postcard-sized brochure for nutrition software. "The pedometer and food log all upload to an app I'll be able to access remotely. Technology, gotta love it. In any case, I'd like to see you every week for the next six weeks or so."

"Oh, I can't do that."

She smiles as she sits there, doesn't seem perturbed as the silence lengthens.

"I mean, I'd love to, don't get me wrong. But I'm just too busy at work to be able to come that often."

"I see."

We both sit there, until I say, "What about every other week, your last appointment of the day?"

"All right, let's try that for now," she says. "Okay, let's talk a little about diet. I'd like for you to go off gluten and dairy for the next six weeks. Both are inflammatory agents, and are likely causing some of the symptoms you're seeing."

"Are you sure? Because they're also both a source of deliciousness."

"I'll have to take your word for it," she says. "I haven't eaten either in about five years."

"Jesus," I say. "What about beer?"

"There are some good gluten-free beers out there."

"What about cheesecake?" I lean closer in my chair.

"I make a very nice soy cake. I can give you the recipe, if you want."

"Chocolate?"

"I don't really like chocolate." She shrugs.

"Dr. Tess, I feel the need to tell you I find this all very disturbing."

"Just call me Tess." She smiles as she flips through the diet journal I filled out for her. "And I bet you do. But let me ask you, why do you eat all this? I mean, it's horrible. Don't get me started on the farming and animal cruelty issues with all this fast food junk, but the reality is there are so few nutrients in this food that you are most likely malnourished. And you don't want us to even talk about the sugar and corn syrup problem you clearly have yet. But I can guarantee you it's affecting your health, your sleep, your headaches, your mood, your everything."

"Crap."

"Crap, indeed," she agrees, tucking some hair behind her ear. "Look, if you really need dairy, you can have a small amount of goat products. But the sooner you start eating clean, the sooner you'll see benefits."

The problem is I don't actually want to eat clean, a terrifying sentence if I've ever heard one. "But food is, like, where I get a lot of my happiness from."

"Okay," she says. "Could you repeat that for me?"

"I get a lot of my happiness from food."

"So, you want to be a director who works all the time and gets most of her happiness from food?"

"Well, when you put it like that," I say.

"You put it like that. It *is* like that. I know it's rough, but you strike me as a fighter. You just need to be fighting on the right front."

There's some more silence after that. "All right," I say, finally. "If it's only for a while. But I probably don't have a problem with gluten anyway. I'm sure I don't. Isn't all this gluten stuff just a fad? I read that somewhere."

"Research has shown that most people with migraine have some level of gluten sensitivity," she says, lacing her fingers together before resting them in her lap.

"Aren't there any, you know, supplements or anything I can take and still eat wheat?"

"No," she says, with a faint smile. "Here's a list of foods containing gluten, and the names it hides behind, like 'natural flavour,' or 'spices,' so you can keep an eye out. Read all the labels when you're in the supermarket."

I take the pamphlet from her. The list is huge, and it goes on for pages: bread, cereals, muffins, soy sauce, pizza, chicken wings, soups, and every delicious thing God put on this planet. Crestfallen is not a bad way to describe how I feel looking at it. Devastated is another word that comes to mind.

She scrawls something on a pad. "Okay, I'm going to start you off with a multivitamin and some magnesium." She punctuates the sentence with a flourish, before pulling a business card from a small pile. "This is a personal trainer I work with. She's currently offering a fitness assessment and a session for free. You should think about calling her." Then she rifles through a bookshelf on her right and retrieves a murky vial that she hands to me. "This is a multivitamin formula."

I try to hide my reluctance as I take the bottle from her. It looks like swamp water.

"You'll want to take that twice a day, before food," she says with a smile, before standing up and shaking my hand. "I'd like you to do something, please. Try to figure out what you want out of our work together. That'll be our roadmap."

I thank her and leave, even though I don't feel very thankful. Food is the one thing I can depend on to try to get some kind of normalcy in my life: delicious, chocolaty, comforting. When I have a migraine pounding in my head, when I've been up for twenty-four hours because I'm in too much pain to sleep, food is the only thing I have to look forward to, and the kick from all that sugar is the only thing that makes me feel better. What else could I use to distract myself? Think about brunch with friends on Sunday, a manicure, a weekend trip away? I can't do any of those things, make plans and cancel yet again, put a deposit down on a weekend getaway I'll never make it to. And I've never really understood manicures. The thing is, after a migraine has rolled out and all that's left is my walloped nervous system, some ketchup chips topped off with chocolate ice cream is the perfect solution. It's the only comfort I can always, always count on.

Crap, indeed.

When I get home the house is pulsing with music. Not hip, vibrant tunes like you'd expect from an urban thirty-something couple living in The Pocket. Bagpipes. Not just a single bagpipe, either. So many bagpipes.

I open the front door. "Nate?"

The music continues, rolling out of the office on the second floor.

"Nate!"

There's no answer as I walk up the stairs. *God, the neighbours are going to kill us.* I knock on the office door. When he doesn't answer, I pull it open. Nate is sitting at his desk, playing video games while altogether too many bagpipes harmonize a melody of torture that makes the headache that's been humming behind my ears all day pop out and say hello. I walk over to his speaker and turn it off, and the sudden silence is as loud as the bagpipes were. Nate is just ever so slightly Scottish and has tossed more than a few cabers in his time.

"Hi honey," I say.

Nate swirls around in his chair and partially blocks the monitor. I can barely make out the images on his screen of a different kind of game. Online poker, maybe. I swallow, my throat suddenly constricted.

"Hi babe," he says, reaching out to kiss me.

I kiss him back and flop on the easy chair near his desk. "The neighbours are going to freak out on us."

"They're gone," he says. "I saw them all pack up the car and leave. I wasn't expecting you home yet."

"Obviously," I singsong. "Is this what you do when I'm not here, play loud bagpipe music?"

"Sometimes," he says.

"Why don't you use headphones?"

"I like to be surrounded by the music," he says. "It's like a great big Scottish hug. And anyway, who cares? No one can hear it."

"I could hear it out on the porch. The house was vibrating."

"So? We irritate a few Jehovah's Witnesses? You're too noise sensitive, Vee."

"You're right," I say. "Sorry."

"How'd it go with the naturopath?" he asks, turning off his monitor. The last flash before it goes dark looks like any other website. Not poker, more like email. Briefly, I feel a twinge of guilt.

I shake my head. "No dairy, no gluten."

"How long?"

"Six weeks."

"Blech," he says.

"Yeah, I know." I reach over and kiss him again, and then I rest my forehead against his. If we get the angle exactly right, our faces fit together perfectly. After a moment I pull away, sit back in the chair. "Dinner?"

"Chinese?" he asks.

"Sure," I say. We watch TV and work after the food comes, and when I go to get a second plate a few hours later, I take in the carnage on the kitchen counters, the graveyard of discarded cartons, the pool of MSG-infused goo dripping on the counter. I don't want to give up Chinese takeout forever, but if things can get better, then why not try it for a little while? I mean, how bad could it be?

Before Nate falls asleep, I ask him, "Do you want to do groceries with me tomorrow? We need to have some non-gluteny foods in the house."

"Sure," he says, reaching out to squeeze me. I wrap myself around him and the two of us sleep like that, perfectly entwined in each other. And each other's problems.

The next afternoon we bundle ourselves up and drive over to the St. Lawrence Market, a bustling downtown oasis of fresh groceries. "What do you want to eat this weekend?" I ask. "Maybe we should do a roast?"

"Sure."

We meander through our favourite vegetable stand, picking up pencil-thin asparagus, red-skinned potatoes and the fixings for a salad. After that we wander over to the best butcher; Nate picks out a roast and some bacon. We make stops at the cheese monger, manhandling a Blue and a Manchego for a few minutes before selecting them and some water crackers. I pick up some Dijon from Kozlik's, and then we head downstairs for dessert, a really good olive oil, and some new Tellicherry pepper, which we ran out of in the spring and I haven't gotten around to getting more of yet. It doesn't take long, but it's nice to do something so normal with Nate.

I try not to watch all the other couples who are walking around the market. Most of them are well-dressed and casually strolling around, like there's no pain hiding behind their ears, nothing bad waiting for them later today or tomorrow or ever. I bet their beds are made and their taxes are up to date and they shop here all the time, holding hands with their perfect spouses. All these rambling thoughts make me almost weak with jealousy, and after a while walking around the market's small maze exhausts me, my ankles even more sore than usual. And goddamn, but I left the stupid pedometer at home. I think about the other part of Dr. Tess's advice, about sending an email to her personal-trainer friend, the one who's offering the free assessment. I mean, how bad can free be? And then, to congratulate myself for deciding to exercise, I get two gourmet cupcakes, red velvet and death by chocolate; so decadent they're almost immoral. When we get home, we drop everything in the kitchen and relax for a few hours; watching TV and working, but not that hard.

At eight-ish we start to prep for dinner. We used to do this all the time when we first started dating, cook together over a good bottle of wine. I attach the pedometer to my waist and press the start button so I can get credit for every single step.

"What's that?" Nate asks.

I show it to him. "It tracks my steps, and a bunch of other stuff. Oh, did I tell you that the naturopath gave me the name of a personal trainer? I'm going to make an appointment."

"Sounds great, honey," he says. "Probably a good idea for you to get some exercise."

I glance at Nate's annually-expanding middle with a meaningful look, but he's already turned away, mincing garlic. I keep working and try not to count the days since my last migraine, because the truth is I'm not throbbing with my usual Saturday headache. There's something squeezing in my head, but it's something tepid and weak and nowhere near as bad as usual, and that small miracle turns the little kitchen and the simple act of the two of us making dinner into something special.

"How long has this wine been open in the fridge?" Nate asks, his nose wrinkled.

"I don't know. Months. Why don't you put a new one in?"

Nate goes down to the basement to grab one off the rack and puts it in the wine chiller I bought for him a few years ago for Christmas. Nate loves his tech toys. After it's cold, he pours a generous glass for himself and when he leans over mine, I cut him off after a small dollop. I don't want to chance a migraine today. Everything is going so well, but it's still so precarious. *No mistakes.*

Nate turns on the oven and unwraps the roast–a gorgeous standing rib hunk of deliciousness. He rubs it with garlic and olive oil, and then mixes up some salt, pepper, mustard, and more olive oil and rubs it into the fat of the meat. I wash and prep the potatoes and then chop some shallots and garlic to throw into the pan. This is the longest cooking session Nate and I have had in forever, and it's still over in minutes. Making dinner has netted me two hundred steps, and it's only a little creepy that Dr. Tess will be able to figure it all out from her end.

Nate pops the roast into the oven before plating the cheese and crackers and the baguette he picked up when I wasn't looking. I watch, wordless, as he puts the appetizers on the coffee table in the living room.

"Oh, God, Nate," I say, finally.

"What?"

I point at the cheese. "Dairy." And then at the crackers. "Gluten." Things I am failing at today: *everything.*

We both start to laugh. "So let me get this straight," Nate says. "We made a special trip to the market, so we could get some non-gluteny, not-dairy food, and that's exactly what we picked up?"

"Indeed," I say, flopping on the couch beside him. "What are we going to do?"

"Well, we can't waste all this," Nate says, "and we can't give it back. Why don't you just enjoy the weekend, and start your diet on Monday?"

Start your diet on Monday, the siren song of everywoman. I sigh. But he's right–there's not much to do but eat the excellent cheese, and the otherworldly baguette and crackers, while Nate and I watch yet another movie we wanted to see in the theatre–we had tickets, even–but had to abandon because of my mangled nervous system. We eat a delicious dinner, he holds my hand, and maybe it's just this simple, for once.

For now, that is.

Monday afternoon, Elliot pokes his head into my office. "Where were you? I came by to talk to you ten minutes ago." He looks down at his watch, purposefully.

"I stepped out to get something to eat," I say, glancing at the salad I picked up for lunch, a task that took way too long because I had to decide what ancient grain to accompany my watercress medley with, a not-so-easy task when your idea of the perfect side dish is chocolate cake.

His sigh is annoyed, his face pursed in *a don't let this happen again* look.

"What's up?" I ask, trying not to worry about Elliot's angst. He's always like this the closer we get to Christmas. And, anyway, my team is on track for all our projects (mostly), my budget for next year has been handed in, and even though I sometimes want to strangle Susie with her skinny jeans, she's been on her best behaviour lately. On the other hand, because all the teams' schedules are so intertwined it's sometimes hard to know when one ends and the other starts, especially if your background isn't in operations.

"I'm worried about our timelines," he says. "Can you walk me through them?"

I pull up my project plan and run down the various schedules. I discovered shortly after I got here that Elliot is a very visual person, so I always have a pretty picture ready, as part of our weekly touch-base meetings. In fact, I showed Elliot this exact timeline last week–he just doesn't remember. His energy is so twitchy, and divided between so many projects, I've spent most of the last four years repeating information to him.

"Joe was saying your team is behind on the Alderaan project," Elliot says.

"Interesting," I say. "Because Joe told me yesterday he appreciated the fact that testing was wrapped up two days early."

"Must be a misunderstanding," Elliot says, standing and brushing something off his dress pants. "Oh, and we've had to move the Q1 meeting to eight o'clock tonight."

"Oh," I say. *Shit.*

"Something wrong?"

Dr. Tess's fitness friend and I emailed back and forth this weekend and scheduled my assessment for tonight. "No," I say. "No problem."

"Okay, Viive. Sounds good," Elliot says. He leans forward like he might want to say something, and my breath hitches in my chest.

"You busy, chief?" Joe is suddenly standing in the doorway of my office.

I chew mightily on an apple while I watch Elliot get up and leave. Then I finish off the TPS reports for the week and review the architectural design for some upgrades to our data centre environment. It's clean and not overcomplicated; no bleeding-edge technology to ruin it. It's exactly the kind of work I want to do when I have my own company.

"Viive?"

I look up. "Yup?"

Elliot clears his throat. "Can we come in? Joe was just telling me about this great idea he had."

"Okay," I say.

Joe leans against the door as Elliot sits down. Joe's looking particularly bug-eyed today, I notice with satisfaction.

"Don't be shy," I say, and after a minute he joins Elliot, sitting down in the second chair in front of my desk.

"So at Joe's last company, he was using a backup solution that sounds like it's perfect for our environment. And since you're doing those upgrades…"

"Mmm," I say, biting into another apple slice. I don't like how comfortable Joe looks in that chair.

"It was a distributed architecture," Joe says, before dropping a vendor name, "And–"

I lift my hand up. "We looked at it for our latest upgrade, thanks. It's not a good fit."

"Are you sure you understood the technology?" Joe asks.

I pause, trying to quiet the irritation rising inside me. "I spent over two years designing and implementing backup systems for one of the companies I worked at. So, yeah, I'm sure."

"Right, but I'm sure things have changed so much since then," Joe says. "In fact, when I was working for–"

"We did a bunch of beta testing," I say, "looked at a number of options. I'm confident in our solution. I'm happy to send you a copy of our report, Joe. Elliot, I sent this to you a while back."

"How confident?" Elliot asks. "Are you 100% sure this will all work out?"

"We have a solution that works and no room in the budget for an experimental build. Maybe next year."

"I know all the right people at the company that makes this product," Joe says, re-crossing his legs casually. "They could walk you through it, since you had so many problems with it."

"I didn't have any problems," I say, more snappishly than I want to. "It's not the right solution."

"Oh, okay," Joe says, peeling the wrapper off a stick of gum and popping it into his mouth. "I was just trying to help. There's no reason to get upset."

"I'm not upset," I say, knowing that I sound upset.

"We're all on the same team here, Viive," Elliot says. "And of course, we want to have an environment where we can share ideas with each other."

"Of course," I say. The two of them seem to be waiting, so after a beat I say, "Thanks, Joe."

"You're welcome, Viive. I'm always here to help you out when you run into trouble."

Elliot nods once, and the two of them leave. On the way out, Joe lobs the gum wrapper into my garbage basket. It bounces off the rim and lands on the floor. He glances at it, not long, just a second, and then continues on his way. Watching him makes my jaw clench.

After they're gone I email the trainer to tell her I have to move the appointment. She answers almost immediately, with a perky, *No problem!* Luckily she has an opening Wednesday night. I can only hope she won't be quite as enthusiastic as her signature line portends: *Abs with Andorra!!! You'll never be the same again!!!* I wonder, momentarily, if I should be alarmed about a trainer who punctuates her messages with that many exclamation points. My gut feeling is yes.

Eight in the morning is not the most fun time to rummage through a pantry, especially since I can't have any of the cereal in said pantry because they're all so very wheaty. I finally give up and decide to skip breakfast. How is it possible that I bought groceries just a few days ago and there's still nothing to eat? I haven't even left the house, and already I'm failing at something.

On the way to work, I stop in at the coffee shop and peruse the hot breakfasts, the muffins, the snack bars. All of them, every one of them, has gluten or dairy in them. Then I inspect the salads. They're wilted and sad, depressing and tiny. I pick up a protein plate with two eggs and some fruit and cheese; I'll give the cheese to Otis. Conveniently, when I get upstairs Otis is sitting at my desk, banging away on his laptop's keyboard.

"What's up?" I ask. It isn't that unusual to find him in my office; once when I was out of town on a business trip he switched our offices for the duration, just to make sure he likes his better. Which, he made sure to inform me, he does.

"They're fixing my desk," he says, hitting the "enter" key with a flourish. "How's it going?"

"I've been better."

"Oh God, you look depressed, come, tell me everything." Otis tents his fingers, uses them to support his chin.

"Take a look at this." I pull the packaged meal out of my bag, the sad-looking eggs, the wilted fruit, the forbidden cheese.

"You're not doing one of those girly diets, are you? Because, and I hate to have to be the one to tell you this, you are not girly."

"Of course not."

"Indeed," Otis agrees, sounding particularly British. "But can you explain to me why you're starving and yet not eating? Because this seems like a pretty solvable problem."

"You'd think, wouldn't you?" I put my head down on my desk.

"Tell Uncle Otis all about it."

"The naturopath, on Friday? She's taken me off gluten and dairy. This is my breakfast."

"So?"

I lift my head and glare at him. "So there's nothing for me to eat–ever again–except salad."

"That's not true, Vee."

"Oh it's true," I say darkly.

"Well, happily, I brought you a surprise," he says, reaching to something on the floor beside him. A few seconds later, a small rectangular box is on my desk, facing me.

"What is–oh my God." I start to laugh. "Only you would do this."

Otis's smile is beatific.

I study his gift for a few seconds: a *Walking Dead* lunch box, with hungry, melted zombie grins splayed across its face. Inside there's a small drink, an apple, a sandwich, and a container of yogurt. When I look up I'm surprised to feel tears in my eyes, which Otis looks slightly horrified by, but is kind enough to ignore.

"Of course, my lovely wife Sylvia is the one who put all this together," Otis says. "But I demand part of the credit. I told her how jealous you were of my lunch last week, and so she made you one. I just feel bad it has both dairy and gluten."

"I'll start my diet tomorrow. Thank you, Otis, so much." It doesn't bother me as much as it should that I've just shrugged off everything my new clog-wearing naturopath has told me to do.

"Anything for you, my sweet. All righty then, get your jacket. I want to take you somewhere."

"I can't leave, Otis, I just got here. I'm swamped."

"Okay, we'll go at lunch."

But lunch comes and goes (and is delicious), and we end up not having time to go on Otis's mysterious errand. At seven-thirty Otis pops his head into my office. Then he propels me up and out of my chair, and out on to the street. He points me left.

"Where are we going?"

"You'll s-e-e-e-eeee," he singsongs. We walk for a few blocks in the biting cold, wind penetrating my sweater. Finally we stop in front of a natural health store.

"Ugh."

"Delicious ugh," Otis agrees. We walk in to the store, which smells fresh and sour all at the same time. He waves at the clerk before directing me down one of the aisles.

"How do you know him?" I ask, even though Otis always knows everyone everywhere.

"I come here all the time," Otis says.

"Why on earth would you do such a thing?" I ask.

"My sister is vegan."

"Oh, I'm sorry."

"I know, eh?" He stops in front of a gargantuan display of protein bars. "I pick up stuff for her every once in a while, because she lives in the middle of nowhere, in a small town where their idea of being vegan is only eating bacon once a day. Okay, let's start reading labels and find you some healthy snacks."

"Oh, Otis."

"What?"

I stand there for a minute, taking in the rack, jam-packed with dozens of healthy–and probably inedible–foil-wrapped nuggets. I shove him a little with my shoulder. "This is the worst nice thing anyone's done for me in forever."

"Steady on," Otis says, shoving me a little back, and then the two of us start going through the rack, looking for sneaky, hidden ingredients.

After a while, the clerk wanders over. "Hey Otis. We have a special on lentils this week."

"Mmmm," Otis says, rubbing his stomach. "Thanks River."

"What are you guys looking for?" River asks.

"Gluten and dairy-free protein bars."

"No problem," River says. "Vegan is probably your best bet. And there are some GF ones over here." He points to a corner of the rack.

"Thanks," Otis says.

Vegan. My God, what a horrible thought. I haven't eaten vegan one day in my life, ever. Estonians are practically professional fish-eaters. I never really liked fish, though, and since leaving home I've branched out to steak and pork, Ontario lamb, Quebec venison, and the delights of Alberta elk. Just thinking about my last good meal makes me hungry. I bring my eyes back to the vegan section. It's a scary place; most of the wrappers seem home-made, like they came out of a cottage industry in a Scarborough garage. Most of the bars are sweetened with figs or dates, and look mysterious and squishy in their little packages.

"Try this one," Otis says, handing me one stamped "Mocha Madness."

"Okay," I say.

"Don't sound so depressed," he says. "Try this one, this one, and this one."

I examine them, trying to fight the revulsion in my stomach. "Are you sure they won't poison me?"

"Um…no," he says.

I read off one of the labels. "Prunes? Ugh. Why are we doing this again?"

"You need to have emergency food, if you're somewhere that you can't find anything to eat. My sister does this. In a pinch she can have a power bar and a salad."

"I want to die."

"You can't complain if you haven't even tried them yet."

"This one is four dollars!"

"Well, welcome to the dark underbelly of vegan culture."

"Oi," I say. Finally I pick a few of them up.

"Well done, you," Otis says.

After that we take a look around the store, and I stock up on food: gluten-free Rice Krispies and cornflakes, almond milk, and some goat's butter. We go to the cash and when I pay for it all it's over a hundred dollars. As we walk back to the office, Otis leans over and pokes me with his finger, and I take the opportunity to hand him some of my bags.

He pretends to be annoyed, and then says, "I was working really late last night, and I heard Elliot talking to Sid. They were outside my office and I think they thought I was gone."

"And?"

"Did Elliot tell you that *you* were going to get the director position, like absolutely?"

"Yes."

"Absolutely yes?"

"How much more of a yes would you like to hear, Otis?" I say, laughing.

"Because they were saying…" Otis, wanker he is, leaves that hanging while we turn around the corner, the office now in sight.

I punch him in the arm. "Don't make me get you deported, Otis."

"Now, that hurts my feelings." He smiles at me. "They were saying that they're just about ready to announce the new director on Elliot's team. That's what I heard, anyway. Obviously, they were talking about you."

I'm not big on jumping up and down, but the thought occurs to me, albeit briefly. I don't want to scare Otis. Instead I smile so wide my ears hurt. *After all that, Elliot just wanted to give me some time off before promoting me.* So I'd be ready.

Sneaky little Elliot.

"Well, I wanted to say congratulations, my dear. I know you've been having a tough time lately, but it seems like things are looking up."

"Indeed they are," I agree, with a grin and a faux-British accent that makes Otis crazy.

When I get home at ten-thirty I make a not-so-shocking discovery: goat butter tastes exactly like being kissed by a goat. Nate eats a metric ton of gluten in front of me ("We wouldn't want to waste food," he says, in what can only be described as reasonable, if slightly heartbreaking logic), while I quietly pine for a bite of coffee cake.

The news of my pending promotion ticks away inside me as we while the evening away. I slant my laptop away from Nate's, so he can't see my screen while I research restaurants we can go to and celebrate. Excitement pricks up and down my spine while I scheme on my side of the couch, excitement mixed with relief and an exquisite feeling of content. I can't *wait* to surprise Nate with the good news.

9 – THIRTY FEET

Unfortunately the personal trainer is a bubbly sociopath. When we started my fitness assessment twenty minutes ago I stipulated that I have no fitness, but she insisted on making me prove it, which I'm currently doing handily. My headache is hiding today, so I had no good reason to cancel, and we've been doing squats and push ups and some horrible thing called the plank for over a half hour now.

"Okaaaaaay!" the trainer, Andorra, yells, jogging on the spot, her blonde ponytail swishing back and forth. If I had to describe Andorra in one word it would be: *bouncy*. "Now we're going to do burpees."

I wheeze, my hand on my waist. "I don't even want to ask what that is."

"No problem! I'll show you." Andorra abandons her jogging and drops to the floor, kicking her legs out and balancing like she's about to do a push-up. Instead, she snaps her feet back in and jumps up, her hands held up over her head. "Okay, what do you think, can you do it?"

"Sure," I say, even though I'm 100% sure I can't.

"Okay, great! Let's get started." She's back to jogging/jumping on the spot again. There's no sweat on her skin, just a creepy, preternatural glow. "We're going to time how many you can do in a minute."

"Is there a particular number I should be doing?"

"It's not a competition, Viive!"

"I know, I'm just trying to do well," I say. The truth is I'm doing horribly, but I don't want to admit it. My hands and feet are oil slicks. I smell rancid, like old fruit and gym socks. I long for an eighties headband.

"You're doing great!" she says, still jogging in place. "Okay, ready?"

I shake out my legs and nod. "Ready." The term *girding my loins* pops into my head.

"Okay, go!" Andorra squeals.

I put my hands down on the ground and try to kick my feet out. *See, this isn't so hard.* I pull them back in and jump up.

"Great job! That's one!"

I do another, trying to ignore the beginnings of a cramp on my left side.

"That's two!"

When I go to kick my feet out this time, my left foot doesn't quite make it.

"That's three!"

My legs weigh eighteen thousand pounds.

"That's four!"

When I'm done with this one I stand up and drink some water. "How much longer?"

"Keep going!" Andorra yells.

The next time, standing up makes me dizzy.

"That's six!"

The next one is agony, my legs are exhausted, I'm out of breath, and I stumble a little when I stand.

"That's seven!"

I gather every ounce of strength and determination I have and do one more. When I stand up, I feel like my legs are going to buckle.

"And that's eight!" she says. "Great job!"

Andorra's pants are practically on fire, but a not-so-small part of me appreciates her amateurish falsehoods. On the other hand, I can't believe a few minutes of exercise have wiped me out so utterly. I used to be active all the time when I was a kid: ski, squash, baseball. But today, here, is the first time I've had to confront the fact that I'm this out of shape. Knackered, exhausted, bone-weary. Old. Finished. I'd go on, but I'm too tired.

Andorra shuffles through some papers. Everyone I meet these days seems to be rifling through something. I don't understand why the health industry is so analog.

"Viive, I'm going to put together an exercise profile for you." She goes on to talk about yoga, Pilates, cardio. There's a second session in the deal Andorra's offering, and she and I talk about scheduling it, which I try to sidestep as deftly as possible. Andorra talks like a tornado, all of her words running together, with so much enthusiasm it's hard to make out exactly what she's saying. Of course, that's probably for the best.

When I get up the next morning, my shoulders, my feet, and everything in between are so sore I can barely walk. I hobble to the shower, my calf muscles pulled tug-of-war tight. My arms start to tremble when I rinse my hair, and I finally just stand under the spray and turn myself over to the forces of gravity. The elevator at the office, of course, has chosen today to break down again, and Hattie actually gets up from behind her desk at reception to hug me when she sees my face.

I'm halfway to St. Barbara's after work when I realize I never actually decided to come to tonight's Migraine Mafia session, and the realization jumpstarts a torrent of anxiety inside me. *If my subconscious is going to get on subways and join groups, what's next? Vetting a cult? Sprouting gills? Becoming a vegan?* I almost get off the subway at that moment, but the car is packed and my legs are exhausted and I just can't make it happen. I'm almost there, so I might as well go, I decide, and so I turn to focusing my energy on trying not to wince as I walk up the stairs to the building.

By the time I finally get to room 237 there's a thin sheen of sweat on my forehead. Ruth and Jaydyn are there, along with someone new, a small, mousy woman in her twenties who's talking quietly to Asha. The lights are off, per usual, and the camp lanterns are almost reassuring against the boring government paint.

"Hi guys," I say, and gingerly sit down in a chair.

"Feeling okay?" Asha asks. She introduces me to the new woman, and I promptly forget her name; there simply isn't enough room in my head for both my self-pity and new data.

"First session with my personal trainer was yesterday. I got on this thing called an elliptical machine, did this plank thing, and jumped up and down for a while."

The mouse has a knowing smile on her face. "It's horrible, isn't it?"

"It's okay," I say. When her expression changes to one of scepticism, I admit, "Yeah, it's horrible. I want to lie down and weep for a bit."

Jaydyn lets out the world's biggest sigh. "Seriously? It's just exercise, dudes."

"When's the last time you worked out, Jaydyn?" the mouse says. Her tone of voice is perfectly neutral, as if she hasn't noticed the extra pounds Jaydyn is carrying.

I wince as I reach for my bottle of water, and I notice Asha looking at me, her eyes thoughtful. "You're lucky," she says softly.

I laugh. "You have *got* to be kidding. Everything hurts, I feel terrible."

"The only exercise I can do are low-impact activities, like swimming or walking. If I tried to jump around and do the things you're talking about I'd be in bed for days with a spectacularly bad migraine. My system just can't tolerate it." She blinks. "The whole family, except for my youngest, skis. I always hated missing out on that. But I was in charge of organizing hot drinks and snacks when they came in. They would take pictures or videos of each other and show them to me. They did that when

I was sick; we have albums full of pictures." She smiles again and pats me on the arm. "But good for you, Viive, it's wonderful that you're trying new things."

Lucky. It's not something I often feel. And even though Asha is sitting here, watching a newcomer get something she probably will never get, and even though she missed out on huge slices of her children's lives, instead of feeling sorry for herself, she's happy for me. Not to mention, she came up with a brilliant solution for her problem. Photo albums, home movies. So simple, but ingenious.

"We should do a class together," the little mouse says. "Something like yoga."

"Yoga is for girls," Jaydyn says.

"Well, you don't have to come, do you?" Paulie says, as she flops into the chair beside me.

"I guess not," Jaydyn says.

"Where's Claire?" Asha asks.

"Migraining," Paulie answers. "I'm going to bring some stuff over to her place after group."

Ruth isn't listening to the conversation, her eyes glazed over, focused on nothing.

"Does everyone want to go around the room and give us an update on what they've been up to? Any new things you've tried?" Asha asks.

Ruth fumbles with her purse, easing out two small pills, which she palms. Her eyes dart around, looking to see who's watching her. When she meets my eyes, she drops her gaze immediately.

Paulie leans forward. "My dialysis seems to keep aggravating my symptoms. My doctors are going to try a magnesium drip."

Everyone makes supportive noises.

"Why?" I ask.

"Dialysis depletes the body of minerals, and magnesium is a key supplement for people with migraines. Most migraineurs–well, I think anyone with headache, really–should watch their intake."

I think about the magnesium Dr. Tess told me to buy. So far I've gotten as far as Googling it: horse-sized pills I know I'll never be able to swallow, which is why I haven't actually bought any yet. I haven't tried the swamp water vial yet either, for obvious reasons.

"Do you really hurt that much?" Paulie asks me, leaning forward. "I haven't worked out in forever." Paulie is so petite she's almost scrawny, although maybe it's because of her kidney disease. I think about juggling two illnesses instead of just one, how Paulie does both so proficiently.

"It'll pass," I say, trying to sound light-hearted.

"Oh, before I forget," the mousy girl says, snapping her fingers. "Viive, do you know about my sister? She's a professional organizer. She volunteers her time with people in our group."

"Oh. Well, thanks, but I'm okay," I say.

"Are you sure?" Asha asks. "Weren't you saying–"

"I can't do something like that," I say.

"Why not?" The new mousy girl asks.

I think about the state of my kitchen, the summer gear still in our front room, the dust in the corners, the quiet sense that something is wrong in our home. I can't show people how bad it's gotten. My mother used to meet me at my place when we had brunch plans, but a while ago I started just meeting her at the restaurant. In fact, I can't remember the last time she was at our house. So I can't have an organizer over; they'll think I'm a slob. They'll turn me over to that hoarders' show. I'll have cameramen in the bushes outside my house, sound booms over the windows.

"It's a little too messy right now," I say, finally.

"Dude, who cares about how your place looks? At least you don't have anyone nagging at you to clean up," Jaydyn says. "Like me."

Ruth drops the pills into her mouth, washing them down with some orange pop.

But I want to clean up. I close my eyes and think of how the house was when we moved in. Simple, clean, a little Scandinavian, a little retro. Now you need a search party to find the ice cube trays. "Hmm," I say.

"Hmm is right," Paulie says. "And maybe you should think about a cleaning lady, too."

"I can't do that either."

"Why not?" Asha asks.

"Well, I mean, it's so much money. Plus, having a stranger come in and clean would be weird. What would they think of me–a woman who can't even take care of her own house?"

"They'd think you're putting their kids through college, is what they'd think," Paulie says, with a wry grin. "The woman I use does laundry, and she can do groceries too."

"Or you could try a food delivery service," the mousy says.

I'm not sure how all the attention–all the eyes, all the energy–in the room got focused on me, and I don't know what words to use to find a new target for everyone. It's all very kind and helpful, but uncomfortable as hell, a disquiet that makes me want to squirm in my seat. They're not pushy, they all just…push. It's some kind of dark art, they way they're so friendly about it all.

Finally I say, "I'd love to, but the problem is I never know when

I'm going to get home."

"What about Nate?" Asha asks.

"Same."

"What about first thing in the morning? Or when the cleaning lady is there? She could put the stuff away." Paulie says.

"I don't know…"

"You need to start accepting help," Asha says gently. "Because things are not going to get easier as you get older. You must have a stable home environment, or you will always be out of balance. And the stress of it all will make your illness worse. You know this, of course."

"A cleaning lady isn't going to fix all that," I say, shifting in my chair.

"No, but it's something," Paulie replies. "Look, we're not here to tell everyone to change everything immediately. We just want people to realize that something little, over time, can turn into something big. I mean, I have to work a full-time job and get dialysis three times a week. When I get home after a long day, I don't want to have to worry about cleaning the bathroom. I just want to focus on living the best life I can."

"But isn't it expensive?" I ask.

"It's worth every penny," Paulie says, her voice firm. "And if you're a manager, why are you worrying about money?"

"Most of my money goes into my mortgage and savings."

"But what are you saving for?" Ruth says, a question that starts something churning in my head. *What am I saving for?* I think about my older Estonian relatives, who were always afraid to spend, just in case another war broke out. I don't want to be like that, but I don't want to be frivolous either. Our mortgage isn't exactly cheap, and what if the roof falls in? You never know what's going to go wrong. *Shouldn't I hold on to my savings, just in case?*

"That's a very good point," Paulie says and everyone murmurs in agreement.

I glance around the room, to cast out for a new problem for the group to focus on. Jaydyn is playing some sort of a video game on his tablet and Ruth just looks defeated. She's wearing a suit that hasn't fit properly in a good long while, and her dishwater-blonde hair is limp and lifeless. Her face is puffy, especially her left eye, and she looks like she's forty going on eighty.

"Are you okay, Ruth?" I ask.

"Hmm?"

"Are you all right?"

"Oh. Yes, I'm fine."

"You look like you have a headache," Asha says.

"It was a hectic day," Ruth says. "I haven't really had time to eat."

All of us, except for Jaydyn, rustle around in our bags. In almost the same moment we find our snacks–me with my squishy vegan power bar, Paulie with a liquid meal, Asha with some nuts, and the mousy girl with a piece of soy cheese and an apple in a zip lock.

"Oh, I couldn't," Ruth says.

"Moooom," Jaydyn whines. "I gotta get out of here." He stands up and starts to walk out of the room.

"Where are you going?" Ruth asks.

"Somewhere that's not here," he says, looking out from underneath his overgrown bangs. His eyes appear tired and bloodshot, like he's all used up at fourteen.

"Let him go," Asha says. "It's fine, Ruth."

Ruth's eyes follow Jaydyn out, and after he leaves, Paulie gets up and closes the door with a decisive *snick*. "Ruth," she says, "we need to talk to you."

Ruth is taking small, tentative bites of the cheese the new girl has handed her. "I'm so sorry about Jaydyn. He doesn't mean it, you know–"

"Sure, sure," Paulie says, waving her hands. "We're all more worried about you, Ruth. Tell me something, where does Jaydyn get his headaches from?"

Ruth stops chewing. "Me. I used to get them when I was younger."

"What about now?" I ask.

"Well, you know. Over the last few years…yes, I guess they've been acting up."

"Why didn't you ever say anything?" Asha asks.

She blinks. "I…I was so worried for Jaydyn I didn't even think of it."

"Ruth, you know when you're on a plane and they tell you to put on your oxygen mask before helping someone else, you know, if there's a problem?"

Ruth blinks again, her eyelashes like hummingbirds. "Yes."

"That's because you can't help other people unless you help yourself first," Paulie says.

"She's right," I say.

"Of course I'm right, I'm always right," Paulie says, with a little smile. "Anyway, we're saying the exact same thing to you, Ms. Viive Las Vegas. All the money you've saved up is going to be wasted because it's not helping you live your life the way you need to. What's the point of a life like that, anyway?"

I look around the room, at all of them, there's something in their expressions that says: *I know you. I am you.* Then I look at the mousy girl and say, mostly to be polite, "Sure, give me your sister's number." I still can't picture me picking up the phone and dialing, but I'd feel better if this conversation would stop.

"Right on," Paulie says, nodding.

It is impossible to keep these people from helping me, I think, and thankfully the conversation goes on to other things, problems with work, insurance coverage, shitty in-laws.

"Viive?"

"Sorry, what?" I say.

The mouse has her phone in her hand, and has obviously been texting. "It looks like my sister is going to be downtown on Saturday, she could just drop by your place. Does that work?"

I feel a small pinch of irritation, but after a minute I think: What's the way out of all of this? If my house is so cluttered that the neighbours might call a reality TV show, then why don't I just get some help with the housework? If I'm worried about what people will think, why don't I just not tell them? It's none of anyone's business what goes on in my home. And I guess that's why I say, "Uh…sure." I scrawl my phone number and address on the back of an envelope from my bag and hand it to the mouse.

"I have to go back to the doctor," Ruth says, sounding like she's just been shipwrecked.

"Yes," Asha says, smiling so big her eyes disappear.

At nine, the cleaning staff comes to lock up, and the group disbands. Paulie asks me if I want to come with her to Claire's condo in Liberty Village. Paulie has a migraine kit with her and wants to bring it to Claire: saltines, Coke, Gravol. It's not on the way for me, but Paulie says she'll drop me off at home afterwards, and I don't think I can face the subway tonight, so that's how I end up saying yes. Her car is a boxy old Datsun, with stuff on all the seats and the sharp smell of stale tobacco in the air.

"Do you mind if I smoke?" she asks me as soon as she cleans off the passenger seat and we get in the car.

"Nope," I say.

Eventually Paulie pulls on to Liberty Street East before winding her way around the ultra-new developments, condos stacked on each other like matchbooks. Paulie and I walk up the steps to Claire's apartment, and her hand is barely raised to knock on the door when it flies open. A thirty-something guy stands there, in old saggy jeans and a dirty white t-shirt. His eyes are dull, his nose is runny, and his hair is matted to his forehead like sweaty blond abstract art.

"Wsup?" he says, taking a sip of beer before wiping the back of his hand over his mouth.

"I'm Paulie," she says. "I'm a friend of Claire's. Can we come in?"

"She's lyin' down. You'll hafta come back."

"She's expecting me," Paulie says. "She texted me."

"Naw. You'll hafta come back." He moves to close the door, but Paulie slides her foot over in a fluid motion and blocks it in a way that says she's no stranger to doors being shut in her face. She holds his gaze for a few minutes before he grudgingly steps back. I wish I could look at people like that, move them with only my eyes. Paulie brushes past him and down the stairs, and I follow.

It's very dim in the basement room, just a flicker of light, really. Claire is curled up on her side, facing away from us, fetal and forlorn on a shitty camp bed. Paulie walks over and puts her hand gently on Claire's shoulder, and Claire twitches a little before pulling an earplug out of one ear, and then the next. She opens her eyes slowly, blinking until she adjusts to the light. Her eyes are puffed and swollen, bloodshot, barely open. When I pull a chair across the floor and the legs screech–unexpected and sudden–Claire's eyes close in pain.

"Sorry," I say, and pity runs through me, even though I absolutely hate it when people feel sorry for me. I think of the well-dressed, successful, together woman I met not that long ago, and I can't reconcile it with the pathetic figure on the bed, even though a small voice is telling me I look *exactly* that bad when I'm sick. It doesn't seem like something anybody could survive. It looks like she's going to die. And then suddenly I'm blinking back tears.

"Hi," Claire says, and she looks exhausted after speaking that small mouthful. She tries to open her eyes again.

"We brought you the stuff you wanted." Paulie says, speaking softly.

"Lifesaver," Claire says, her voice slurred just like mine when I have a migraine, like a drunk on a three-day bender in Vegas. Like someone who's barely verbal, barely somebody. She squints at me. "Who's that?"

"It's Viive," Paulie says. "The new chick."

"Sorry. Eyes."

"It's okay." Paulie slowly helps Claire sit up, in a way that lets you know Claire's going to throw up if she has to move too fast. "What do you want to eat?"

"Saltines," Claire says, her head leaned back on the wall, her eyes closed again. "Can you get a new icepack? Please?"

"You got it," Paulie says. Beside the cot is a jumble of discarded icepacks, a small mountain of blue gelatin-filled bags. Paulie collects them all and takes them upstairs.

When it's just the two of us, I run my eyes over the basement. The condo is new, but the room already looks shabby. I'm surprised at how cluttered it is, since Claire looked so together when I met her. The basement looks worse than my living room, in fact. Maybe I'm not the only one hiding something.

Claire is watching my eyes. "I sleep down here when I'm sick so I don't bother Raymond." After Paulie comes back, Claire takes some Gravol and then eats the saltines–one at a time, every movement laborious. And none of us say anything about the fact that we're doing all of this, and not Raymond. After about ten minutes, Claire motions to the side table. "Paulie, can you get me a triptan?"

Paulie deconstructs the tangled nest of packaging for the migraine medication; a box, then a sachet, then a blister pack with a single sugary-sweet wafer–the same one I take–a task so arduous I'm perpetually amazed the drug company thought we could cope with it during a migraine attack. It almost has to be a joke.

Claire takes it, her eyes closing in relief. "Thanks so much, guys. I've been throwing up all day. Couldn't keep my meds down."

"It's okay, Claire. We're here." Paulie reaches over and holds her hand. After a little while, Claire is asleep, her chest falling and rising peacefully. At least for this moment, she's out of pain. For a minute I feel like I'm watching a miracle, and that's when I notice I've been holding my breath, trying to be quiet. When I exhale, that's when I realize how angry I am. I hate the mean-nothing, well-intentioned platitudes you read in campaigns about chronic illness, or on online forums, the pink-ribboned, cheerleadery talk of flourishing and triumph. There's no wisdom to be gained at Claire's bedside, other than thinking about the bared-knuckle, enduring-a-marathon-from-hell gumption that someone in her position has to summon every single minute, just to survive. Watching my disease play out in someone else's body is a nightmare, and as Paulie and I sit there quietly, in our miniature vigil, the room is full of a breathless kind of misery. My stomach knots itself so furiously I start to worry that I'm going to throw up too.

After a half hour of this, Paulie nudges me, and the two of us leave, silently, ignoring Raymond as we go. On the drive home I'm quiet, thinking about everything Nate does for me, so many things I probably don't even see, without ever complaining, and I still feel so sorry for myself all the time. Claire doesn't even get to suffer in her own bed, and lives with an asshole.

Paulie drops me off on my front steps, lights a cigarette off the one she's already smoking, and waves as she peels off. Nate is still at work so it's just me in our small living room. If you look at it, really look at it, it's not so bad. Our to-be-read piles might be overflowing, there's dust everywhere, and about six spots that need to be spackled, but there's love in the room, in the pictures on the walls, in the knickknacks on the mantle that Nate and I have bought each other over the years. So I can't really understand why I'm crying, sitting on my couch, if I'm crying for Claire and her loveless house or if I'm crying for all of us. I feel impossibly spoiled, like a bratty rich kid with too much money and not enough sense. But the truth is that even though I'm so spoiled, and so lucky, I'm still going to fail. With all that extra help, it's always going to end the same, a dark room, a dark pain, loneliness, and silence.

I don't know if I can survive the group, with their optimism in the face of all the things that are waiting to go wrong, when I feel a raw, aching vulnerability in saying just a handful of words. I don't want to spend every week confronted with things that can't be changed, not really. My old way worked perfectly fine, if you want the truth. No delusions, no nonsense. No laundry list of doctors with me in their clutches, telling me what to do all the time. No false hope.

But then I think of the promotion headed my way, the reward for all that work, and I think about being in a spot where I can take a breath, for once. The chaos will have to stop, then, and once I've gotten to where I'm going, everything will change. It has to.

A good day at work, hitting the gym, home for dinner, weekday sex, sleep: that's what life as a director will be like. Nothing else to push for, everything in its place. It's a hazy success story, and there aren't a lot of details, but in my mind all of those things have always all gone together. And it's all right around the corner.

The professional organizer, one Lily Tidwell, is supposed to be at my house this morning at eleven. I mean, what better way to spend a Saturday? But s*upposed to* is the key here, because I've been throwing up since three and I need to send her send her a message saying I can't meet her because my cranium is going to erupt like Eyjafjallajökull, the Icelandic menace that brought air traffic to a halt a few years ago. What year was that? I can't remember, the detail gone, swimming in the soupy glop inside my brain.

The real problem is that her email address is on my phone, and my phone is downstairs, and the stairs are pretty hard to face right now, especially since my legs are floppy like a pair of deboned fish. Herring, maybe. It's not a lot of stairs, that's true, but they still require a strategy, a mini-summit meeting between my cranium and my feet, not to mention everything in-between.

My brain is straining with the effort to stay focused, just for a few minutes, just until I can send the email, and the only way to do that is to break the problem down to its smallest components. First step: sit up. That's not so hard, is it? Billions do it every morning. *I can do it if I count, I can.* I count slowly; one, two–at three I stop for a rest–at ten I grab on to the bed frame. Glaciers have moved faster, but this small movement utterly saps me. I sit there until I catch my breath, heavy metal playing in my ears. There doesn't seem to be a way to survive all this, to live through this kind of pain.

I float away for a while, try to pretend this isn't my life.

Focus.

Next step: stand up, walk to the door of Nate's office–I moved here a few hours ago–go down the stairs, go left to the living room, get the phone, send the email. It's a huge task, one I don't know if I can carry off or not. But I do know I can have a rest on the couch, thank Jesus Christ and any other deity who might be listening (because, you know, I'm not picky). The squirrels start to bounce around under the eaves, like it's their personal rumpus room. Time to go.

I struggle to my feet, wavering a little when I'm finally vertical. *I can do this.* I've done this so many times before. The blood pumping through my head is an ocean, a tsunami crashing up against my skull, tipped with razor-sharp shards of glass. It's a bad one, the pain so violent it's hard to breathe.

When my heart rate is finally equalized, my feet start shuffling. It's seven steps to the door, where I take a rest. It's hard to see anything because the room keeps sliding in and out of focus, but the next step is down the stairs. I take them one at a time: my left foot on the first step, then my right. Then the same thing down one more step. My brain pulsates with every step, the cluster of nerves on the left side of my head hammering against my skull, my heartbeat squeaking in my left ear. It's so loud it drowns out the *waah waah waah* of the car alarm going off in front of the house, the sound so close it feels like someone's pouring all the noise into my ear. Nate and I still haven't figured out who owns that car.

I'm almost at the bottom of the stairs now. All I have to do is turn and go left into the living room. My hands track my progress by holding onto the wall. I like this colour–I painted it myself. Later, when I'm better,

I'll probably be irritated by all the smudged hand prints from this trip, but right now it's the only way to balance. I wonder: *What colour should I paint the walls to hide my migraine handprints?*

It's so important not to cry. The amount of self-control it takes to keep from crying is enormous; a boulder I have to push. The phone is beside the couch, so I can sit down when I get there. *Couch–phone–sit.* I can do this, especially the sitting part, which is where I'll really shine. Halfway there, my dizziness goes nuclear, the floor gyrates underneath me, the air grabs at me. I take the last few steps in one big lurching stumble. The sofa is victory; the crowd goes wild. The furnace is off and the house is cold, and it makes me shiver. I pick up my phone, find the address, and send the email before wrestling with the wrapper for my migraine meds, the same triptan Claire couldn't open last night. The scene in Claire's basement feels like it just happened, probably because it did. It's funny, how quickly things can change.

I take one, and then put the phone and the pills down and sink onto the sofa. The wafer is a sickening sweetness on my tongue, and after I take it, I'm engulfed in that old post-marathon, squashed-lungs kind of exhaustion. Somewhere in the back of my head the thought is thrumming: I thought I was getting better. I thought I was making things better.

And out of all of the bad moments I've had this is one of the worst, because now all I can think is, *I'm supposed to be getting better better better.* All those doctors, all that therapeutic chit-chat, all that medication has gotten me nowhere. I start to shiver, my skin suddenly overrun by sweat. The blankets are in a tangle beside the couch and I pull them over me, my movements jerky and awkward. You could surf on the waves of pain in my head, long board it all the way to China.

It's the deepest, ugliest, reddest moment in a migraine attack, when I'm nothing but breath and bones and pain. Every iota of my focus is on getting to the other side of the next exhale, trying to find the end of this agony. Time is so full right now, like it's slower or bigger than it usually is, and all I can think is: *How much longer?* Every new throbbing wave in my head means *not yet not yet not yet.*

There is no way I can make it back up the stairs. I've probably only walked thirty feet, but I have absolutely nothing left inside me.

Nate is standing over me, and the room is flooded with morning light. He's shaking me lightly.

"Nate, stop!"

"Sorry babe," he says. "But don't you have that meeting in an hour? With the organizer?"

"I had to cancel," I say, moving so I can sit up.

"Shit. I'm sorry I woke you up. Can I do anything?"

"Water?"

Nate goes to the kitchen and pours a glass for me. "How bad is it? Out of ten?" He reaches out and holds my hand, his eyes on me. For a minute, I wonder what he sees when he looks at me when I'm like this? A sad wreckage of a person? A life sentence? I ease two Gravols out of a blister pack and take another triptan. "Bad. Nine-ish."

"I guess we're not going to that thing tonight, then."

I have no memory of whatever *thing* Nate is talking about. "I'm sorry."

"It's all right." His shoulders slump as he says it, or maybe I'm just imagining it.

"I'm sorry. You should go."

"It won't be fun without you. It's okay. Did you do something yesterday? Did you not eat?" He tucks my hair behind my ear. I can feel every strand pull at my scalp.

I nod because suddenly I'm all out of words, like I've come to the end of the English language.

After a while Nate says, "Can I do anything for you, babe?"

"Help me up?"

"Okay." He puts his arm under mine and gently steers me upstairs.

"Slower, Nate. Please."

"Sorry." The two of us shuffle like geriatrics up the stairs and back to the bedroom.

"Can you get me…" The room moves two inches to the left. I grip Nate tighter, hang off him like he's a life preserver. "An icepack?" I think of Claire on her tiny camp bed, her eyes swollen shut, sickness swelling out of every pore in her body. I know I look like that, that my voice is thick with sleep and stupid thoughts and I'll never find the right words for Nate.

"Sure."

He comes back in a few minutes with one of my favourite icepacks, and I slide it under the left side of my head and over my face and forehead. My left eyeball starts to turn numb.

"Anything else, sweetie?" Nate asks, holding my hand. He sits down on the bed.

"No, thanks. Love you. Sorry."

Nate rests his forehead against mine, snugs the bridge of his nose into my face and stays there for a minute or two. Our neighbours are all out at brunch, or hockey, or naked skydiving, while Nate and I sit here like two lovebirds in a Victorian sickroom. After a minute Nate kisses me and goes, leaving my phone on the bedside table so I can text him if I need anything. The room feels empty after he leaves. The light is off, and my blinds are blocking out the light from the window, but I can still see a small sliver of sun, if I look. There are just the muffled sounds of the next-door neighbours living their lives, and the faint noise of traffic coming from the street. I think about all the mundane things people are doing to make all those noises, right outside my window. A life like theirs has never felt further away. I try to slow my breathing because my oldest, best rule is about to be broken. I'm going to cry during a migraine.

Breathe, hingata, breathe, hingata.

I force air through my lungs while a few tears escape out of my eyes. I think about chocolate ice cream and promotions. My new title is the one shining success on my horizon, the reward for all my overtime and work and study and sacrifice. Just beyond that is the next, perfect phase of my life; my own company, my own way of doing things. No more meetings about how to push staff beyond the point of no return, no more conversations with people who can't even tell what operating system they're looking at, no being forced to buy shitty technology because your boss plays golf with the CEO of a company staffed by morons.

I have to have that one success. I have to.

I've been telling myself this story forever, and saying it often enough has become its own kind of truth. There's no pain and sickness in that future; the only way to make the churn of all that worry quiet is to think about my promotion. I can't be losing ground, if that's the destiny about to meet me. So, I can survive this moment. I can make it until this is over, until my future begins. Today is just one more step towards where I want to be.

My breathing is calm now, my mind fuzzy with the medication, my stomach finally settled, the pain in my head muffled. The pillows are soft against my skin, the blankets the perfect kind of warm. Outside, a horn sounds, and then the squeal of brakes. The next-door neighbours' dog barks. A group passes, a family maybe, small children chattering, on the way to something they've probably looked forward to all week. The wind kicks up.

I hear it all.

I'm able to get out of bed on Sunday and eat something (ketchup chips, ice cream, chocolate–all terrible for me, but gluten-free, and the dairy in the chocolates can't possibly count) but on Monday my legs are still rickety after two days off my feet. There's something familiar and old about facing a Monday with a weekend headache hangover, a sense that it should still be

Friday, that the weekend has somehow vaporized.

Nate has an early meeting, so he gets up and bounces out of bed, showers with the enthusiasm of ten men, kisses me everywhere and then leaves. After the tornado of Nate is over I glance at the clock. It's early, so I go downstairs and get some of the gluten-free, high-protein cereal I picked up with Otis, pouring some almond milk in the bowl and going into the living room. The news is on with the volume muted because the female host's voice is so deranged it's practically a yodel, and it's just too much for me to face right now. I check the weather channel, and when I see the date, November 4th, I realize that Nate never decorated the house this year for Halloween. So not only have I missed my weekend, I've completely skipped October 31st. The stores will already be full of Christmas decorations. Briefly, I think about my winter coat.

The cereal is awful; squishy, clinging to my gums like barnacles. It smells like a bog. I put the bowl down on the coffee table, still half full, before going upstairs and brushing my teeth with an energy I'm surprised I'm able to summon. After that, I examine myself in the mirror. I don't normally wear makeup to work, but today I put some concealer under my eyes before swallowing two painkillers, whites. The remnants of my weekend headache still thrums through me, and my balance is still not quite drunk-looking, but not quite right-looking either, like I'm gearing up for my third martini. I think about the subway, the streetcar, the jumble of people, the smells, the noise, the crazy commuter who'll try to sit on my lap and bamboozle me with talk of eternal salvation, for a small price.

I dial a cab.

I'm in my not-an-office before Otis, sipping tea and burping up terrible breakfast smells. I'm not hungry, though, not light-headed or distracted like I get when I haven't eaten, and then I curse the healthy cereal, which I know I'm going to have to eat more of. I keep my door shut and pretend to be engrossed in work.

Later, Otis knocks quietly and lets himself in. "How's it going, my dear?"

"Good," I say, trying to shrug off the weekend and all the things which can't be changed, and focus on right now. "Is it time?"

"It is," he says, and I palm two more whites before we walk down the hallway to the dreaded management meeting. It's the same crowd as always, the team managers and Elliot, everyone sipping on an overpriced, overcaffeinated beverage, including me. Elliot starts off the meeting, talking briefly about some exec concerns. He's doing a preview of the year wrap-up, talking about how Christmas this year is going to be huge, and all that jazz. Not much of his speech is new to me; a lot of his data comes from information I emailed him last night after he called me on my cell and woke me up, in fact.

About halfway through, I notice Joe, who's smiling at me in a disconcerting, sly kind of way, his eyes more focused and googly than usual as he shifts around in his chair non-stop, which is particularly annoying because his chair has a squeak.

"…I also want to talk about some critical initiatives we're going to be working on in the new year," Elliot says.

Squeak.

Bug-eyes.

Squeak squeak squeak.

"The exec has done a lot of strategizing with regards to organizational objectives and structure…"

I perk up. This is it, my promotion. I casually reach up and neaten my hair, so that when everyone looks at me I'll look all right.

"We're going to be introducing a new position, a director-level position, the first in this team…"

I sit up straighter, my breath coming short and fast, my pulse ratcheting up. I try not to smile and give away the fact that I know what's coming.

"As you're all aware, we have a recent addition to our management team, but he's become a critical asset to the organization. He'll be assuming this position immediately. Congratulations, Joe."

Oh holy Jesus Christ and fuck.

10 – No, Timmy, It's Not Just a Headache

Somehow Avery is in my kitchen. I'm not sure how this happened, how she got past my perimeter defences. I feel betrayed. Violated. It isn't just that Avery is in my kitchen, but rather that Avery is in my kitchen at six o'clock, especially considering the fact that Nate and I don't usually get home until much later.

And exactly when the hell did Nate give Avery a key to our house?

I was out the door at 5:01 today, for obvious reasons, banging down the stairs (goddamn elevator is out again) and slamming the front door. Twice. I brushed off Otis's offers to go to a pub and wallow so I could try to blow off some steam before Nate gets home from work. So I can be calm when I tell him that Joe has stolen my promotion like a dirty thief in the night. I got off the subway three stops early so I could stomp my anger out on the sidewalk. Instead, I ended up walking twelve blocks with a roaring in my ears, the ocean come alive in my head. When I trudged up the walkway to my house, there was a black squirrel dancing on the railing. Taunting me. Now my insides are a twisty nest of snakes, the back of my neck is slick with sweat, and I feel like kicking a stranger.

"So what do you think?" she asks.

Actually, I might feel like kicking Avery.

"What do I think about what?" My heart thumps once, and then twice, out of sync, like it's forgotten how to beat.

Her eyes narrow. "About the boat."

"What boat?"

"The boat Nate saw a few weeks ago."

"What kind of boat?"

"A sailboat. Thirty-four feet."

"Why?"

"Well," Avery says, speaking very slowly, her head tilted to the side. "Because he wants to sail. We used to sail all the time when we were kids."

Goddamn thirty-four feet? Who needs that much boat? One day I'm going to come home to an empty lot, because Nate will have gambled away the house.

"I see."

The front door opens. "Hi honey," Nate yells, before the usual noises of Nate dropping his shit beside the door ring out.

"You're early," I say, trying to keep the tension out of my voice.

"We lost power, so they sent us home. I still have a bunch of stuff to do." He walks over and kisses me on the head. I don't lean toward him like I usually do. I don't kiss him back, and I don't pat his hair down, which looks like someone has run an eggbeater through it. All I can think of is: *When did he give Avery a goddamn key? How long has she been creeping around my house? What else is going on I don't know about?*

"Hey Avery. What's up?" Nate says.

"Well," she replies, like she's about to announce she just won an Oscar. "I actually came over to discuss Christmas, but we ended up talking about the boat we went to see, instead."

Avery and Nate went to see a boat together without telling me? My stomach is a fist, a rock. I stare out the window; I want it to storm, I want things to crash around.

Nate looks exasperated. "It's supposed to be a surprise, Avery."

She smacks her forehead. "Oh my God, I'm such an idiot."

"It's okay," Nate says.

"Are you sure?" Avery answers, all wide-eyed innocence.

"Of course," Nate says, before turning to me. "Dinner?"

"Pizza?" I suggest, and he nods, so I go upstairs to order from Mystic Slice, the local organic/alternative pizza parlour; one pepperoni and one Hawaiian, both on a rice crust. If you close your eyes and think of England when you eat that crust, it's not so bad. But it's also not enough right now. *Sugar*, my brain sings, *salt*, *potato chips*, *sugar sugar sugar*.

"Anything else?" the pizza guy asks.

"Something with chocolate. Please," I say, my voice almost husky with need.

He laughs, a silvery peal of teenage noise, before hanging up. *His worst problem is probably that he can't find enough hours in the day to watch all the porn he wants*, I think sourly. I sit on the bed for a minute. I don't want to go downstairs, and I don't want to go to work, and frankly I don't know what the hell to do next. *Just breathe*, I tell myself. *Worry about your job tomorrow. Eat the chocolate. Don't kill Avery.*

The three of us sit in the living room while we wait for dinner, and no one mentions anything else about the boat while Nate and Avery chat about nothing. I sit on the couch, looking at job listings on my laptop.

When the pizza is delivered, Avery squinches her face into a displeased pucker. "What's up with the crust?"

"It's rice," I say. "It's gluten-free."

"Why?"

"My doctor told me to try it."

"Isn't it just some kind of fad, all this gluten stuff?" She laughs.

"It's supposed to help Viive's headaches," Nate says, putting his hand on mine.

"Really?" Avery says, like: *Really? You were born with a tail?* "I think people who go on and on about all these food sensitivities are only looking for attention."

"What?" I snap, unlooping my hand from Nate's.

"It's just, you know, people make such a big deal about it. It turns into a hassle to everyone."

"Yeah," I say, "I'm sure all the people with Celiac disease do it just to hassle everyone."

"Well," Avery says, opening the other pizza box. "You don't have Celiac's, do you, Viive?"

"Ease up, Avery," Nate says.

"Don't help me," I say.

"What did *I* do?"

Avery sighs, her arms crossed over her chest, scowling. There's a silence in the room, and if I close my eyes I can imagine things crashing around, a deeply satisfying thought.

Eventually, she roots through my dinner a bit more. "Is that all?" Avery hates both pepperoni and pineapple.

"Oh, *no*," I say, not bothering to flatten the sarcasm out of my voice. And then I smile. I can't help myself.

Avery sighs, hard and annoyed, like a child. "Well, I'm starving, so I'm going to head home. Viive, I'll call you later this week. We need to finalize Christmas plans."

"I'm not hosting Christmas," I say flatly. "So there's nothing to finalize."

"Well, hang on a minute," Nate says.

"Hey, if you want to make Christmas dinner, you go right ahead," I say.

"I've done it for the past four years," Avery says.

"I know." I pinch the bridge of my nose. "And everyone appreciates it. But we don't know how I'm going to be that week–and I refuse to ruin Christmas for everyone because I have a headache."

"Can't you just, you know, make sure you don't have one?" she asks.

My jaw clenches so tightly I hear a popping noise. "No."

Avery turns to Nate. "I don't want to do it this year, our kitchen is being renovated, and frankly, I think I've put my time in."

"Nate and I would be happy to host dinner at a restaurant. Isn't that right, Nate?"

Nate shifts in his chair.

"Isn't that right, Nate?" *Thud, thud, thud;* my heartbeat is surround-sound in my ears.

"It won't really be Christmas without a home-cooked meal," Avery says, her face in a practiced pout.

"It'll be Christmas," I say. "Because God and the calendar will say it's Christmas." I love Nate's mother, but I'm 100% sure that this home-cooked meal shit is just some nonsense she told her children when they were growing up, like life can't possibly be happy unless you baste your turkey with butter and love and your own tears. I'm about five seconds away from saying: *In some countries they can't even afford turkey,* just like my mom would. I pinch the bridge of my nose again.

"Can't you take some time off work?"

"No."

"Why not?"

"Because I don't have that kind of job," I snap.

Nate is still standing there, saying nothing. *Oh, Nate.* Finally, he says, "Viive and I will talk about it and get back to you, okay?"

"Well, I hope you do the right thing. I don't want Christmas to be ruined."

"And I do?" I ask.

"No, of course not," Avery says, in an *of-course-you-do* voice.

"Bye Avery," I say.

Her expression falters. "What?"

"You heard me."

"Okay, Viive, you're obviously having one of your difficult days," she says, gathering up all her shit. "I'll talk to you when you feel better."

"I feel great," I say.

She turns back, leans against the doorframe. "You know, I don't understand why you always have to make such a big deal about it. I mean, it's just a headache."

If I close my eyes I can see my mother telling me, like I'm watching a movie, Pere on kõik: *family is everything.* Ours was so small, so few people got out, we can't take family members for granted. I always believed her. I still do; I want harmony in my home, to get along with Nate's family, that we all live our quirky little happily ever after. But if Avery can't start doing the same for me, then maybe we're going to have to make some changes. *Be careful*, I can hear my mother say, but then I think, *Maybe today, maybe we'll be a little less careful.*

"Let me ask you something, Avery."

She tilts her head to the side. I can tell she's aching to roll her eyes at me.

"What do you do when you have a headache?" I ask.

Her face is blank.

"No, really, what do you do?"

"I take some Tylenol."

"How many?"

"Two."

"Extra strength?"

"No…regular usually does it."

"Must be nice. And then?"

She shrugs and looks away. "And then I feel better."

I wait until she meets my gaze again. "Do you really think…do you *really think* that if I could take two regular-strength Tylenol and feel better, I wouldn't do exactly that?"

She squints at me, tugs the corner of her shirt down.

"There's no pill, don't you get it? There's no pill that works for migraine. I'm pumped full of medicine for *epileptics!* I'm waiting for results from an EEG given to me by the angriest woman *ever*, so I can find out if I had a seizure last week because of that very same medication. The painkillers I take aren't even painkillers, and they take hours to work. *Sometimes days!* And that's *if they work at all!*" I'm on my feet now, my guts churning, and I'm walking toward Avery, even though I don't remember telling my legs to move.

She backs up. "It's just…you don't really say much about it… I mean…"

"I don't want to make everything about me being sick all the time, Avery, but my disease is just as real as cancer." I look back at my to-be-read pile, at the jumble of brochures Dr. Throckmorton gave me. And then I cross the small room again, pick them up, and hold them out to Avery. "I'm sorry that me being sick impacts other people, I really am. I wish my life were different. And I'm trying to make things better. But I don't want to see you again until you read these, and do some research, and figure out that it's not just a fucking headache."

Avery's skin is pale as she takes them from me, and then she mumbles a quiet goodbye.

Nate and I sit on the couch, listening to her go. Outside, a wind has sprung up. Inside, my chest rises and falls, my heart a hammer against it.

"You okay?" he asks me.

"To be honest, I'm starting to feel better than I have in a long time."

"Well, okay, then, I guess everything is settled." Nate shrugs. God, I hate it when Nate shrugs like that. When we have a problem, he just shuts down, making it impossible for us to solve anything. And then I remember the huge yacht, and the Christmas nonsense, and everything else that's waiting for me to tell Nate. Sometimes I feel like if I pull too tightly on my marriage that it'll all come loose.

"You know what?" Nate says. "We both make good money. You save every single penny you make, and I save *almost* every penny I make. Why can't we enjoy it? Why can't we enjoy *anything*?" He runs his fingers through his hair. "And what about Christmas? Avery has a point. It should be perfect."

"Christmas isn't about perfect cooking or perfect anything, Nate. Sometimes Christmas is just about survival."

Nate makes a pissed-off noise in the back of his throat. "Well, whatever," he says, getting up and leaving. His pizza gets cold on the coffee table after he goes upstairs and does whatever he does in his office. Probably gambling away the yacht he hasn't even bought yet. *Thirty-four feet. Jesus fucking Christ.*

I want to quit everything: my job, putting up with Avery, trying to keep my brain from exploding out of my ears. I feel exhausted, like I walked home from work, like I'm all used up. I want to call Ruby, but I can't, because I still haven't talked to her since her birthday, and I can't call her up to complain about Nate, who she loves, or about my job, which she's been telling me to quit for years.

After Nate leaves, I'm alone in the room with the almost-impossible-to-eat pizza and the chocolate surprise the horny teen at the pizza place sent along for me. Flourless chocolate cake. I eat it with a glass of milk, and when that's done, I eat Nate's too. It's not bad for gluten-free. The frosting lingers on my tongue, the sugar tucking into my bloodstream, my energy level surging. I pull up my laptop and write an email to Elliot, telling him I'm taking a personal day tomorrow. Everyone on staff gets two of these a year, but I've never taken one before. Then I call Manjit and ask him to take point on everything until Wednesday, and then I shut off my work phone, something I've never done before either. It feels awesome to watch the screen fade into nothingness, like Christmas and Thanksgiving all wrapped up together with a side of really good chocolate. Godiva, maybe.

My throat is sore as I surf some of the silly Internet sites I never have time for, before sending an email to Lily Tidwell, asking her if she's free tomorrow. She fixes Christmases for a living, I'll bet. And then I see the stack of email from my mom, so I send her a message, to see if we can meet for lunch.

I need my mom.

The lump in my throat is too big to swallow. After a minute, I wipe some tears off my cheeks, even though I didn't know I was crying.

As my stomach eases into that tired old post-carb floatyness, I spend a little more time doing nothing, but what I'm really trying to figure out is: *What am I going to do next? How can I explain to Nate that change feels like standing at the edge of a cliff?*

The conflict Nate and I have is in all the things we don't say to each other. I hate that.

And I hate that the Yuletide season leaves such a bad taste in my mouth, but my shitty knack of getting migraines as soon as I'm on vacation has made Christmas a nightmare of a holiday. Which makes it the perfect goddamn event to cater. I ruin so many things; the last thing I want to do is ruin Christmas.

Again.

I've never taken a personal day. So it's a little surreal to be sitting with my mom at lunch on a Tuesday, at a funky eatery near her office, a little ethereal and strange and reckless. We're sitting in the window, looking at the passers-by; the sunshine is aggressive today, a last stand against winter. I examine the menu with trepidation while I ache for pancakes smothered in maple syrup and walnut butter, my very favourite culinary indulgence. I can't remember the last time the two of us didn't order it when we came here.

"What's wrong?" my mom asks, looking at me over her bifocals.

"Nothing, Ema."

She narrows her eyes and nods, as if we've just agreed on something.

The server comes by and asks us what we'll order. Her hair is an almost-white blonde like my mom's and mine, her cheeks are pale, and her wrists are small and delicate. She looks like the other kind of Estonian; super tall, thin, and dainty. My mom and I definitely run to the other type; thicker, shorter, burlier. One generation from the farm. My mom smiles at the young woman and then glances at her nametag: Tiiu, the Esto equivalent of *Jane*. There are less than a million Estonians in the world, but Toronto is the largest centre of expats, and it's not that unusual to stumble over a Tiiu or a Toivo every once in a while. The three of us smile at each other, a quiet *I know you.* In Estonian, my mom orders Lady Grey tea like always (her act of feminism for the day, she likes to say), and then pancakes for both of us, with a side of bacon.

I exhale. "Actually, I'll have the omelette," I say, also in Estonian. "Without the cheese, please."

"How can you have an omelette without cheese?" my mother asks. "She'll have the cheese," she says to the server, who's no stranger to Estonian mothers.

"No, no cheese, please," I say.

"She'll–"

"Run," I say to the server, who takes the opportunity to withdraw.

"No cheese, hmmm?" my mom says. She takes off her bifocals and then puts them down on the table the way she does most things, purposefully. "You're not on some silly diet, are you Viive?"

"Nope," I say, pushing the bread basket over to her.

Her answer is a raised eyebrow and a quiet, "Hmmm."

Tiiu brings the tea, along with milk and sugar and another smile. When I pour some of the Lady Grey for myself and then a cup for my mom, her eyes narrow again when she sees I'm skipping the milk.

"Okay, I'm on a little bit of a diet," I say.

"A mother knows."

I try not to sigh; my mom never takes well to melodrama and the truth is I don't really want to talk about the sage smudging and the dairy embargo, and Dr. Tess's little clogs. "It's your fault."

"How is that possible?" she says, smiling as she takes a bite out of a scone.

"Bad genes?" I say, grinning.

"Oi," she says, trying not to smile as she looks at the ceiling. *What have I done to deserve this?*

"I'm seeing a naturopath, who thinks it'll help my headaches if I cut out dairy and gluten. And she made some disturbing comments about sugar, too."

"Naturopath," my mom says, her nose crinkling.

"My neurologist gave me a bunch of diet recommendations too," I say.

"Well, that's all right, then," my mom says. "How do you feel?"

I think about confessing everything about my recent medical merry-go-round. Not telling her about it is the first big secret I've kept from her, although I guess you could say that Joe stealing my promotion is the second one. It's been a big week, apparently. "Okay." I don't mention the little voice in my head that's sprung up ever since I started stuffing myself with salads, boiled eggs, and misery this week, a siren song for sugar and salt, preferably in the same mouthful, preferably right now.

"This will pass," my mother says, echoing one of my grandmother's favourite expressions.

I take a sip of the tea, aromatic and sweetly spectacular. "Maybe," I say.

We both chat about the weather (mildly disturbing global-warming-type weather) until our meals come. My mouth waters at the sight of my mother's lunch, and when I lift my fork, my hand pauses mid-air while I watch her tuck into the fluffy, syrup-soaked flapjacks. My not-really-an-omelette looks nude on the plate, eggs put together in a way that only suggests an omelette. But when I finally bite into it, it's delicious, full of sausage and sweet peppers and onions. The salad it comes with is equally tasty; field greens and a champagne dressing. Mom decides to order another pot of tea, and the two of us sit there, together, after most other people have cleared out. I feel a small jolt of pleasure, seeing her ignore her work cell, which buzzes every few minutes. My mom is an important person, and it always gives me a warm feeling when she puts me ahead of everyone else.

"Have you talked to Martin lately?" she asks, casually.

"No, I had to cancel plans with him a while back," I say.

"You should call him," she says, equally casually, and the two of us finish our tea while she chats about work. My mom has always been a workaholic, up all hours of the night, trying to squeeze teachable moments in between business trips and no vacations. When I was six, she brought Martin and I downstairs to our laundry room and explained centrifugal force while we sat on the dryer, Martin poking me in the ribs when he thought she couldn't see. My mom ignored him while she opened and closed the door to the washing machine, explaining why the clothes were flung against the sides of the washer, what scientific forces were at work. Which goes a long way in explaining my lifelong obsession with machines and electronics, and my belief that they're more than just a bunch of parts.

My headache is in abeyance, a small thump behind my left temple that's strong enough to remind me it's there, but weak enough to lull me into thinking it's going to go away. I try to ignore it and focus on my mom, but as she's telling me a story about her work, the strangest sensation starts to creep up my lower back. In a tight band around my waist, under my skin, I feel something strange. Something like…tingling.

"…don't you think?" my mom says, in Estonian.

I rub my lower back, trying to banish the pins and needles. I don't know what's going on. I've never felt like this before. "What was that, Ema?"

"I said, it's ridiculous. The mother of one of my junior engineers called me when he had to stay late. She asked when he was coming home. She's deranged, don't you think?"

"Yeah," I say, pressing my hand against my waist and then scratching.

"What's wrong with you?" she asks. "You look like you have ants in your pants."

"I don't know."

Tiiu comes back over. "Veel midagi?" *Anything else?* She sees me grabbing at myself. "Are you okay? Are you allergic to something?"

"No," my mom answers.

"I can't figure it out," I say.

"Dairy, nuts, gluten?" Tiiu asks. It sounds funny when she says it in Estonian: *gluteeni.*

"There was none in my meal."

"Oh, there's gluten in the sausage that was in your omelette," she says. "I'm so sorry; I didn't realize you have an allergy."

"I don't," I say.

"It's okay," my mother says. "My daughter is fine. We're sorry to bother you."

The server nods, but looks concerned as she leaves, probably thinking: *God, don't let me kill an Esto. We're probably related.* My mom is so upset she forgets to organize her silverware on her plate, and the moment for me telling my mom about what's going on with me is gone.

I sit back in my chair. The tingling isn't painful–it wouldn't even register on my pain scale–just weird and distracting. It's the newness of it that bothers me, the perpetual sense that I'm going through a different kind of puberty every day when I'm trying out new meds. I just want to stand still, for once, and be where I'm supposed to be, somewhere peaceful and quiet and calm. The problem is I don't quite know how to find out where that is.

The organizer, one Lily Tidwell, is a formidable woman. Right now she's sitting on one of the comfy chairs in my living room, sipping tea and extolling the virtues of the "organizational sciences," as she puts it, a term I'm 99% sure she just made up. She showed up shortly after I got home from lunch with my mom, and so far I've learned that my kitchen needs a total re-org because it's the nexus of evil, and that the mousy little woman from the group's name is Shirley.

"I adore these old houses," Lily says, smiling over her mug. "But the one problem with these places is lack of closet space." Earlier, I took her on a tour of the house. I thought she might cry when she saw there's no closet in the master bedroom and just a tiny one in the office.

"I know," I say.

"But there's things we can do," she says. "Maybe we should back up a little and I'll tell you about myself and my company. We offer a variety of services for the working wife and mother. You know, it's so hard to find the time to do all the things we need to do; make sure we're eating properly and getting enough exercise, let alone spending quality time with our loved ones. You don't have any children, correct?"

"No." I've never been referred to as a *working wife or mother* before. Although, I don't know how much longer I'm going to be a *working* anything.

"Good stuff. Okay, well, what I do is co-ordinate services for the busy professional woman. Have to work late and need to get groceries? No problem. Need to find the perfect cleaning service? No problem. Need travel arranged? We love arranging travel!" She looks down to her lap and tidies a pile of brochures. "Here. Just so you know, I offer a free organization plan for people with chronic illness. That means I help you go through your closets and kitchen and figure out how best to organize it. For people with migraine we put together a collection of food that's accessible and easy to make if you're incapacitated. My time, a few hours of it, anyway, is free, but any equipment we need, shelving units, that kind of thing, would be purchased by you."

The pamphlets are glossy and professional and promise they'll take all my problems away. On one, there's a chef lovingly plating some desserts. "You do catering?" I ask.

"Yes! We have a range of food services. And if you're looking for something we haven't done in the past, we'll find someone who can do it." She smiles again, her enthusiasm for her work plain on her face, like a beacon of helpfulness. I find it hard to imagine a task Lily Tidwell can't execute efficiently. It all sounds so alluring. Send an email, get a healthy dinner delivered. Pick up the phone and the house will be spotless. Guarantee an awesome Christmas.

"Okay," I say. "You've seen the house. What would you estimate for cleaning services?"

"Eighty-five dollars." There's no pause when she answers me, years of muscle memory kicking in.

I do some rough math: *If I can get her down to $75, every other week, that'll be $150 a month.* I wonder, *Is my piece of mind worth $150?*

"Seventy," I say.

"I can't do seventy," she says.

"It's such a small house."

"True, but you have the same rooms everyone else has," she says with a smile. "What about seventy-five?"

My mother is a senior engineer at her firm, with a team of thirty. She made it to the top of her field at a time when there *were* no other women in her field. She holds patents on six industrial engineering designs. She's won awards for her work. She never had a cleaning lady or a grocery delivery service or any kind of help, and I want to be just like her. And besides, all this feels like a cheat.

But then I wonder what it would have been like if she did. I wonder if home would have been different. Easier, maybe. I close my eyes. *I need things to be easier. I want to choose easier.* And that's when I think about what the Migraine Mafia, and Dr. Tess, and Lily Tidwell's company are really all about: choice. I never really wanted choices before, I just wanted to follow the rules, do things the way they've always been done. But if a little bit of choice could get everyone what they wanted without a ton of pain and drama, then maybe that's the better way. I can't help but glance around the living room; I'm embarrassed at the dust on the TV, the slipcovers that haven't been washed in forever, all those murky corners. And the truth is, I want better than this for me and Nate. I want to choose better.

"Sold," I say, and we shake hands. "When can someone come?"

She looks at her iPad, swiping the screen until she gets to where she wants to be. "One of my regular clients is out of the country and I have an opening tomorrow afternoon. How does that work for you?" She continues without waiting for my answer, "One thing to keep in mind–your place won't be spotless on the first day. They need to do some overall maintenance, wipe down the baseboards, that kind of a thing. But it'll be a start."

"Okay," I say. "They'll be gone when I come home, I guess?"

"Yup," she says.

"I see."

After a moment, Lily says, gently, "I just need the keys, Viive."

"Oh, sorry!" I scramble to my feet–too fast, so quickly that my not-quite-there headache starts to bubble to the surface–and I have to slow myself down before unlooping the spare key from the hook near the front door. I walk carefully back to the living room, and by the time I sit back down, it seems like I've tricked the headache back to sleep for now. "Here you go."

There's a moment before the key drops out of my hand into hers, but then she closes her fingers over it, slides it into her purse, and gets up.

On her way out, she steps into her shoes, moves a few errant sneakers into a small pile, and straightens a picture, all without breaking stride. It's a starburst of productivity, an almost disconcerting feeling, that level of efficiency, one that makes me wonder what other changes Lily Tidwell is going to bring.

11 – My Own Kind of Poker

Everything is exactly the same as usual when I'm back to work on Wednesday, in a creepy and not-quite-real sort of a way. Elliot is out of the office at a work retreat until Friday, meaning, *drinking in the woods with a bunch of executives.* He's left me a few emails overnight, pushed three new jobs on me and said nothing about Joe's shiny new title. I scowl at his message. My team is already at capacity, and he knows it, so I send him a return email, pushing back on two of the tasks. I'll figure out how to fit the third in to my own schedule, somehow. Or maybe I won't do it at all. That'd be a new one.

"Got a sec?" Otis is standing in my doorway, wearing plaid suspenders and a saucy look. He's holding two coffees. *Goddammit, now I'm behind again.*

"Thanks Otis."

"Let's go to Elliot's office," he says.

"Why?"

Otis looks up at the space where my ceiling should be. "Because he actually has an office."

"It's that kind of talk, huh?"

He nods and then stands back so I can go out the door first. On the way, he hands me my coffee, and once we get to Elliot's office, the two of us sit in the chairs in front of the desk. Elliot doesn't mind if we come here to have private conversations when he's not around, but he doesn't let anyone sit in his Aeron chair, although I know that the quality assurance manager comes in here and farts on it every chance he gets, an unsavoury habit I discovered one day when I interrupted him

Once we're seated, Otis smiles smugly and hands me a pastry-thing, a mangled lump of coal that looks like it was tortured before being run over by a car.

"Er…thanks." I'm not actually sure if I'm seeing it properly. I'm in a mini-stupor, an odd sort of malaise. My headache is quiet behind my ears but my head feels swollen, bloated, and I feel strange, not quite myself. It's too early to know if this cotton-ball-cranium feeling is because of the

Xamaxia, my daily ball-and-chain preventative, but I can't remember ever feeling like this before. I try to sift through some memories but I come up with nothing.

"Anything for you, my sweet," Otis says, interrupting my thoughts.

"What is it?" I ask, trying to focus.

Otis laughs. "The health food store I took you to is trying their hand at gluten-free baking."

I look at it again, squashed flat, with slivers of coconut emerging from the wreckage like sugary tentacles. It's dotted with what could be prunes. *Christ, is there anything worse than prunes?* I bring the pastry close to my nose and sniff, and take a small, tentative nibble.

"I wanted to talk to you on Monday," Otis says.

I take a bigger bite. There's a squishy molten goo inside the pastry-thing that spurts into my mouth with an almost audible *pop*. I can feel the sticky ooze splash on my face at the time that a large glob arcs gracefully over Elliot's desk. Both Otis and I track its progress with our eyes, helplessly. Before it lands, it seems to hang in the air like some sort of culinary extra-terrestrial.

And maybe it's the leftover tension from Monday, or the fact that I didn't really sleep last night, or maybe it's the look Otis and I share when we face each other–horrified–but suddenly Otis and I are laughing so hard we can't speak. We both examine where it landed, a not-so-small splat on the middle of Elliot's desk.

I try to put my coffee and the pastry on the floor without causing any more carnage, but the little lump lets loose another volcano of goo on the floor. My mouth is covered with it, my fingers are sticky with it, and I still can't stop laughing.

Otis gasps, his hands over his stomach. "I–just–just couldn't…look away."

This starts us off laughing again, tears in both of our eyes. When it seems like we're going to wind down, one of us starts up again. Finally, he hands me some tissue so I can wipe myself off. "Otis, I have to say, I really needed that."

"Oh my Christ," Otis says. "I just couldn't take my eyes off it. It was like a car accident."

"Elliot is going to kill us," I say, my voice still shaky from all that laughter.

"Who cares?" Otis says, his eyes narrowing. "He can kiss my arse."

I raise my eyebrows at him.

"Vee, what the bloody hell is going on? How is Elliot giving out a directorship–the first one ever in our team, as he so nicely put it–to Joe, and not you?"

I wipe at my fingers with the napkin. "It's an excellent question, my dear."

"What are you going to do? What did Nate say?"

I pull off the top of my coffee and take a sip. Caramelo, one of my favourites. "My sister-in-law was over on Monday, and Nate worked until really late last night, so I didn't get a chance to tell him."

Otis tilts his head to the side, gives me a suspicious look.

"I'll tell him tonight." I shift in the chair. "Elliot hasn't said anything to me about it, and he's out of town. So I'm not sure what's going on. If it makes you feel better, I'm super pissed about it."

"Hmmm," Otis says. The two of us drink coffee in silence, while I wonder if it's the last time I'll be in Elliot's office. *Would it be okay if it was the last time? Am I done here?* I've always just quit if I had a serious problem at work; all of my job stints have been from one to two years. This is the longest I've ever worked anywhere, and I helped build this company. I love my team and the work we do. And I can't leave now to start over somewhere new at a time that I'm–and I'm being generous here–not at my best. At a time I can't even remember the last time I *was* at my best. I need that title so Nate and I can launch our own start-up, but I need the last four years to be a success too. I need to know it was all worth it.

After that mildly depressing thought, Otis says since he bought the pastry, he'll clean it up and I take him up on his offer, leaving so I can make a pit-stop and wash the goo off my hands. Back in my office, I finish off my coffee and check my voicemail: there's a message from my GP's office to call them back. I dial the numbers, my hands suddenly sweaty. Her receptionist puts me on hold, and when my GP gets back on the line, she tells me in a few clipped sentences that the EEG was clear–no seizures. After she hangs up, my stomach hollows out, my throat goes dry, and I drop the phone on my desk, where it lands with a metallic thump and a bounce. I'm already crying, tears coursing a warm trail down my cheeks. I try not to make any noise, so Otis can't hear me, and I have to put my face in the crook of my arm to muffle the noise. I didn't even know I was holding on to all of it so tightly, that there was a thump of worry under everything ever since my EEG. Within five minutes my throat is strained from all the crying. There's relief behind the tears, before I realize that, for now, I have to live with not knowing why I've been fainting. Of course, now I have a carousel of doctors to chose from; maybe one of them can figure it out.

I don't bother to look at myself in the mirror after I'm done. I know I'll be a pink puffball. Yet another problem with being so fair-skinned is that every emotion I'm having shows up on my face as some shade of red. I take a deep breath and then another, trying to detach myself from everything that's happening.

I want this to be any time but now; the before-time when I understood all the rules, or the time after this when I have everything figured out. I'm sick of all this change, of failing at all the newness in my life. Sitting there, my face still red, my breathing jagged in my chest, all I want is to be normal and thirty-four, with a thirty-four-year-old's problems; chastising myself when I splurge on lattés, reminding myself to go to the gym, figuring out where to spend my vacation. Over the years I've taught myself not to want those things, all those boring, normal things, so it feels supremely unfair to be saddled with it all of a sudden. Like a practical joke, or the world's worst punch line.

Somewhere inside, I know that's not really how other people live, from one manicure to the next, solving marriage problems with a rom-com-aw-shucks kind of sensibility. But it looks so shiny from where I'm sitting, I can't resist glorifying it, just a little bit.

My bad mood lifts a little when I get home and discover that my kitchen table is magnificently perfumed with lemon oil and the room is spotless, the dishwasher emptied and the counters barren. Magical Maria (I know her name is Maria because she left me a very pleasant note) has even washed the dishtowels. I have to walk through the house twice, glorying in the clean, fresh smell and the vacuum lines in the carpet in the master bedroom. In the entrance way, on the coat rack, is my winter jacket. *Like magic.* When I open the refrigerator door, the groceries I ordered online last night are all there, in neat rows–two salads, some green beans, two pork chops, some new potatoes. The pantry and fridge are full of breakfast and lunch items. I marvel at the sight of it for a while longer before taking the chops out of the fridge and getting started with dinner.

I text Nate and tell him to come home early.

Getting ready for supper is easier than usual, thanks to Magical Maria, but I still have to contend with the jumbled silverware drawer and the overstuffed pantry. It's still impossible to find anything, and so I decide to email Lily Tidwell, so we can get started with organizing the kitchen. It's a small, spontaneous moment, over before it really starts, but once it's finished I feel a fuzzy sense of pride, that maybe I really can embrace change after all.

"H'llo?" Nate calls, before dropping all of his work stuff with a series of thuds.

"In here," I answer.

Nate takes in the dinner prep with a whistle. He kisses me carefully, staying away from my chef's knife, which I put down so I don't accidentally chop off a finger. It's a good knife, sharp like a scalpel. I haven't used it in forever.

"What's all this?" he asks. His voice is normal, not angry after our fight the other day. Nate never stays angry and is perpetually befuddled that other people feel the need to hang on to ugly feelings.

"I wanted to do something nice for you."

"You do nice things for me all the time." He kisses my forehead.

I snort.

"What?"

"Oh, please, Nate. I spend half my life in bed, and not in a good way."

"It's okay, babe," he says. "It's not your fault. And anyway, I like my women quiet." He squeezes my shoulders as he kisses me.

I want to tell Nate about all the guilt I feel, every time I'm sick, every time I ruin our plans, our weekend, all the little slices of our life that go wrong. I've always thought that Nate doesn't need to hear that kind of truth. But maybe I've been wrong. Maybe admitting it would be a kind of freedom.

Nate rustles around the refrigerator, emerging with a bottle of wine, and then the moment's gone.

"Well, it doesn't really help things," I say, as I fill a wine glass with Perrier, for myself; I'm still shaky from the weekend and I don't want to chance another headache. The two of us sit sideways on the couch, our legs crossed over each other's.

"Would you like to tell me what happened here?" Nate asks.

"What do you mean?"

"I'm assuming you didn't clean up the house."

I laugh. "Oh, that. Remember the organizer? She was very persuasive. So now we have a cleaning lady. Her name is Maria and I'm madly in love with her. I guess I should have talked to you about it first."

"Well, I think it's a good thing, Vee. I don't think we should work super-long hours and then have to do a bunch of chores when we get home. I want us to enjoy our life, and…well, you don't have that many good days. I don't want you to spend them cleaning." He squeezes my toes, and then takes a sip of wine. As he drinks, I catch him up on Joe's sudden rise to power.

Nate finishes his glass of wine and goes to get another. From the kitchen, he says, "It's basically a slap in the face, Vee. Elliot is promoting someone over you, and he's been dangling that director position in front of you for a year now. Now the whole thing with him making you go on vacation is even more suspect. I mean, what if they *are* setting you up to be fired, after all?"

I rub my forehead with my palm. "Yeah, well, that's the thing I'm worried about."

Nate sits back down on the couch. "What did Elliot say to you?"

"So far? Nothing."

Nate twirls the wine in his glass and looks at the clarity pensively. "Maybe this is a good thing. We'll just set up shop a little earlier than we thought we were going to."

"We're not ready, Nate. My dad says–"

Nate puts his hand on mine and squeezes gently. "Why don't we talk to your dad when he comes home for Christmas, and make a new plan?"

"Look, speaking of Christmas, can we not come to a compromise about dinner?"

"Yeah, I've been thinking about that, and I'm sorry about the other day," Nate says. "Sometimes the idea of things seems more important than the actual thing, and that's stupid. We always had a home-cooked meal, and that feels like the only way to do it."

I exhale. "So can we talk about getting it catered?"

"How about we talk about getting it catered if you come see the boat?"

I smile as I squeeze his foot; Nate and I have a long history of odd marital negotiations. "You're a tricky one, you know."

"The thing is, Vee, we need to change how we're spending our money. A little bit on cleaning ladies, a little bit on a boat, a little bit more on stuff we want to do."

I take a sip of soda water, and look at Nate. Normally I love his sure-footed happiness, his just-right way of looking at things, except with money. But maybe he's right about this. "Why a boat?" I ask.

"We need somewhere to unplug, to relax. And Estonians are natural sailors, so I don't see the problem." His smile is cheeky.

"I don't know if I can commit to a boat."

"You'll love it, there's lots of nice people at the club. Nice couples and families."

"We're not like other families," I say.

"No, we're not," Nate says, and he pulls me close to him. "And that's just fine with me. I love you so much, Vee."

"I don't know why."

"You're perfect, you dolt. You just don't get it yet." He smiles at me, one of his best smiles yet. "Everything's going to be okay. I promise."

I drape my arms around him and squeeze. "I love you too, honey." I feel awake, for the first time in forever. Nate's neck is right there, so close and tantalizing, and all I can smell is his skin and his shampoo and that other smell, the one that's only Nate. I can't remember the last time he put his hand on the small of my back exactly like that. Before the run-in with Sid and his bowtie, before all this started, definitely. And then suddenly we're kissing, his hands on my face, my hands untucking his shirt, and then we're a jumble of arms and legs and couch, his skin against mine, his breath hot against my neck, and I'm thinking: *I'm still here, I'm still alive.* It's not the whole world, and it won't fix everything, but it's the two of us fitting together perfectly, raspy breathing in my ear, my lips on Nate's, his arm around my shoulders.

Afterward, we lie together under his grandmother's quilt (lovely woman, great quilter), and hold each other, quiet, but not really silent. There's something simple and safe and perfect about the curl of Nate's arms. I don't know what's going to happen next, with my work, with my health, with the rest of my life. But this is the moment when I start to think everything is going to be okay.

A Kelly green sweater I haven't seen in forever–because it was wedged at the bottom of my laundry basket before being liberated by Magical Maria–is on the top of the clean laundry pile in my room. I love this sweater; it's soft and warm and comfortable. I rub the sleeve against my skin, and then I put it on.

Nate pokes his head into the bedroom. "Done in the bathroom, babe."

"Thanks honey."

He leans in to kiss me. "Are you wearing a colour?"

"Yeah. What's the big deal?"

"I haven't seen you wear anything but black in…a year or so, I guess. Since last Christmas, I bet."

"It can't be that long," I say, but even as I say the words I know I'm probably wrong.

"Liar," he says, with a smile and a kiss.

After Nate leaves I take two mouthfuls of that terrible cereal (barnacle bites, I've nicknamed it), strap on my pedometer, grab my winter jacket, and hit the subway. This morning I have a meeting with the senior management team, and I head to the conference room after dumping my stuff off at my desk. This group gets together once a month, a cross-functional infantry that tries to avert looming screw-ups, especially the kind that erupt out of a company moving so quickly we don't have time for the basics. There are seven of us, and we've all been here for at least a couple of years, except Joe, who's shown up today, even though I doubt he's been invited.

It's Denise's turn to chair the meeting, an arbitrary title that simply means she's the one who brings the cupcakes, but Joe hasn't let her get started yet, not even to distribute any of the sweets, which would make me sad if I was able to actually eat wheat, which, of course, I can't. Denise looks tortured, like she's ready to start wailing if Joe doesn't shut up. They're standing at the front of the meeting room, the pastry boxes still in her hands, while Joe rails on about something to do with his parking. Now that he's a director, he gets a free parking spot near the building. Denise is the senior manager of HR, which is why she's currently embroiled in this less-than-scintillating topic. Of course, the more people Joe pisses off, the better it is for me, and since I'm still wrapped in a post-coital glow from last night's romp on the couch, I find it a little more amusing than I probably should.

At one point in the conversation, Joe rubs his temple and says, "God, I have such a migraine." I don't think it's an accident that he glances in my direction as he says it, the lying little schemer, a small hiccup of movement that sets my nerves on edge.

Finally, Richard from finance liberates the cupcakes from Denise, which makes her snap out of her funk. "You'll have to excuse me, Joe," she says. "You can come speak to me about this later. Okay everyone, let's run through the minutes from last meeting." She turns on the projector and, not particularly subtly, turns her back on Joe, who looks around the room and then parks himself in the seat across from me.

My pulse quickens as he sits down. I look back at him, remember all those bouncy schoolgirl thoughts I had when Otis told me Elliot and Sid were getting ready to promote someone to a directorship. And then I think: *Am I really so off my game that I thought Elliot was trying to help me? Am I really so off my game I didn't see Joe coming?* It's embarrassing, to be honest, that I've let all this get as far as it has.

Joe's watching me, with his big blue bug-eyes. His terrible tie winks in the fluorescent lighting.

Denise switches slides. Joe's eyes stay on mine, his head cocked, now.

It really is rude, the way he looks at me all the time, and to be honest, I've had enough of it. I think back to my fight with Avery this week, and a small voice inside me says: *Nice to see you still have a little fight left in you.* I smile at the thought. I feel like having a few more fights, actually. I hold Joe's gaze while I think about how the two of us ended up here, in this room together. And then it occurs to me that Joe is just like those bullies in school who push you into the dirt and then tell the teacher you hit them first. But here's what Joe doesn't realize: this is my schoolyard. I got here first, and, frankly, I have no intention of leaving until I've finished what I started. I am a start-up survivor, and I've survived alpha-geeks much, much, smarter than Joe, ones with even bigger hero complexes. I've lived through worse than this. I didn't see it coming, not from someone with googly-eyes and bad neckwear. That's true. But I see what's going on now. I'm ready now.

Looking at Joe, I feel perfectly clear-headed, for the first time in a very long time. I've been chugging away here for so long I never stopped to think about doing things differently. About choices. I notice, as I think all this, that my thoughts feel clear and unmuddied by pain or side effects or anything else. It's just clear sailing, and focused thoughts.

Joe's brow is knit, now, like he's trying to figure something out.

It's not much, of course, that I'm sitting here without any pain, but sometimes things that seem like not much have their own kind of momentum. It's like what Paulie said, about small things becoming something big.

Denise flips another slide: *Internal customer satisfaction.* Internal customers, meaning employees. I've always liked that idea, that you have to treat your staff as well as your clients. It is, as Sid would say, one of my core values. Denise sighs when we get to this slide, because as someone in HR she knows how poor this number is. The pie chart shows 47% of the staff are either a little or very dissatisfied with the company, their jobs. It's so close to fifty percent, so close to failing.

My mind continues to wander. You know, growing up in a healthy family, no one ever taught me the rules for being sick. But maybe the rules are*: Just do the best you can and don't get stepped on by assholes like Joe.* I look around the room. I like everyone here, veterans of layoffs and disruptive technology and lunatic executives, all of us. Probably everyone else here thinks their life was supposed to be a little bigger, too. A little easier, a little less confusing. Maybe I'm not so lost after all.

Joe's squinting at me now.

And then I meet his gaze. There's a quick moment where he sees me looking at him, and when it's over he leans forward a little in his chair, as if he wants to say something. I tilt my head to the side, meet the angle his head is still cocked at. He blinks a few times, waiting. My heartbeat has calmed, and the lashing against my chest has eased. I feel a floaty kind of peace inside, something clean and new and good. I lean forward in my chair, and Joe watches me as I do.

And then I smile.

I smile an invitation at Joe: *Come and get me, you absolute asshole.* I smile so widely my cheeks hurt. I smile like a wolf. I smile for what feels like forever.

And as I smile, Joe's expression falters. He looks, to be deliciously honest about it, unsettled, at least for that moment. And then his mask slips back into place, and he looks down at his lap, at his phone.

It's something like victory, that small moment. But it's the moment I realize that Joe is just one other thing I'm going to have to survive.

The meeting grinds on, new slides, new metrics, chasing the next-quarter results. I lean back in my chair, enjoy the relative quiet of a meeting where I don't really have to say much, and glance over at Joe every now and again. He doesn't look back over at me, and it is all deeply, deeply satisfying.

On Friday afternoon I knock on Elliot's door. He's lost in thought, going through something on his laptop. I glance at the place on his desk that was recently decimated by my pastry, and try to hold back a smile.

"Got a minute?"

He doesn't glance up. "Not right now, Viive, I'm in the middle–"

I close the door behind me, and Elliot shifts his gaze to my face. "I have five minutes," he says.

I stay standing. "That's it? Really, Elliot?"

"What?"

"Don't you think you owe me a little more than that?"

"What do you mean?"

I take two steps, sit down. "I'd like for you to explain to me how you've been promising me a directorship for over a year and you hand one to Joe after he's been here for five minutes."

"Well, that's different. And it's not going to affect you." He sighs. "Well, not so much."

"Elliot, I'm happy to agree to disagree with you. I think it has a lot to do with me."

He taps a pen on his desk and then drops it. It skitters over some paper before getting buried. "Joe is going to be taking over some of my duties. I'm out of the office all the time these days, and I need someone I can rely on to back me up."

There's a beat.

"He's the one who went to you and said I've been lying down in the nurse's office every day, isn't he?"

"No comment," Elliot says, but his throat flushes red, his version of *Jesus Christ yes*. "Let's talk later Viive. I'm really swamped." He turns away and picks up a piece of paper.

None of this is going the way I thought it would, and maybe that's why I get up, go to the door. My hand reaches out and holds on to the doorknob. I think about what it would mean to turn it, and then I think about what it would mean to sit back down. It's the most delicate kind of triage, this moment. Do I do what I'm told, or do I forget about being afraid and do what's right for me? I think about Paulie, for some reason, who's so good at sticking her foot into doors that are being closed in her face, and then I think: *I want to be just like that.* After a beat I release it, and another second later I'm settled back in the chair.

"What about my promotion?"

He sighs, looks up from his papers. "We're still looking at the budget, but it should be soon, Viive."

Budget, Viive. Soon, Viive, the same thing he's told me for the last year. And it's not like I barged in his office one day and demanded a promotion. He raised the issue with me last year, at my review. I meet his gaze with a look that says, *I know what game you're playing.*

"Viive, we need to keep growing, keep building. Joe has a lot more experience than you with enterprise environments. He worked at Google, you know."

Google, the goddamn holy grail of the tech industry.

"I can't believe you want to promote someone who behaves like Joe. He's totally unprofessional–"

"It's really hard to believe that someone who worked at Google would be unprofessional."

I inhale once, and then twice. "You know it's a lie, eh? You know that what he told you about me lying down all the time in the nurse's office is not true."

Elliot meets my eyes, and for the first time, he looks like he might actually listen to me. But then he says, "I don't even know why you're getting so upset about this. You have to try harder to stop letting emotions get in the way of everything all the time. Your work is excellent, but Joe has the perspective of a large-scale expert. He can't be bothered by all the little details you get hung up on. But I'll talk to him. He's new, you know. He can't be expected to know how you run things."

"I run things according to industry-standard, engineering best practices, and he cowboys shit. And worse, when he does, he gets rewarded. And I'm not sorry that affects me emotionally. I care about my work, and this job, and it's all nothing but a pit stop for Joe. He'll be gone before you can blink twice, to a better opportunity. Or back to Google, for Christ's sake. I mean, why would anyone ever leave Google anyway?" I should call Jimmy, I realize, a buddy of mine who's worked there for a couple of years.

"All right," Elliot says, holding up his hands. "The truth is, I wanted to thank you for getting that customer back up and running so quickly last week. Their contract is in the process of being renewed and they made a point of telling their sales guy how happy they are with our service; by the time they'd figured out there was a problem, it was already fixed. It's a big win for us. I know what happened with the outage last week was not optimal."

Be smart. Don't be stupid. I exhale, stare at Elliot's ear, so I don't have to look him in the eye. *Nah.* And then I decide to lay my best card down; play my own kind of poker. "Not optimal? Remember what happened the last time someone cowboyed code into production?"

Elliot pauses, his hand straightening out his collar. "Oh, it's like that, is it, Viive?"

The last person who put rotten code up on the Internet was Elliot, who took down an entire bank of servers with a cluster of programs that had failed quality assurance testing. It was an accident, but it came after a sixteen-hour day when Elliot was pushing everyone to complete our rollout within the scheduled maintenance time, instead of increasing the window like I wanted. His literal last words to me before promoting the code were: *This isn't brain surgery, you know. I'll show you how easy it is.* The only people in the room were Elliot and myself, so we're the only two who know he's the one who took everything down. It cost us the client, one of our biggest.

In the incident report, I blamed it on a junior staff member who I refused to name, even though Sid squeezed me as hard as I've been squeezed in my career. Elliot didn't ask me to do any of this, but he sure didn't step up to the plate and admit anything, either. That was the last time Elliot stuck his hand into production systems. Part of me knows I'm playing that card now, and part of me just wants to remind him that slow and steady sometimes trumps new and flashy. Neither one of us might like where we are right now, but we still know each other, Elliot and I.

"Oh, it's like that," I say. "Look, if I don't have a future here, tell me I don't have a future here. Don't force me to take a vacation I don't want to take and then give me this bullshit run-around crap about Joe. A few months ago you had no issues having a plain discussion with me. Now you're all over the place. If I'm done here, that's cool. But I'm not going to live like this any more."

"No one's saying anything like that."

"I think you are," I say. "I think when you promote a weasel like Joe instead of people who've put their time in here, then it's nothing more than an insult. A public one. You think other people don't see that their loyalty isn't being repaid?"

He tents his fingers. "I have a problem with the budget."

"Then fix it."

He looks at me.

"Or don't. But let me tell you this; either I get my promotion by Christmas, or I'm out of here." My stomach is empty of butterflies, my breathing calm. I think back to the other night, when I was entwined with Nate and the knowledge that everything is going to work out just fine. If this is my last time in Elliot's office, then that's okay. There are other offices, other places for me.

"Oh, don't be like that, Viive."

"It's exactly like that, Elliot. Just exactly like that." I get up, get ready to leave.

"I thought I was doing the right thing, you know," Elliot says, not looking at me.

I pause, right before the door. "What do you mean?"

"I thought you were in trouble, that you could barely make it through the day. I thought I was helping."

"Maybe next time, ask me."

"Viive." He drops his pen on his desk. "All you ever tell me is that everything is okay."

I pull the knob, and then turn around, face Elliot. "Well, I'm working on that." As I walk back to my office, my legs feel loose, like those speed walkers, the ones with the wobbling hips and comical gaits. I feel like I'm at the end of some kind of marathon. Electricity pricks up and down my spine, the beginning of something else. I feel warm, my insides churning with adrenaline afterglow. I know I'm smiling.

I'm at Otis's office now, leaning against the doorway, when my cell rings.

"Hi honey," Nate says. "How are you?"

I blink while I take stock. "You know, I feel awesome. I just talked to Elliot."

Otis looks up from his laptop, a grin on his face.

"How did it go?" Nate asks.

"Very well."

"That's great, honey," he says. "Look, let's go out for dinner. Let's have drinks. We'll leave early."

"What time?"

"Leave at five. Hell, leave five minutes to five, that'll show them." He laughs. "We can go to The Black Hoof."

I love The Black Hoof, pleasantly cramped, designer drinks, gamey main dishes. "I'd make a reservation, except they don't take reservations. Honey?"

"What, babe?"

"I love you."

"Suck up," he says, with a laugh. "I love you too."

And at 4:55, Otis and I zip out for a quick drink before dinner. His wife is coming to meet us at the restaurant, later, just like old times. With all the new things that have happened lately it's nice to return to something old. And I definitely feel like a good dinner and a kick-ass cocktail. I feel great, in fact. I really do.

And there's lots to celebrate.

12 – Life Is

The next week I send an email to Martin, with a single word in the subject line: *Laiskvorst*. The English equivalent would be "lazybones," but literally translated, it means "lazy sausage." This was our code when we were little and one of us needed something (generally when we didn't want to do it ourselves), like our very own ethnic version of the Bat Signal. Martin answers almost immediately with an email that says: *Where and when and how much vodka should I bring?* I reply with the dates for the next Angry Bridesmaid's concert, because I've bought tickets for just the two of us. I smile as I send it. Of course, money is sometimes just that easy; the rest of it, I'm still figuring out.

After that, I do all my new usual morning things: pills, pedometer, barnacle bites, office. At lunch I go back to the hippie store with Otis. He and I both have a goal this week to find beans or lentils we like. So far he's found seven; I've found none. I finally settle on a chick pea salad while Otis spoons beets into a biodegradable container. Then I pick up the magnesium I'm supposed to buy; the oversized horse pills I'm terrified to swallow. On the way back, Otis tells me about his poodle, Gloria, and her most recent tryst; apparently she and a pug are behaving inappropriately and might be asked to leave doggie daycare. Otis and I eat lunch together, and I crack open the swamp-water-multivitamin tincture from Dr. Tess and take some, to Otis's great hilarity. Later in the afternoon, when I feel hunger start to pull at me, I eat a vegan wedge of pretend protein. And I guess it's not so bad.

After work I leave the office at a gloriously reasonable time, and I'm the first one in room 237, before the rest of the Migraine Mafia. As I wait for everyone to show up, it occurs to me that I'm looking forward to it, this hour of people just like me. I shift in my chair, recross my legs. For the first time in forever, nothing twinges as I move, there's no pain in my ankles or my feet. I open my eReader, the screen frozen at the book I bought last night, but I look up almost immediately, my thoughts bouncing around about everything.

Before, I never really asked myself what was at risk if my health didn't get better. It's hard to admit you need help when you come from a DIY, duct-tape-solves-everything kind of family, but this is the year my illness became something I couldn't hide any more. I used to think it would be nice to edit out that part of the story, but lately I've been thinking maybe it's more like a gift, having nowhere left to hide. I know now that things have to change. I have to make my life a little bigger; more time with friends, a little less stress, maybe a hobby, even. I close my eyes and let my thoughts run to the things they always do when I daydream: dinner out on a Friday with Nate, going to a movie theatre, reading in the park. Boring, domestic bliss. It's such an easy thing to want, that luring maybe-life. And sitting here, today, I feel like I can have it, at least a little bit of it. It's a moment that feels sustainable, like a bunch of good days are lined up right in front of me, just waiting. They're not, of course. That nagging tension between what I *want* to do and what I *can* do, all that ugliness, will always be there. But maybe the worry about the things that are going to go wrong is just a little quieter now, maybe my *just in case* is just a little bit smaller.

I don't know what's going to happen with my health, but I know I'm never really going to be fixed. And maybe that means that success for me is just that my bad days won't be quite so bad, that there will be fewer of them as I get older. Maybe success is all those times you put one foot in front of the other, the times you don't give up.

My mother's favourite expression is Elu on. Literally, *life is*. In English you might say: *Such is life*, but Estonian has an elegant kind of directness about it, and that's why it's simply *life is*. Life is friends you need to call, squirrels that need to be extricated, a work nemesis to be thwarted, gambling habits to be corralled. And I know I can't keep leaving early (well, early for me), shipwrecking my staff, but there's nothing wrong with a few days of hooky. Next week, I'll start leaving on time again, but I'm also going to start delegating more, hand off more to Manjit and Brian, maybe promote one of the team members to help them out more. So I can let go a little.

My thoughts turn to the Migraine Mafia, to the quiet wisdom that happens in this room when they *push*, their sense that words can be their own kind of medicine. I've never asked anyone in the group why they chose to give themselves such an odd nickname, but I don't really need to. They did it because we're all members of a community we can't ever leave, because we know each other, even if we're virtual strangers, because we're our own peculiar kind of family. I can't depend on my medication to always work, for my doctor's office to actually listen to me, but I can depend on the Migraine Mafia to be there.

This is the year I learned that I'm not alone.

I work in an industry obsessed with upgrades. Rebooting. The next big thing. If I use a tiny bit of that ingenuity in my personal life, I know I can make things better. Not perfect, just better. There's a breathless sort of uncertainty about the future, about how things will be tomorrow, but I'm not afraid any more. Everything will work itself out.

A smile spreads across my face when the thought completes itself in my brain. And then I realize: Jesus Christ, you know what I've caught from these people? *Optimism.*

Maybe.

"Hey there." Paulie strides into the room, her gum snapping. She looks like she has a story she wants to tell.

"Hey, yourself," I answer, matching her grin.

And then we start talking.

About The Author

Maia left the tech sector to write about sock thievery, migraines, and...the tech sector. She is Estonian-Canadian and lives with her better half, John, on the Danforth in Toronto. She was diagnosed with migraine as a child, and has cycled between episodic and chronic periods for most of her adult life. These days, she's doing pretty well.

The Migraine Mafia is her second novel. Maia's debut novel, *The Sock Wars*, is a story of love, loss, and sock thievery, and is available as an ebook and in print. You can find Maia online at www.maiasepp.com.

If you enjoyed *The Migraine Mafia*, please consider leaving a review at your point of sale, or on a review site such as Goodreads. Thank you for taking the time to read and review Maia's work.

Acknowledgements

Many thanks goes out to all of the friends and family who have supported my writing over the years.

Special thanks to über awesome author Shanya Krishnasamy for all of her feedback and support. Muchos gracias to my other beta readers: Carolyn Taylor (twice!), Aisha Khan Alam, Fran from *Skulls and Ponies*, Tania Monaco, and Ella Peters.

Thanks to Judith Harlan of Lucky Bat Books for her publishing assistance and support, and to Theresa Rose for her awesome cover design work. Many thanks to Gary Smailes of Bubblecow (Bubblecow!) for the structural edit of my final draft, and also to Sarah Kolb-Williams for her awesome beta-and-backflap (say that five times fast) work, as well as Alexis Arendt for her copyedit/proofreeding kung fu.

I'm very grateful to all the Spoonies who have shared their stories, and shown us that people living with chronic illness are not alone. I'm also profoundly thankful for my crack team of quirky medical professionals; Dr. Ravinder Gill, Dr. Imelda Gunawan, Sophia Boulos and Amber (who I miss). They all know how to squeeze 70 minutes out of an hour, how to unmangle a pinched nerve, how to get to the bottom of things with a smile. To help.

Finally, I am eternally grateful to my better-half-and-sometimes-sugar-daddy, John, who let me leave the rat race and become a starving artist. Woo! *Ma armastan sind, kullake.*

Maia
December, 2013